Beau's Redemption

My Brother's Keeper Series

Blue Saffire writing as Royal Blue

Perceptive Illusions Publishing, Inc.
Bay Shore, New York

Royal Blue /Perceptive Illusions Publishing, Inc.
PO BOX 5253
Bay Shore, New York 11706
www.RoyalBlue.com

Publisher's Note: This is a work of fiction. Names, characters, places, and incidents are a product of the author's imagination. Locales and public names are sometimes used for atmospheric purposes. Any resemblance to actual people, living or dead, or to businesses, companies, events, institutions, or locales is completely coincidental.

Ordering Information:
Quantity sales. Special discounts are available on quantity purchases by corporations, associations, and others. For details, contact the "Special Sales Department" at the address above.

Beau's Redemption/ Blue Saffire writing as Royal Blue . -- 1st ed.

ISBN 978-1-941924-57-0

You will always arrive where you need to be when you need to be.

−Royal Blue

Broken

Beau

The crowd has fallen completely silent. Moments ago they were all screaming for blood. They were cheering for us to tear each other apart. No... correction. They were screaming for me to tear apart my opponent.

None of them understand how wrong this fight is. It never should've been. I never would've signed up for this. I didn't know I had until it was too late.

Now, I've lost everything. I drop to my knees beside the lifeless body at my feet. I never should've stepped into this ring.

I don't care who's watching. I scoop his lifeless body up as I sob. I did this. In just one blow, I destroyed everything I love.

Everything starts to spin; the crowd starts to laugh and mock me. They jeer, relishing my loss. I look down at my hands and blood covers them. Roman's body is no longer in my grasp. I see nothing but blood and darkness before me.

I look around and everyone's pointing at me. I can feel their accusations. This is on me, all on me. I should have hung my gloves up and let this fight go. I knew Roman wasn't ready to step in the ring with me.

I knew this would end badly.

"I've told you before, I'll tell you again. You have to trust your gut, son." My father's voice pierces the air, but I can't see his face.

Pain and loss consume me. I feel it deep within my bones. This hollow feeling threatens to pull me under.

"Why?" I bellow out. My throat burns, stripped raw.

Gasping, I sit up in my bed, soaked in sweat, tangled in drenched sheets. It's the same dream every time. The same damn nightmare.

"Fuck." I rub at my tired eyes.

The dreams have been coming more often in the last few months. I've tried to ignore them, but they just won't quit. It's been so long since it's been this bad.

I look over at my phone on the nightstand. I should call my sister, Emma, but I don't want to bother her with this. Wiping a hand across my forehead, I try to focus and clear my mind.

"Fuck," I mutter again. "A shower. That'll help."

At least I hope it will. I need some fucking sleep. I can't keep going like this. Six years and I'm still trying to keep my head above water.

I know I'm in survival mode. I've been this way since.... I close my eyes against the memories. The nightmare isn't so far from the truth.

God, please just let things be some type of normal again.

Angel

"Shit." I grunt as I pace the tight space in my brother's guest room. "I can't do this." I run a hand through my hair. Andres means well. He doesn't want to see me living on the streets, but this isn't working.

I can't breathe. This bedroom is like a cage. I need to be in the open. I need more space. Too bad I can't afford a fancy apartment to spread out in. I can barely keep a job, and my benefits aren't doing much to help me live in the heart of New York City.

"Fuck." I grab my bag and start to throw clothes inside.

I'd rather roam the streets. Andres will never understand. I've tried to explain it to him, but he will never know what it's like to live in my head. My mind isn't the same as it used to be. I'm not the man my brother used to know.

I'm grateful that he wants me safe and has offered me a place, but I can't stay here. It's making my skin itch. I need to see my surroundings at all times…. I just can't be confined like this.

I pull on my shirt and toss my bag over my shoulder. I'll stop by Andres's work tomorrow or something. This won't be the first time I've had to get away. We've tried this before. It never lasts long, not that I don't want it to.

God, do I want to be normal again.

I just can't keep going like this. I'm tired, I'm just barely holding on, and I'd love to finally have a good night's sleep. At this point, I feel like I'm fighting for my life and my sanity.

It just won't be happening here. Not tonight. Not in this tight room.

CHAPTER ONE

Crush

Beau

"Looking great, Josh. Just watch that left," I drawl as I walk through the gym.

"Got it, Beau," Josh huffs out, continuing to pound through his workout at the heavy bag.

I get to the front desk, grabbing a clipboard to look over the day's schedule. A glance at the clock tells me my favorite part of the day is about to begin. The hiss of the doors opening followed by the sound of passing cars and a stream of voices and laughter confirms the time.

I turn to watch as a group of kids from Savanna's House, the orphanage, walk into the gym. That place has become my brother and best friend's pride and joy. The happiness and well-being of these kids means everything to Kyle. Secretly, it's the one project I'm most proud of. We did the right thing by these kids.

My sister brings up the rear of the group. It's Emma's turn to bring them down to the gym every Tuesday and Friday. When her eyes dance around the gym, I chuckle to myself.

I know exactly why she so graciously volunteered to be their twice-a-week chaperone. My sister has a big crush on one of my trainers. Andres has been with me for two years now. He broke his collarbone in an MMA match and decided to become a trainer after.

He was a great fighter. The break just didn't seem like it was ever going to heal right. When he came here, he blended into the family. Still, I think my sister wants to make him a bigger part of our lives.

I chuckle again and shake my head as I saunter over to where she stands staring at Andres's back. Tugging at a strand of her long dark hair, I grab her attention. Those bright gray eyes that are so much like mine swing my way.

"You're going to cause one of my fighters to slip in that puddle if you don't stop your drooling," I tease.

"Shut up, Beau," she hisses and pouts.

After wrapping an arm around her shoulder, I give a gentle squeeze. I love my little sister. We've been through a ton of ups and downs, but we know we can count on each other. I'd give my life for her happiness. "I've never seen you shy about a thing in your life. What's it about him that has you twisted up in knots?"

"Ugh, really? Am I that obvious? Maybe I should stop coming so often. I could switch out with Andy," she rambles nervously.

It's cute. A hint of her Southern accent flares up. Daddy used to tease that she'd be the one to become a true New Yorker. My smile wobbles a little as thoughts of my father creep in.

"You own the place. You're welcomed here anytime you want," I reply as I nudge those feelings back.

"I'm part owner, and we both know you do all the work to keep this place going. It's your life blood," she says, looking at me with those sad eyes.

I know what she's thinking. I know that look like the back of my hand. I'm not in a good place to think or talk about why I won't get back in the ring to do more than train a few fighters and some kids.

Speaking of kids, I turn to the group and give them a once-over. I don't discriminate. Boys and girls alike have entered this gym, and we train them just the same. That goes for the group of kids that signed up to come down here from the orphanage.

My focus falls on Mason. My nephew. Well, technically he's Kyle's nephew, but since Kyle is my adopted brother, Mas is my nephew in my book. I dare anyone to say differently.

My lips twitch with a smile as I see what has Mason's concentration. Or should I say who. Billy.

Her little sad almond-shaped brown eyes and pretty brown face have captured Mason's attention in full. She's a tough little girl. Billy is the epitome of why we started Savanna's House. She needed a safe place in her life. Her short eight years have made her a little fighter. The kids call her a tomboy, but all I see is a little girl who says what she feels and does what comes naturally to her.

"Yo, Andres. I'm here," Billy calls, ignoring everyone else.

You would think she owns the place. She's taken a liking to Andres. Her hard shell started to crack when I introduced her to boxing. However, the day Andres took her and the others into the cage to talk about mixed martial arts, her face lit up like never before.

"I just love her," Emma says beside me. "I want a home and family for all of the kids, but I really want something special for her."

"Yeah, you and Mas both," I say, nodding to our nephew who follows Billy at a distance.

Mason's not going to join her lesson. He's there to protect. It's been interesting to watch this new development. Mason is now eight, but his perception of others is profound. I truly believe he sees Billy's vulnerability that she tries to hide from others. He wants to be her friend and protector.

"So it's not just me?" Emma giggles. "Look at him."

"Nope, not just you at all. I've been watching."

Mason picks up a rope a few feet from where Billy and Andres stand. He starts to jump rope as he keeps an eye on his friend. At least Mason wants to be friends. Billy hasn't been very receptive of any of the friendships she's been offered by the other kids.

"Remember when Kyle was just like her?" Emma asks.

"Yeah." I nod. "I was sure we were going to bump heads forever."

"It didn't take long for him to warm up to us. I think she'll come around too," Emma muses.

"Not too sure about that one." I snort and turn to look at Emma. "You hanging around to wait?"

"Yeah." She nods. "I'm going to hit the weight room. Why not take advantage of the free membership?"

"Sure, just so happens Fridays are the days Andres takes Billy into the weight room."

"It's Friday?" she says and strolls away.

I shake my head and turn my attention to the kids who are waiting on me. As I watch them talk among themselves, flexing their muscles and shadow boxing, a surge of energy hits me. I may be sleep-deprived, but I'm making it through the day. These guys are going to help me sprint through my afternoon.

"All right, guys." I clap my hands together. "You know the deal. Drills."

I laugh at the mix of groans, mumbles, and cheers. I was the same way when I was their age. Eventually it all becomes a part of breathing. Like Emma said. This place is in my life's blood. I can see it will be the same for a few of these guys as well.

Angel

Soaked to the bone, I've been pacing in front of the back door to the gym Andres works in. It's pouring. Rain has been falling in sheets, beating down around me, but I haven't committed to calling on my brother yet again.

"Make a choice, Angel," I chide myself.

I need an actual shower and something other than a street dog to eat. I didn't want to come to him. It's been a week since I left his place in the middle of the night.

I know I said I'd come check in with him, but the texts he sent me the next morning left me feeling like I needed to give him time. I know he's getting fed up with this. I'm getting tired of it.

We're twenty-eight. Life should be shaping itself into something that promises a future by now. I think in Andres's head, because we're identical, we should have the same life. He was so pissed with me when I joined the Marines. In high school, all Andres could talk about was going pro in the ring. Boxing and MMA were his life.

"We're going to take them by storm, *hermano*," he would say with that gleam in his eyes.

"Yeah, sure we will."

That was always my reply. I wanted to box, but I didn't want to make a career out of it like our father had after marrying our mom. I wanted to be a Marine like Papi. That was what I admired most about our dad.

I thought being a Marine would prove I was a man. Yeah, I'm good with my hands, but to be a hero? I thought being a hero would take that look out of Papi's eyes.

I shake my head and bounce on my toes. I'm not going to fall down that rabbit hole. I'm out of money until next week, and I lost the key to Andres's apartment. He's going to have a baby about that one. I'll pay for new locks when my check comes in.

"*Coño*," I mumble, hitting send on my phone. I purse my lips at the device. It was a "gift" from Andres. More like he made me promise to take it so he'd at least be able to always keep in contact with me. I'm not mad that he wants to keep tabs. I'm furious that he spent so much to do so.

I don't know how long I'm standing there before the back door opens and Andres pops his head out. He looks just like me. Long dark hair, whiskey-brown eyes, and full lips that give us the biggest smile when we choose to show it. We both take after Papi.

Although our red-clay skin is a mix of our Puerto Rican mother and half-African-American, half-Puerto-Rican dad.

Angel and Andres: we look just alike, but we're like night and day. My mother calls me the defiant twin.

"Get in here, man," Andres grumbles.

I look up at the sky that has opened with no mercy. Lightning flashes, and something inside me shifts as I blink through the raindrops. It's my instinct to challenge what's before me.

I ball my fists and head into the gym as my brother opens the door wider. The warmth of the place massages my bones and seeps into my muscles as soon as I step inside. I drop my duffel bag to my side and turn to my brother.

He has that look on his face. The one that I hate seeing. Like his big brother failed him. I'm older by an entire ten minutes, but at the moment, he makes me feel like I'm younger by ten years.

"I just need a shower and something to eat, and I'll be out of your hair," I say tightly.

"Angel," he says and sighs. "You can shower at my place anytime you need. I've told you this."

"Yeah, I know, but I lost my keys," I admit, running a hand through the front of my hair.

He groans and tosses his head back. "Come on, man. This is the third time."

"Look, I'm not doing it on purpose. When I—"

"I'm not saying you are. I know things can get a little... I get that you lose things during your episodes."

Crazy. I'm crazy. That's what he wants to say. It's what everyone thinks. Hell, I'm starting to think I am too. I've seen things I can't unsee.

I've lost friends moments after we were just joking together. Like, walking to the water pallets with Green as he talked shit about going home to get his girl pregnant on her living room floor. I teased him about doing it before her parents walked in on them since his girl still hadn't decided on the house she wanted. In the next breath, a bullet burst through his skull. He was right in the middle of his retort.

I've held others in my arms as they've taken their last breath. I've spent the night not knowing if I'd make it through to the next morning, but that last ambush…. I can't unlive that last mission.

The one right before my time served. Two hundred and ten days to go, but I didn't think I was going to make it to two hundred and nine. None of my brothers did. My team… the ones who gave their lives protecting mine and this country. Yeah, I'm fucked-up, but I'm not crazy.

"I have to lock up for the night. Why don't you go shower in the locker room? I'm going to run out and get some roti and plantains from the Jamaican spot up the block. My boss just left, so you should be cool," Andres says. He looks at my soaked duffel bag. "Come on." He waves me to follow him. "I have some things in my locker."

"Thanks, Andres."

"You're my brother. I wish there were more I could do. This shit kills me."

Emotions fill his words, delivering them tightly from his throat. This has been hard on my entire family. When I think of all the misunderstandings we've had over the years, I wish I could turn back time. I'd gladly argue over silly things at Thanksgiving dinner.

Too bad I can't stand to be in my parents' small Brooklyn home longer than ten minutes. We're a family of five, and with my sister's husband and kids and Andres's ex-wife and daughter, the place can get crowded fast. Not to mention the closed-off layout of the old house.

"If I could make this all go away, I would," I say through tight lips.

"Bro—" He spins to face me. "—I get that I'll never understand what you went through out there, but I need you to remember you have a life here. Nieces and nephews that love you, a sister and brother that are here to help you.

"Dude, I thought my life would fall apart after breaking my collarbone, and Tati filing for divorce out of the blue. I had my little girl, and I just wanted to be a good father and husband. I had no idea my wife was so unhappy," he says, looking down at his feet.

"Tati was out the door long before she walked. You were too in love to see it," I say before I can choke the words off.

"Yeah, that's my point. Sometimes it takes a push to show you life can offer you better," he says. "I've been trying to give you that push. Then again, I thought living on the streets would be that push. I mean, you're Angel. There was a time when you needed to be fly every moment of the day. This… this just isn't you."

Tears build in my eyes, but I fight them back. There are those who accept their circumstances and fall to what's handed to them, and then there's me. Standing out there in the rain tonight, I identified my battle. I just need the time to pick my weapons and scope the terrain.

"I know, Andres. I know. I just need to figure some things out. I need some place with more open space. I can't afford that in New York," I say.

"Well, your whole damn family is here. Your ass ain't moving down South or some shit. Maybe we can get a place together," he says hopefully.

I scoff. "Neither one of us can afford five-thousand-dollar rent or more for a place big enough for me to breathe in."

"Hey, it sounded good when I said it. I'm sure it would be way more."

I scan the open space of the gym. I wish I could find a loft or something that was as open as this place. Andres looks around as if reading my mind.

"I have an idea. I've been on the closing shift. When I lock up at night you can come in the back door and sleep here. The shower stalls are huge. Man, your freak-outs… you know what I mean. You can chill here…."

"Yeah, I get you," I say, staring at the ring.

My mind fills with what-ifs. What if I turned to boxing? What if I had a place like this to hold me down like Andres? What if this plan of his works?

Sleep. I'd sleep right in that ring.

"You sure that will be okay?" I murmur.

"As long as you're out of here by six in the morning before the boss arrives, we're good. You just said you need more space and to figure things out. Take some time here and do that. You can beat this. I know you can."

I nod, wishing I had the confidence that my brother has in me. However, it sparks a new fire inside. He's putting his job on the line. He has a little girl who he has to support.

I can't fuck this up.

CHAPTER TWO

Close Call

Angel

"Fuck," I hiss again as I rush around. I don't know how I overslept this morning. For three weeks I've been sleeping at the gym, and I'm up and out of here by 5:00 a.m. Yes, I've been sleeping.

I don't feel closed in. I don't know if it's the mirrors that give me a view of almost all the angles of the gym or the workouts before bed that actually allow me to pass out. This place has offered me a sense of peace I haven't been able to acquire in a very long time.

However, this morning I'm running behind by a half an hour. I need to clean up after myself and get out of here. I shove my blankets in the locker Andres assigned me and close it.

I look around for anything I may have left out of place. I don't have my usual time to double-check. Grumbling with frustration, I toss on my hoodie and head for the back door. However, when I get to the door, keys jingle in the lock.

I don't panic.

I go into Marine mode. I have two choices: stand here and get caught or double back for the front door and slip out once whoever is on the other side of this door disarms the alarm.

Andres could be in so much trouble for this. I have a key to the place and the code to the alarm. I've kept the key on a string around my neck so I won't lose it. I once thought that would be my biggest worry. I always leave an hour early so this would never happen.

I move stealthily to the front of the gym and hide in the shadows. Heavy footfalls enter the gym, and the back door closes with a loud slam that makes me flinch. I grit my teeth to keep my mind from throwing me onto a battlefield and in the center of the war zone in my head.

"I don't know who you think you're fooling with the bullshit," the guy says with a heavy Southern accent.

His voice is rich and deep. The hairs on my arms stand at attention and my belly tightens. I'm surprised that I take notice of the sexy timbre of his voice. It's been so long since I've had interest in anyone. My life hasn't been in the greatest order to think about starting a relationship or even a casual fuck—something I'm not that big on anyway.

"Whatever you say," he scoffs.

I hold my breath as he comes to the front of the gym and unlocks the door. I'm out of sight, but all it would take is one slight turn to the left, and he would see me in my hiding space. Luckily, he's too engrossed in his call.

I wait until he enters the back office before heading the few feet to the front entrance. I'm out of the door faster than I can take my next breath. I take about three steps before colliding with a tall brunette.

"Hey, you," she coos. "You can't stay away from this place can you? I get why Beau values you so much."

It takes me a few seconds to realize she thinks I'm Andres. Knowing she had to have seen me coming out of the gym, I think fast. I don't want to say the wrong thing and fuck this all up after getting out of the gym without Andres's boss seeing me.

She's pretty with her dark hair and gray eyes. Definitely among my brother's many types. I get the feeling Andres is her type as well from the way she's batting her lashes and the blush that stains her cheeks.

Fuck. Oh hell nah. I'm not about to flirt with this chick.

"What are you doing here this early?" she asks when I don't reply right away.

"Needed to pick something up. Hey, talk later. I got to go."

I realize after the words are out and her face falls that I may have said that pretty harshly. Yeah, just my luck I'd encounter some chick my brother's involved with. What's done is done.

If I try to say any more, I know I'll blow this. I need to get out of here before anyone else who knows Andres comes along. It wouldn't take long to tell the difference between the two of us if I have to interact for more than a minute.

I step around her quickly and take off before she can say another word. Damn, I hope I didn't cause a problem. I've been the most relaxed I've been in two years while staying in the gym at night.

Time to figure shit out, Angel.

Beau

Hearing the front door of the gym close, I walk back out to the main area. I ignore Kyle droning in my ear to smile as Emma walks through the door. That smile falls at the look of confusion and disappointment on her face.

"Hey, Kyle, let me call you back," I say into the phone.

"Always avoiding the hard topics. You called me about the dreams. I'm just telling you what I think. You miss the ring," he replies.

"No, that's not it. I mean, Em just walked in the gym. She looks…. I'll call you back," I repeat.

"Let me know if she needs me," Kyle says, going into big-brother mode.

"Got you." I hang up.

I walk over to her, and she looks up at me. I tense, ready to beat the shit out of someone for upsetting her.

Emma is always full of humor and life. Seeing her like this raises the hairs on the back of my neck. "You okay? What's going on, darlin'?"

She gives me a weak smile. "It's nothing. Just a lot on my plate. Kyle's schedule seems more busy now than it ever was when he played ball," she says and shrugs. "I think I'm just nervous about the wedding and making sure everything is just the way Kyle and Andy want it."

Emma has been Kyle's personal assistant since she decided college wasn't a fit for her. She's a bright girl, maybe too bright. School just didn't call to her. She's been happier helping Kyle keep his life in order.

"Um, sure. Now tell me the truth," I say.

"It's nothing. Let's get to planning this bachelor party. I have a ton of things for you to look at," she says, waving me off and heading for my office.

I reach for her arm, causing her to turn. Searching her eyes, I try to read her for the source of the hurt I see. She shuts down, locking me out.

"You know I'm always here when you need me," I say.

"Yeah, I know. Trust me, this is nothing. Just me being naïve." She shrugs.

I go to make a comment, but I know my sister. I'll give her space to deal with her feelings first. When she needs me, she'll let me know. Still I tug her into a hug before I release her and lead her to my office.

CHAPTER THREE

Beau

"No!"

I jump out of my sleep, bellowing into my darkened bedroom. As usual, I'm covered in sweat, my chest heaves, and I'm gasping for air. I run a hand through my damp hair and close my eyes.

That's a mistake. I pop my lids back open to erase the images trapped behind them. The ring, the blood on my hands, the body, it's always the same. Pain sears through my chest. I draw my knees in, wrapping my arms around them. I start to rock back and forth, trying to find the comfort that will never come.

"I'm sorry," I breathe out. "I should've protected you better."

The pain threatens to consume me. I need to get out of here. The room feels like it's trying to cave in on me. I toss the sheets and climb my exhausted body from the bed.

Finding a pair of shorts and a T-shirt, I throw them on and shove my feet in a pair of runners. With my keys, phone, and wireless earbuds in hand, I make my way out of my apartment. A run should help me fight these demons back.

I pound the pavement as Brett Eldredge croons "Go on Without Me" in my ears. My face is wet with a mix of sweat and tears, but I keep pushing. I try to get lost in the words of the song and the run. When the song changes to Snow Patrol's "Chasing Cars," something inside me breaks. It's speaking to my soul.

Memories of lying on the canvas beside Roman flood my brain. He was gone. There was nothing anyone could do to bring him back. I just needed to be there, to lie there and beg to go with him. As if my heart could just stop beating in the center of that ring.

It still feels as if it did. When I walked out of that ring, my heart didn't come with me. We'd been dating for four years. Roman was my first love. He gave me the confidence to be in a relationship and own it. Before Roman, I questioned everything. I fell in love with his carefree attitude. I grind my teeth against my thoughts.

I don't know why all of this has started to surface so strongly now. I thought things were finally getting better. I don't want to believe it's what Kyle thinks.

"Maybe the ring isn't done with you. It could be calling you to deal with the past so you can return where you belong," he suggested.

"That's not going to happen," I replied. "Besides, I'm twenty-nine, going on thirty. That ship has sailed."

"If you say so," Kyle said knowingly.

When I look up at the sign to my gym, I wonder if Kyle was so wrong. I hadn't realized my feet were leading me here. Now that I'm here, it's like I'm itching to be in the ring, but I know in my heart that's not going to happen. That's a bitter pill I don't want to swallow.

So much has changed. Kyle has a family. It seems like Javier has been throwing himself into the club more, as he talks of wanting to retire soon. I can't even think of what the world of baseball will be like without him.

Everyone else is either busy with their careers or family lives. Some have both. *Careers.*

Sometimes it's hard to watch my friends in their success. Not because I don't want it for them, but because they're out there. They're pursuing what they love.

"I don't have that option," I snort, pulling out the keys to the gym.

Angel

I should've known my peace wouldn't last for long. The gym has been a place of comfort for weeks, but tonight nothing has worked to settle my nerves. Something just feels off.

The mirrors that give me a panoramic view of my surroundings have done little to calm me the way they usually do. If anything they may have heightened my anxiety.

It seems they've rearranged sections on the gym floor, obstructing my view at certain angles. Shadows that weren't there in the past now lurk, throwing me off. The lights seem to hit the mirrors in a way they haven't before.

As a combat engineer, it was my responsibility to take care of roadside bombs. The reflection of light keeps triggering a memory I'd rather forget. For hours I've kept looking and waiting for some hidden threat to come storming in.

They were just teenaged boys, but they were coming at us hard and fast. We didn't have time to assess their age; they were a threat. It was only moments after I'd just defused a bomb blocking our passage and seconds before another was detonated.

I still have that sick feeling in the pit of my stomach from after it was all said and done. I couldn't bring those boys back, and I couldn't stop them from making the choices that lead them to lie at our feet, lifeless. Yet I felt the relief of not losing my life or, better yet, one of my brothers that had my back. At least we didn't lose anyone that day.

I've struggled to keep visions of that day away tonight. I tried to use the gym to my advantage. Working out to the point of exhaustion. First, I started on the weights. Then I moved to the heavy bag to punch myself out. All I did was work up a sweat.

Sure, my body is exhausted, but my mind is still racing with a jumble of thoughts and anxiety. I'm even more on edge than when I first started the workout. I drag my tired bones into the locker room for a shower.

Stepping under the warm spray, I welcome the steaming water as it beats down on my skin. Pulling the tie from my hair, it falls around my shoulders. I adjust the water to cool it down just a bit.

When I release the knob, I stare at the tremor in my hand. The feeling of drowning takes over me. My airway tightens, and I try to swallow past the knot building in my throat.

"I can't keep going like this," I push out, wanting to sob, but not knowing how to release the emotions.

Instead I let my head fall forward against the shower tiles. Reality sets in. This isn't the life I wanted for myself. This isn't the life I'm going to allow myself to keep living. I have to find a way to get through this... no... I need to get over it.

Just like me and my brothers got over so much shit together. I have to do it for them, because I'm the only one still breathing. I have to figure out how to live again. If not for me, for them.

But how?

I close my eyes and let that question ring in my head. I have to find an answer, and I have to find it soon. I have to get out of here before I cost my brother his job.

Suddenly, I stiffen. Someone moves behind me. My gut tells me it's not Andres.

Beau

I guess I subconsciously knew I'd end up here. After unlocking the doors, I push inside and turn the alarm off. My brows draw; a few things are off.

Some of the lights have been left on in the back of the gym. The locker room is illuminated, and light is shining out from the staff break room. Andres should've turned out all of the lights when he locked up this evening.

As I move farther into the gym, there are blankets and pillow in the center of the ring. My fists ball at my sides, and every muscle coils for a fight. It's clear someone's camping out here inside of my gym.

Yet the alarm was on from the inside. That doesn't make sense. My mind shifts through a million scenarios as I move toward the back of the gym.

The sound of one of the showers running pulls my attention, causing me to head into the locker room first. I step inside the shower stalls and freeze. There's a guy standing beneath the spray with water crusading down his back. His head is bent and pressed to the wall as long locks of dark hair fall in sheets around his shoulders.

At first glance I would have called out Andres's name, but I pause as the water slides down over the intricate tattoo on this guy's back. The man standing before me is a Marine. The eagle, globe, and anchor tattoo that spreads across his shoulders, down to the center of his back, tells me that much.

I've seen Andres shirtless in the gym a million times. He doesn't have a tat on his back. Yet this guy has Andres's build, long thick hair, and the same red-clay-colored skin.

As if sensing me behind him, he turns abruptly. His stance screams that he's ready for a fight. I, on the other hand, stumble back in shock. Now that he's facing me, I'm stunned. I know this is not my employee, Andres, but he looks just like him.

"Fuck," he blows out, reaching for a towel to wrap his waist.

Once covered, he throws his head back and pushes a hand through his hair as if he's in prayer. I shake off the shock and fold my arms across my chest. When he looks back at me with those whiskey-colored eyes, identical to his brother's, something shifts in the air. I ignore the feeling and get right to the point.

"Get dressed and call your brother. He has some explaining to do."

CHAPTER FOUR

Family

Beau

Ten minutes ago Andres stormed through the front doors, looking as if he just rolled out of bed. I stood in front of his brother with my arms folded over my chest. His brother who has dressed in jeans and a T-shirt and perched his big body on the side of the ring. For almost thirty minutes we waited in a tense silence for Andres to arrive.

"I'm so sorry, man," Andres says for the millionth time since his arrival five minutes ago.

I still can't get over how much these two look alike, down to the dimples in their cheeks. I'm six three, Andres has to be an inch shorter than me, but his brother, on the other hand, meets me eye to eye. If I look closer, I can see other little differences.

Mostly in their demeanor. There's something intriguing about Angel.

Angel.

He sure does look like an angel. If you think of angels as gorgeous, brooding avengers. At least that's what comes to mind when I look at this one. Those long, dark, thick lashes frame his mysterious eyes, completing his handsome face.

"Listen, this isn't on Andres. I'm having a hard time, and he's trying to help me out," he says.

"Explain this to me. Why are you living inside my gym?"

Angel runs a hand through his damp locks and blows out a breath. So many emotions run across his face, causing me to wonder if he'll answer. Andres seems to look like he's not going to be the one to furnish me with an answer. He looks to his twin with sorrow in his eyes.

"I'm a vet. My last mission left me a little fucked-up in the head. I have a hard time remaining in tight spaces for too long. Andres's place is too... I can't be confined there. Work has been hard to come by because of my episodes," Angel says after a beat.

"He's been living on the streets, man. This is my brother. I know I should've said something, but this was the first time in two years I've seen him look so rested. It was working. He's been sleeping," Andres adds.

"Yeah, until tonight," Angel mutters to himself. Then he raises his voice for us to clearly hear him again. "I've felt safe enough in my own skin to sleep for a few hours. This was only temporary until I could figure my shit out and get my head together. Listen, don't punish my brother for this—"

I hold up my hand to cut him off. My jaw works. I know what it's like to just need a break from your own mind. Listening to Angel, something tugs on the inside of me.

It's as if I want to help him because I don't know how to help myself. Selfishly, I want to offer him a reprieve to somehow redeem myself and get the peace I need to get rest. Or at least, that's what I try to tell myself as my thoughts drive me to make a couple of swift decisions.

Decisions that are so unlike me. I don't trust people easily, but as my gaze sweeps over Angel, something tells me to have faith that he'll be as honorable as his brother has been up until now. I should be pissed at Andres, but I'm not. I would've done the same for Kyle or Emma, no matter the cost. I know they'd do the same for me.

"Family is important. You should've come to me. I thought I made it clear that you're family around here," I say.

"Yeah, you have always treated me like family. I just didn't know what to say," Andres replies.

"I'll get my things and head out," Angel says.

"Now hold on a minute. I didn't say you had to go."

Angel

That voice and drawl. The hairs have been standing up on the back of my neck since he found me in the shower and told me to call my brother. Beau is a fine-ass man. Those gray eyes and that dark hair are just the tip of the iceberg.

He's paler than my usual type, but it compliments his eyes and dark hair. A low beard highlights his full lips. The T-shirt he has on stretches across taut muscles, revealing a fit body beneath. His running shorts showcase long legs with a slight bow to his right one.

This dude is a fucking collision begging to happen. I've tried not to think about that. Especially given the circumstances. Something in the way his gaze has lingered on me makes me question if he might swing for the same team.

I shove those thoughts back to focus on the words he just drawled out. I cock a brow. Surely he didn't just offer for me to stay here.

"I'm not following," I say.

"Andres is family. That makes you family. You said you need some time to figure things out. Now that the shock of finding you here has worn off, I want to find solutions," he replies.

"I don't want to be a burden, man."

"You won't be. You'll work for your keep," he replies. "You're Marine?"

"I am," I nod and narrow my eyes.

He nods, and I can almost see the wheels turning in his head. My body is tense with apprehension. I'm not going to make any assumptions, and I'm too frustrated with the situation to get my hopes up.

"I've been looking for a replacement for the self-defense class. Kimberly's pregnant. She let me know a few weeks ago that she'll be leaving."

"I noticed she hasn't been as hands-on in her classes," Andres muses.

"Yeah, I had a feeling it was coming sooner rather than later after her wedding," Beau says and shrugs. "The classes are three times a week. If you want to take over for her, the job is yours."

"You're giving me a job?" I ask with my brows furrowed.

"That I am. There's also a loft upstairs. We used to use it as a private training room. You can check it out and see if it's open enough for you," he replies. "Not sure if it will offer what you need, but the space is pretty open. If not, you do what you need."

He leaves his statement open as if to say I have the run of the place if I need it. I'm blown away. I was sure he was going to fire Andres and call the cops on me for trespassing or something.

"That's a great idea," Andres says to Beau before I can react. He turns to me. "Maybe this is the break you needed. This place is so laid-back."

"I need time to think about it," I blurt out to stop my brother before he gets ahead of himself.

"Think about it? He's offering you a place and a job. What do you need to think about?"

I give him a sharp look. He knows me better than this. I don't know this guy, and he has no reason to help me out like this.

"It's okay, Andres. Teaching self-defense can be challenging. If he's not up for it…." Beau says. There's a taunting note to his voice. He's setting a challenge for me as if he knows me well enough to know I'll take it. Something about the sparkle in is gray eyes has my mouth moving before my brain can catch up.

"I'll do it."

A ghost of a smile turns up Beau's lips as Andres slaps me on the shoulder. I ignore my brother as I tilt my head in curiosity. I'm even more fascinated by this dude.

However, that all takes a back seat when it hits me. I have a job, and I get to stay in the one place that has offered me some sense of peace for the first time in longer than I want to remember. This is where the real fight begins.

I have a shot to make this right. Now it's up to me.

CHAPTER FIVE

Chemistry

Angel

"Hey, Hernández."

I turn to one of the other guards as I stand outside of Club Refuge.

"Javi wants to see you inside."

I nod and start into the club, wondering why someone didn't just relay the message through my earpiece. I look around the place as I move to the private area my boss is supposed to be in tonight. I still can't believe that within a week I got two jobs, not just one.

Over the last month, I've continued to question why Beau has gone out of his way to help me. The self-defense classes and the chance to stay at the gym were just the beginning. Not that those were such small offerings.

Beau informed me and my brother that we would have to keep things quiet about my living arrangements until he could get a certificate of occupancy for the second level at the gym. The gym is zoned to be a commercial space. To convert the second level would change the upper floor into a residential space, which requires new certificates and zoning.

Not that I stay up there much. There's something about sleeping in the center of the boxing ring on the main level that soothes my soul. I haven't had trouble sleeping as much as that one night. After finding out that I'd lost comfort in the gym because of the shift in the setup, Beau had it all returned to the way it had been when I first started staying there.

Yet Beau still has had a contractor come in to add a bathroom and kitchenette to the second level. He has also applied for the permits for me to legally occupy the space. I mean, I don't even know how long I plan to stay, but he has insisted that this is something he had already planned to do.

I call bullshit.

I've been observing Beau Dalton closely. He works hard and cares about the people who come into his gym. When he talks to you, he gives you his full attention. I always get the sense that he's looking through to the core of me, not at me. Not just with me. I've seen him do the same with so many others.

Which is why I shouldn't have been shocked when he handed me a card and told me to go see his friend. I didn't put two and two together until I stood in front of Javier Salvado. Javier Salvado, the baseball player.

Man, that was the shock of my life. I had to fight not to fan out. My family is as big on baseball as we are on boxing.

Turns out Javier needed a few new guys for security at his club. Several things about this job offer have surprised me. The first one being the extensive background check and amount of paperwork I had to sign.

I seriously think I signed an NDA for each level of the interview and hiring process. Call me crazy, but four NDAs seemed extreme to me. Once I started my first day of work, I began to understand why. While I mostly work the front door, I've seen enough to observe the fact that this isn't your ordinary run-of-the-mill club.

"Hey, Angel," a guy dressed in pink chaps and a corset purrs.

Reaching out he slips something in my pocket as I pass. It's not the first time someone has done this. At the end the night I've found tips, lube packets, and condoms in my suit jackets. This guy usually gives me the latter two.

"How you doing?" I nod and keep it moving.

"I'd be better if I spent the rest of the night with you, gorgeous," he calls after me.

I grin but don't turn to entertain the comment. He's a decent-looking guy, but not my type. Besides, I'm working. I'm not here for pleasure.

It's funny how everyone seems to already know me by name. At first I thought this place was just a sex club. By my second night, I realized it's a queer country club with extras—yeah, sex club. My suspicions were confirmed on my fourth night of work.

This place is a private getaway for the elite of the elite that just might not want the world to know their secrets. My gaydar has always been pretty stellar. I guess in my case, I know my reflection.

I haven't been surprised by a single guest I've come across here. I smile as I walk past a famous black actress and her voluptuous Latina dance partner that looks awfully familiar to me. Two gorgeous women. Neither here for the men. Not that they'd get much male attention here anyway. Most nights there are only guys here. Tonight seems to be a special night, though, from the guests I've seen arrive and the size of the crowd.

I can't help but smile when Javier comes into view, sitting in a small group at his private booth. He's a real down-to-earth guy. Everything about him has been genuine. He makes me feel like family just as much as they do at the gym.

"Here he is," Javier croons, causing me to come to a dead stop.

My gaze lands on Beau and I'm slammed with surprise. When it comes to Beau, I've been telling myself that I'm not catching the vibes. That I've only been wishful thinking.

Seeing him here, in the middle of this club could change everything, because if I'm honest, I have a thing for my other boss. He's at the top of my list for reasons why I enjoy my day job. That drawl is something I look forward to hearing each day.

My stomach coils with heat as his gray eyes land on me. It's as if everyone else disappears from the club. His gaze is heavy with appraisal.

He looks good tonight. It's the first time I've seen him in something other than workout clothes. The gray suit and black dress shirt cause his eyes to look sharper, more striking. His easy aura fills the space and draws me in.

That is until another guy at their table leans in and whispers something in his ear. He's an old, nice-looking guy. With a frown I don't bother to suppress, I turn to Javier. I force my feet to continue moving in his direction.

"You need me for something?"

"Beau here was asking after you," Javier says with a grin on his lips.

I become hyperaware of Beau's presence. Not like before when our eyes locked. No, this time when I face him it's as if we're having a silent conversation.

Still, I don't understand our dialect just yet. I think I'm still in denial. Or it could be that I don't want to be wrong. From the way our eyes are trained on each other, I know I've been right about Beau from the start. I never miss, and this hasn't been the exception I've tried to convince myself of.

"I just wanted to make sure things were working out for you. I didn't mean for Javi to disturb your night," Beau finally says.

"It's cool. It's been pretty quiet out front," I reply.

I pause in thought once the words are out. I've been on the door since we opened for the night. Of all of the A-listers and guests that came through, Beau didn't pass me. I look around at Javi's table, and none of the men sitting here did. They had to arrive before opening, or they came through some other entrance I'm unaware of.

"Take a load off for a few," Javier offers.

"I should probably get back," I say, jiggling my work keys in my pocket.

I'm starting to feel a bit cagey as I stand here. I'd rather be out front. There are too many rooms, too many unknowns within this place. The sweat on the back of my neck proves I'm overstaying my welcome as it is.

"Nonsense—"

"Leave him be." Beau glances at Javier. "This place isn't for everyone."

I feel a surge of jealousy as I think of why Beau is here tonight. His words feel like salt in my open wounds. Not wanting to dig too deeply into those feelings, I shove them back, fisting my hands on my pockets.

"I'll get out of your hair. You all have a good night," I say more tightly than I mean to.

Beau

"I think he's gay," Javier says as Angel moves back toward the front of the club.

He looks damn good in that suit. He's dressed in all black like the rest of the security staff, but Angel pulls it off like a model on the cover of a magazine. My fingers itch to pull the band from his hair to watch it tumble over his shoulders.

Not happening, Dalton.

I haven't dated in six years. I don't plan to start now. I try to push my newest obsession from my mind, but I can't seem to tear my eyes from his retreating form.

"I know he is, and if he isn't, I'm pretty damn sure he would be for Beau," Darwin says at my side.

"I told you both, I don't care if he's gay. I'm not interested," I mumble.

"Bullshit," Javier says. "I just watched you eye fuck him in front of all of us. Or did you forget we were here?"

"I don't know what you're talking about."

"Honey, please. I had to fight to not fan myself. You two were sending sparks and flames back and forth with just your eyes. For a minute there, I thought he was going to break my neck for whispering to you," Darwin says with too much joy in his voice.

Leave it to Darwin. For as long as I've known Dar, he's made it his mission to be a matchmaker. Not sure why I expected this to be any different.

Leaning forward for my scotch, I think back to the look on Angel's face. Maybe they're right, but I'm not ready to start a relationship. Besides, Angel is now one of my employees, and he lives in the gym.

Nope, I'll be keeping my distance.

"You'll have to live again someday," Javier says more seriously.

"I'm living," I reply.

"No, you're surviving. You, my friend, haven't lived in six years. You have a thing for Latin men. I say Angel is the universe dropping a sign in your lap that it's okay to move on," he says.

"This conversation is over."

"Fine, but you won't be able to avoid this forever. Trust me, life has a way of kicking in doors when it's time for change," my friend warns.

I don't reply. The only thing kicking my door in is a nightmare I can't seem to stop having. The last thing I need is the complication of a relationship with someone that seems to have just as much shit going on in his life, if not more.

"He's gay," Darwin says one last time.

I scoff and take a sip of my drink. I make my mind up here and now. Gay or not, Angel is off-limits.

CHAPTER SIX

A Night Out

Beau

"You've been avoiding the gym. Is there a reason why?" I say into the phone to my sister as I spray on cologne before walking out of my bathroom.

"I've been busy with the wedding and helping Kyle and Andy get settled into the new place," she replies.

I can hear it in her voice. Something is off. I think back to that morning almost two months ago when something had clearly upset her. She never did cough up what was going on, and she hasn't been back to the gym since now that I think about it.

I've been pretty busy with the gym reno and some other ventures I'm thinking about getting involved in, but I've noticed she hasn't been the one to bring the kids down. She's been getting everyone to cover for her. That's not like my sister. If she commits to something, she's committed.

I normally would wait her out. However, I have this feeling something has been going on with my sister. Running the place may not be her thing—you don't get much more of a silent partner—but once she devoted her time to the kids, she's been there.

"Did something happen I should know about?"

"No," she says, but her voice betrays her whether she knows it or not. "Beau, I'm fine. I truly have been busy with the wedding. I'll get back to my usual schedule in a few weeks."

"I hope so. You bringing the kids down has been a part of their routine. They need that," I say.

She gives a heavy sigh. Maybe I shouldn't lay the guilt trip on so thick, but I'm sensing a lot of what my sister isn't saying. I figured mentioning the kids would at least get her to open up.

"Yeah, I know," she says softly. Another red flag. This isn't my sister. "I'll be back to my old schedule as soon as I wrap a few things up."

"I'll see you at Mama's this weekend at least?"

"Of course," she says, the real Emma coming through this time. "She's making chili, and I promised Mas I'd pick him up and take him over."

I make a mental note. It's something at the gym that has ruffled her feathers. I'll be having a talk with Andres. After all, he's the reason she decided to spend so much time at the gym in the first place.

"I'm looking forward to that chili," I laugh, patting my stomach, hoping to keep her in this better mood.

"You and me both," she says. "What are you up to tonight?"

"Javier's having a little get-together at the club."

"The club again. That's the fourth time this week. You've been going there a lot more than usual."

I'm officially talking to my sister, Emma. I can hear the mischief in her voice come across the line. Looking at my reflection in the mirror, I let her words sink in.

I have to question the extra effort I just put into dressing in a pair of jeans and a T-shirt. This is a more casual event, and I've questioned my choice a million times. Blazer, no blazer. Stetson, no Stetson. I don't know what's gotten into me.

"You should come out," I say to avoid the probing I feel coming.

"I haven't been to the club in so long. That actually sounds like fun."

"Last I heard, Kyle and Andy might be there. It's more of an intimate set up. I don't see why you shouldn't come," I reply.

"Awesome. I'll meet you there. I swear Tara has taken over being bridezilla for Andy. I could totally use a drink." She laughs.

"Use the underground entrance. The front won't be open since it's all family tonight," I inform her.

"Got it. I'll come through the Batcave," she says.

I snort. "See you later."

I hang up and run my hand through my hair. Emma is right. I've been spending way more time at Club Refuge. I try to convince myself it's because I want to have a better social life and get out more, but I know that's a lie.

I've started to enter through the front door whenever I go, which is something I've never done before. I do now for one reason and one reason only. That look on Angel's face whenever I show up.

It's a mix of surprise and... irritation? Almost as if my being there makes him jealous. At first I'd started to enter the club through the general entrance just to see Angel in his suits, but that look. It drew my curiosity and has only continued to do so.

Tonight's event was Javier's idea. Having an understanding that Angel isn't too big on crowds and tight spaces, he stopped trying to get him to join us at our booth at the club. Instead Javier had the main dance floor on the first level set up for a private event tonight.

With the open views and wide space, it's Javi's hope that Angel will accept the offer to hang out. He also gave him the night off but asked him to stop by to pick up his check and have a talk.

Leave it to Javi to come up with an elaborate plan even after I told him I'm not interested in dating. I'm quite sure Darwin is in on this one as well. I still don't know why I'm going along with it.

"This is a very bad idea," I blow out.

Angel

"You've done a great job here over the last month. I like your style. The guys speak highly of you as well. This could be great for you," Javier says with a smile. "If you want to take your time and think about it, go ahead."

"It's a great offer. I could use that kind of money. I'm just not sure if it's for me." I've adapted to being a bouncer here at the club. I like it. It's been a good way for me to get to know the other guys and ease my way back into some semblance of a normal life.

Still, I'm not ready to take this kind of leap. Thirty grand per gig to travel with Javier as well as getting to see games would've been my dream job three or four years ago. Today, I have too many demons riding my back.

"Just think about it," he repeats.

"I will," I say, clenching and unclenching my fist.

This could open so many doors. I can get a place that I can breathe in. I'd be confronting my anxiety instead of allowing it to cripple me.

Yet this is a man's life, and that's where my hesitation lies. I don't know if I can be responsible for another life just yet. Not like this. Being a bouncer, a gatekeeper, keeping danger out, that's one thing. Taking on sole responsibility for another human being, I can't do that.

I can't fail another mission.

The voices and yells of my fallen brothers start to fill my head. My vision blurs. I'm sinking into my past quickly just from thinking about this offer.

Walking through the small town, it's hot and we all can't wait to get back to camp. A group of kids runs by laughing and playing. I smile. Suddenly, a herd of goats ahead grab my attention.

A few of my guys are only a few feet away from the herd. "Goat, goat. On your six, there's a bomb on that fucking goat. Johnson, move, move, move!"

I grab the small girl wandering away from the other kids in the direction of the goats. I shield her with my body as the bomb explodes, thrusting me and the girl in my arms forward.

"Angel." Javier calls my name sharply.

My gaze clears and he comes back into focus. Releasing my hands from their biting grip into my palms, I root myself to the here and now. I tighten my jaw and suppress the trembling that tries to take over.

"If that's all I'll get out of your hair," I say.

"Wait, what's the rush? Come down and have a beer with me," he says.

I narrow my eyes at him. Javier is a good-looking guy with his hazel eyes and pretty face, but I like him as a boss. I can see us becoming friends, maybe, but nothing more than that.

"You need to relax sometime, amigo." He grins. "I'm having only friends over tonight. Have a drink, shoot some pool. Relax."

I think about his words. It's been so long since I've kicked back, but the one word that catches my attention first is *friends*. I can't help but wonder if that includes Beau. As much as I hate the choppy layout of the VIP section Javier and Beau always seem to hang out in, I try to tell myself I can grit my way through it for just a bit to get to know more about the gray-eyed quiet storm named Beau.

"We'll be in area B," Javier says as if reading my thoughts. "Instead of a dance floor, we're using it for a few pool tables and a little dancing if anyone feels the need. It's extremely low key. Just some friends. Come on, Angel," he coaxes.

"I'll hang around for a beer," I relent.

"Magnífico, let's join the others," he says.

We make our way down to the main level, and I tell myself this is what I need. I need to get back to interacting with people, forcing myself to settle into a room and get absorbed in life.

However, the moment I step into the main area, I become absorbed in one thing. About twenty people are hanging around, but just one of them sucks me in. I only have a view of his profile, but it's enough to send my heart racing.

Beau has on a black T-shirt and fitted blue jeans. He's wearing a pair of cowboy boots, a black cowboy hat finishes the look. He's with the older dude from the first night I saw him here. His head is bent to listen to whatever the shorter, older guy is saying.

Suddenly, his head lifts, and he turns in my direction. With his eyes on me, I'm at a loss for why I shouldn't be here. All at once I dig deep to push through to find the old me. The Angel that would pull up and holler at a dude I'm interested in without a second thought.

"Come, let's get you a beer. Then we can go chat up Beau and Darwin," Javier offers.

"Cool." I nod and follow him to the bar.

With a beer in hand and my mind set on my mission, I turn to head over to the other side of the transformed dance area. I bump into Beau, those intense eyes locking with mine.

"We were just coming over to say hello," Javier says as he pulls Beau into a one-armed hug. "Angel, I want you to meet Darwin."

"Hello there," Darwin says. "Welcome to our little family."

"Nice to meet you," I reply cautiously.

"Listen, I need to steal Javi away for a bit. Why don't you two go play a game of pool? We'll catch up with you in a few," Darwin says, grabbing a hold of Javier before anyone can protest.

"Do you have time for a game?" Beau's voice vibrates through me.

I turn my attention back to him to find him watching me closely. It's the uncertainty in his eyes that makes me say yes. It's as if he's just as unsure about this as I am.

I can't help but wonder where his uncertainty comes from. From what I can see, Beau has his life together. Sure, he often looks like he could use more sleep, but up until now I've written that off as him working tirelessly for the gym and everyone whose life it touches.

Before I can place the mix of emotions that filter across his face, the shutters come down. Little does Beau know, I'm not one to back down easily. I'm just as curious about him as I am attracted. A game of pool will get me those answers I've been looking for.

"I have time," I reply.

We fall into step with each other as we move to one of the open tables. I sit my beer down and pick up a pool cue. Beau removes the rack and retrieves his own cue. I watch as he finishes his beer before sitting it down. He nods for me to break, and I get the game started.

We fall into a comfortable silence as we make it through our first game and a few rounds of beer. It's a welcomed silence. Not as awkward as it would seem for such a long period of time. Actually, it's as if our auras speak for us.

Each time our bodies move past each other, they call us closer like magnets. After a while, I begin to loosen up, looking for the right thing to say. It feels like it's been so long since I've put myself out there with anyone. I wonder if I still have it.

"How are things going?" Beau asks as we start our second game, breaking the silence.

It's a relief as his words slice through the tension that has started to build to a crackle between our bodies. I feel it. I know he has to. I wouldn't trust him if he tried to deny it.

"Pretty good. I'm not complaining," I reply as I knock two in.

"Sorry I couldn't tell you more about this place before you were hired. I hope you weren't put out," he says, eyeing me closely.

I stand up straight, place my stick on the floor, and lean in against it. I tilt my head to study Beau more closely. A smile comes to my lips as anticipation rolls off him.

"You mean all the gay shit going on around here?" I say with a straight-as-fuck face.

Beau's lips tighten, and I almost let out a laugh. His jaw works and his nostrils flare. I swear dude is about to spit fire at me.

"Maybe this isn't the place for you. I'll let Javi know you're not interested in stayi—"

"So you *haven't* figured out that I'm gay?" I laugh, reaching for my beer. I take a sip and narrow my eyes at him as he takes my words in. His entire demeanor shifts after a few beats. A small smile kicks up the right side of his mouth.

"I try not to assume things about people. I can only know what you tell me."

"I'll give you that. I appreciate all you've done for me. Javier's a good dude."

"That he is. I figured you'd make the decision for yourself about the job once you got to know him and the place," he says.

"Took a minute to figure things out fully, but I'm good. Javier is a great boss. No one causes any real trouble around here. Unless you count getting my ass pinched once or twice." I shrug.

Beau tenses up. "You should talk to Javi about that."

"It's cool. It was a regular that's been flirting. He was a little drunk the other night."

"That's no excuse. There are rules around here," Beau says tightly. He signals for another round of beers, picking up the one resting on the table to drain it.

"I'll take care of it," I say with a smile.

Beau nods. I can tell he doesn't want to let it go, but he does. I'm beginning to like the fact that he's so quick to be in my corner.

"What about the classes at the gym? Are those working out?"

"Yeah, it's cool. Some of the ladies there may not appreciate the fact that they'll never have a chance with me," I say and wink.

Beau gives a hearty laugh. The rest of the tension seems to melt away. He has a warm laugh and an infectious smile. I take a chance and walk closer to him.

"I don't want to make assumptions either. I'll come right out and ask. Do you come here just as a friend or for the lifestyle?"

"A little of both," he says with a smile.

I let my eyes roam over him from head to toe. Biting my bottom lip, I grin at him and lean in. His cologne fills my head. The energy rolling off him is so strong I can taste it on my tongue. "I don't know if I like that answer," I say.

"Oh no?" His brows lift into his hairline.

"No, I'm not into sharing."

Beau rocks back on his heels and folds his arms over his chest. My gaze is drawn to his muscles as they flex and bunch. When I force my eyes back up, his smile is now on full display. He leans a hip against the side of the pool table.

"Sharing? Looks like we jumped over an entire conversation," Beau says.

"You don't like to assume. I don't like to waste time. If I see something I want, I go after it," I reply.

"Is that right?"

"*Sí, hermoso.*" I pause and lick my lips. He's definitely beautiful. "Unless I missed something. You're feeling me too."

The heat in his eyes tells me I'm not wrong at all. I put it out there. Now the ball is in his court.

Let's see if you can accept a challenge as well as you can set one, Beau.

Beau

I should walk away. This isn't the simple flirting I'd planned on. Although Angel's forwardness is a total turn-on. From the white T-shirt that's stretched across his chest to the loose-fitting jeans and tan construction boots, we're a complete contrast of each other, but that's what draws me to him.

I love that New York edge he has. Angel is my type and so much more. Those whiskey-brown eyes have taken on a new light tonight. I like this look on him. The dark shadows still haunt him as usual, but all of that's not sitting in the forefront.

Although a bit of mischief I've never seen before sparks to life. It's a bonus that I can stand eye to eye with him to observe all of this. My gaze drops to his turned-up lips. That smile and those dimples are almost my undoing. My cock twitches in my pants as his tongue darts out to drag across his lips for the second time.

"You're asking for trouble I don't think you're ready for," I murmur, pushing off the pool table to close the distance between us.

"Trouble is all I know," he says with that heavy New York, Spanish accent.

"But let me be clear. I'm not looking for a relationship," I say. "I'm not... it's just not a good idea."

A frown rushes across his face, but he quickly shuts it down and schools his features. Features that draw me in no matter the expression. Just when I think he has changed his mind, he reaches up to snatch my Stetson off my head and places it on top of his own.

His full lips turn up higher. His eyes roll over me. Reaching to hook his finger into my belt loop, he tugs gently.

"What are you waiting for, cowboy? Come and get it," he croons low.

Placing my fingers under his chin, I tilt his head and move in for a kiss. I'm thrown the moment our lips touch. I know it sounds cliché; I want to snort as the thought pops into my head. Yet when our lips meet, sparks fly.

Angel's tongue glides across the seam of my lips, and I open for him. He goes to deepen the kiss, but I take control. After lifting a hand to curl my fingers into his thick, long locks—the way I've wanted to for so long—I shift his head for better access and devour him.

My Stetson tips off his head and lands on the pool table with a small thump, but that's not enough to stop this collision that's threatening my sanity. The mix of beer and something uniquely him favors his tongue. I groan, searching every corner, taking every breath I can. I plan to leave him breathless.

Angel hums into my mouth, making me realize it's him bouncing in place that's causing the vibration between us. At least I want to blame that for the way I'm feeling. I wrap an arm around his waist and tug him in, holding him tightly. He relaxes into my hold, lifting a hand into my hair.

I break the kiss before I lay him out on this pool table and take him right here. Placing my forehead to his, I allow us both to catch our breaths. Angel gives a small laugh.

"Damn, Papi," he pushes out.

"My place," I grunt.

"You're wasting time even saying it. Let's go," he replies.

Everything except for getting to my place is forgotten. I even manage to block out my demons with the aid of the beer I've consumed throughout the night.

CHAPTER SEVEN

Just This Once

Angel

I was a little thrown by the fact that Beau had a car waiting for him in the underground parking garage. I know he owns the gym, but I never thought about how much that place brings in. I certainly didn't think it would be the type of money that supplies a driver.

However, once in the back seat with Beau's tongue down my throat, all of that was forgotten. After all, he only wants one night. It's not my style, but this dude is not a regret I'm willing to have. I want him more with each passing second.

"Damn, you're driving me crazy," Beau grunts as I claw down his back, and he struggles to unlock his front door.

He has me pinned to the door, with one hand shoved down the back of my jeans and the other fumbling with his keys. The sound of our open belt buckles knocking against each other fills the air, pulling a laugh from my lips. Beau hisses when my nails bite into his ass as I shove his jeans down his hips and nip at his neck.

"Focus, Papi. Get us inside," I croon in his ear.

I pull back to look into his eyes. He blinks seemingly to focus. I love that I have him this dazed. I can't wait to have that gorgeous face twisted up from pleasure. I'm going to bring the Latin spice to his country ass all night.

If all I get is one, I'm going to make it worth it. As if reading my thoughts, he turns his attention to the lock and opens it quickly. We push through the entrance, joined together once again. I tug his shirt over his head and toss it behind me.

He drags my shirt up next and sends it flying through the air. Beau shifts me in a swift motion. My back hits the now-closed door, this time with us securely cloaked within his dimly lit apartment.

His lips are on me again, kissing and nipping at my chin. I love that he kisses like a starved man, taking with every caress, nip, sip. I'm used to topping, but I like this power play we're having. Beau makes me want to see where he'll take me. It excites me in a new way.

We lock lips, teasing each other with our tongues. We both toe off our shoes, causing our kisses to become sloppy and clumsy. Laughs leave both our lips, pulling me further into the comfort this man has wrapped around me.

I want to bask in the attention and security being with him provides. I feel renewed. I dare to grasp that feeling, even if it's just for tonight. It's like a lifesaver I hadn't known I needed so badly.

"Lube and condoms are in my room," he pants, flicking my chin with his tongue.

"I've got us," I reply.

He pulls back and gives me a questioning look. A smile plays on his lips. I shrug my shoulders.

"Someone slipped them in my pocket at the club. I tucked them in my wallet," I offer.

"You're making me hate the fact you work at Refuge," he grumbles and frowns.

"Just one night, remember," I say more bitterly than I mean to.

Beau takes a pause, his eyes searching mine. I see the chance at tonight slipping away fast. I'm not having it. Grasping his hips, I flip our positions until his back hits the door. I take his mouth and don't allow him to take over the kiss this time. He tries, but I'm not giving in.

Biting his lower lip, I tug. He groans, shoving his hands in my hair. He has a tight grasp on the strains he released from my hair tie in the car on the way here.

My hands glide over his heated skin, moving up his ribs. I revel in the shiver that wrecks his body. With a grin, I start a trail of kisses from his jaw to his neck. I love his cologne. It makes me want to eat him up, a mix of something citrusy and clean. My mouth waters at the scent.

He reaches for my hand, pressing my palm to his hard dick. I release a short laugh and look into his eyes. I caress his cheek with my free hand, dragging my fingers down his throat. "I think we're both used to taking the lead. What are we going to do about that?"

"I say we take things as they go," he says huskily and swallows. "It's been a while since I've... I've gotten the occasional blow job."

"You're doing better than me, Papi," I snort.

"So why are we talking?"

"Not sure," I murmur against his lips, squeezing a hand full of thick dick in my hand.

Beau

I groan as his fingers flex around my cock. I want the fabric between his rough hand and my waiting erection gone. I need those full lips wrapped around me.

I want this. God, do I want this, but I'm feeling too much. This reads of more than just a one-night stand. His touch keeps sending bolts of lightning through me. His kisses are intoxicating. I want to make this last, but that's scaring the shit out of me.

A time bomb ticks in my head. Somehow this is all going to blow up in my face. Random blow jobs are one thing. Tonight, I plan to cross lines I haven't dared to since....

Don't, Beau.

I close my eyes and try to breathe. Angel's banter and directness are something I crave. He's making me wish I could have more, take more from this than just a single night. I just know I can't.

"Stay with me, Poppa," he whispers in my ear. "I'm here with you."

The way he says the last part tugs at something deep. I've seen Angel have to take breaks at the gym. I've watched for moments when he disappears into himself right before everyone's eyes. I know being present is something that takes effort for him.

"I'm with you," I say as a promise I shouldn't be making.

But I am. I'm here, and the fact that I want to be screams warning. Angel starts to kiss his way down my chest, pulling me further into his spell. His tongue flicks out against my skin, and my hips buck.

I shove my hands into his thick hair and grasp a tight hold. I watch his descent with my lips parted. I think my heart might burst from my chest before he gets where I need him.

I grunt with tortured frustration when he changes course and starts to lick back up my body from my pelvic bone to my nipple. Angel bites down on my nipple and lifts those brown eyes to mine. He wants to show he's in control.

Not for long.

I push my jeans down my thighs, letting my cock spring free. Angel pulls back and looks down. I grin when his brow lifts. It's clear he wasn't expecting so much from what he could feel through the confines of my boxer briefs and jeans.

That mischief plays on his lips. He looks at me in challenge, pushing down his own pants and boxers. My mouth waters as his thick, long cock comes into view. We both have more than average offerings.

The question is who's taking? I know I said we'd see how things go, but I can see we're going to have a battle of wills tonight. That knowledge alone thrills me and has precum glistening from my tip.

After reaching around him and grasping his ass, I shift our bodies again, his back to the door, my hand kneading his tight ass. My other hand cups his jaw as I sip from his lips. The kiss is demanding and coaxing. Our trapped cocks pulse against each other's bellies.

He smiles into the kiss, revealing that he's enjoying this power play as much as I am. He locks his hand in the top of my hair and tugs my head back, breaking the connection. His tongue and lips seize my throat.

"You like that?" he croons.

"Yes," I bite out.

"I've been wanting to fuck that pretty mouth of yours all night. You gonna let me stick my dick in that mouth?"

His breath fans my ear and neck. It's like my entire body comes alive. I'm used to being the one doing the most dirty talking. I welcome this change. Especially as I think of his thick cock in my mouth.

"Only if you're sucking my cock at the same time, darlin'. I believe in pleasure for all. I want to hear you choking on my cock while I drain you dry," I say.

"Fuck." He groans.

I lower my head to see the need in his eyes. I think we're both going to explode before we get started. I can't remember being this turned on before. The thought is startling, and I slam the door shut on the memories that try to rush me with that revelation.

Stay in the now.

I blink back my thoughts and focus on Angel's large bright orbs. Those whiskey eyes root me to where I need to be. We may sear right through each other tonight, but I plan to be here for every moment of it.

Angel reaches out to wrap his hand around me, but suddenly everything changes. A loud bang from the street beyond my apartment shifts the atmosphere on a dime. Angel's eyes glaze over. He stands frozen.

Angel

I flinch and spin. Bombs are exploding, rapid fire is moving closer and closer. They're coming at us, and they're coming hard. I can't see a thing. Smoke and fog surround me. I can hear my team in my ear, but they're in a panic.

"Hernández, I have you covered," Bachman calls into the earpiece. "I'm wit—"

Another explosion sounds, and Bachman's words are cut off. I don't have time to process the sense of loss. I know... but I can't let that distract me from covering those that are still with me.

"Baby, baby, look at me. I'm right here. Look at me." Beau's voice pulls me back to the present.

I'm shivering and sweating and not from the pleasure we were just about to give each other. The gray gaze staring back at me holds panic and worry. I swallow hard, tasting the bitterness of my life.

"I'm sorry." My words come out a near whisper.

"Never, ever apologize," he says into my hair as he pulls me close.

I'm limp in his hold. I feel like the life has been drained from me. All thoughts of fucking float out of my head. I need to get out of here. My chest is already tightening.

"I can't do this," I mutter, pulling away.

I collect my clothes and start to drag them on. Beau just stands there watching me, wordlessly. I can't look at him. I just need to go.

Thankfully, he doesn't try to stop me. I pull the door open and stand there with my back to him. I try to find the words to say, but nothing comes. Instead, I rush from his place like I have a fire lit under my ass. This was a bad idea.

I'm never going to get my fucking life back.

CHAPTER EIGHT

Too Much

Beau

I've been calling my sister since last night, and she hasn't answered a single one of my calls. She's probably pissed that I bailed from the club before she arrived, but I need to talk to her. Last night was…. I don't know what has turned me inside out more, Angel's freak-out or the haunting dreams I had once I finally fell into a fitful sleep.

I would be drawn to the guy that's just as fucked-up as I am, if not worse. I rub at my chest. The look on his face, the panic in his voice— I know that look of loss. Angel has had more than his share, I'm sure.

My office door slams, causing me to turn around. Emma stands in my office, glaring at me. I lift a brow. I know I left the club without a word before she got there, but it wouldn't be the first time. I can't count the amount of times I've arrived at a party before Emma and Kyle decided it wasn't my scene and left.

Okay, I usually text, but I still don't think this warrants the look she's giving me. Her cheeks are red, and her chest is heaving. I fold my arms across my chest, waiting for her to explain.

"How could you?"

"I forgot to text you I was going to cut out early. I'm sorry," I reply.

"That's not what I'm talking about." She scoffs bitterly. Tears fill her eyes, and I start to get concerned.

"What are you talking about?" I ask, dropping my arms and rounding my desk.

"Don't come near me." She throws her hands up. "I never thought you would do something like this to me. I feel so stupid. I mean, he flirted with me for months. If I would've known, I wouldn't have embarrassed myself. But you... I feel like such an ass."

"Darlin', I'm so confused," I say as I watch her with concern.

"Bullshit, Beau. You knew. You knew I liked him. How could you? We kissed. I... I... shit. I don't know if I kissed him or he kissed me. I'm an idiot. It all makes sense. The cold shoulder the next day. He's not into me. I've been staying away because I really like him, and I... I was so confused, but you go and pounce as soon as I'm out of the picture."

"Em, I have no damn I idea what the hell you're talking about."

"Don't do that. Don't make me feel stupid. I saw you. I know," she says brokenly, tears spilling down her cheeks.

"Em, I *don't* know. I don't understand what you're talking about—"

My office door bursts open. "Beau, you better get out here. It's Angel." Rustle, one of my fighters, rushes out.

I look at my sister and purse my lips. I'm torn, but I need to know what's going on in my gym with my employee. I squish the tightness in my chest as I think of the employee in question. I try to tell myself that my worry is just for the safety of all under my roof.

"I'll be right back," I say and rush from my office.

I jog to the front of the gym where the self-defense class is held. The view through the classroom's glass reveals a crowd has gathered. Making my way inside, I push through everyone gathered in the room to make my way to the front.

As the path opens up, Andres and Angel come into view. The blood drains from my face as Angel stands just like last night. His face is soaked in sweat, and his eyes are glazed over. His chest is heaving, and he looks like he's staring down a ghost.

"Angel, hermano, it's me," Andres says calmly.

His words aren't getting through. I clench my jaw tightly. I'm beginning to understand why Angel has had such a hard time keeping a job and reacclimating to civilian life. It shreds me to pieces because this isn't the confident man that was in my apartment last night before things went left.

"Everyone out," I bark.

People murmur around me, but I can hear Emma and my staff ushering them out. I don't take my eyes off Angel. Andres reaches for him, but before I can warn him not to, Angel strikes out. Thank God Andres is quick on his feet. Angel would have taken his head off if that hit connected. I can see the sheer force behind the strike.

"Don't, Andres. Let me," I call out.

"This is bad," Andres says. "I haven't seen him like this… it's been awhile. He's been doing so much better."

"I've got it," I bite out. "Baby," I call to Angel.

"Holy shit," Emma breathes out behind me. "Twins."

It hits me what the hell she was freaking out about in the office. She must have seen me with Angel at the club. I'd laugh my ass off if this wasn't such a fucked-up situation.

"Sweetheart, it's me. I'm here, Angel. Come here, baby," I say, ignoring everyone else.

"I need backup in here," he bellows.

"No… no, you don't, darlin'. I'm here. It's me, Beau. Listen to my voice, baby. Come back to me."

His eyes start to clear, and I take the opportunity to move in. He looks at me, still disoriented. I wrap him in my arms and place my lips to his ear.

"It's me, baby. You're safe. I've got you." I start to rock him in my hold.

Angel clings to my T-shirt with a grip so tight, I think he might tear the fabric right from my body. His sobs rock right through to my core. I close my eyes, knowing that everything has changed.

I want more than one night with Angel. I want to know how to restore the man I started with last night. I want to show him how to survive. I'm just barely making it through, but I want to offer him that at least. A way to endure and survive.

Can I offer that?

I don't know if I can, but I damn sure want to try. As this big, strong man sobs in my hold, I know I need to try. It doesn't have to be a relationship, but a friendship.

Yes, I can offer a friendship.

Angel

"It's okay, baby." His words coax me closer to reality.

Panic sets in as I look around. My brother looks pale and worried. There's that dark-haired chick again, standing with wide gray eyes bouncing between me and Andres. I can't help but wonder what I've done. None of my eleven students are in the room.

Dios. *Did I hurt one of them?*

I've grown fond and protective over all of my students. From the teenaged girls to the single women and soccer moms who come in to learn or just get away from home for a bit. They've all shared their stories with me and have given me their trust.

I'll never forgive myself for harming one of them. Will he fire me?

I can't lose my job. Beau allows me to stay here because I work for my keep. I want to work for my keep, but I just fucked that up. I don't even know what triggered me. One minute I was teaching a simple self-defense move. The next, I was in the middle of a war zone.

Beau's voice calling me back to the present for the second time in less than twenty-four hours shook something in me. I've been avoiding him all day. I'm still so embarrassed about last night. Now this. He's going to let me go. *Dios mío,* if he tells Javier about this, I'll lose that job too.

"Everything is fucked-up," I sob. "I need to just end this shit. I shouldn't be alive anyway."

"The hell." Beau cups my face. "Bullshit. You're stronger than that. That's not the answer. We'll figure this out. You can make it through this."

Those eyes. Such sincerity in his words. I try to tug away and shift my gaze from his.

"Look at me, baby," he says gently. "We're taking the rest of the day off. I have a friend I want you to get to know. After, we'll get something to eat, or we can come back here when the gym closes and blow off some steam. Whatever you need."

Looking into those eyes, want to tell him that I need him. His calm, his presence. When I'm around him I feel the most safe and secure I've felt in so long. Instead, I nod and vow to push through.

He's right. I'm a fighter. I want to fight this.

"Okay," I say simply.

I'm still visibly shaken. My hands are trembling. Beau pulls me into a hug that's so tight, I can't help but absorb the support he's giving me. Melting into his embrace, I close my eyes and hold on to him like a lifeline.

"I'm here."

I nod my head at his words, not sure for how long they'll be valid. Still, I appreciate them in this moment.

I need to fight this.

Beau

I haven't taken my eyes off that door since Angel followed Eric into his office. I've been rooted to this waiting room. If anyone can help Angel, it's Eric. I'm so grateful to him for fitting Angel in.

I'll never forget the first time Darwin ushered me into this very same office. Eric was able to help me before I completely lost it after Roman's death. I wince as I think of my own festering wounds.

Eric's a great therapist. He got me through the first three years. He's been trying to get me to start back with my sessions, but I haven't been able to force myself to that point yet. However, I just knew it was the right thing for Angel.

I bounce my leg as I rest my elbows on my thighs and cover my mouth with my cupped hands. They've been in there longer than an hour. Yet I've committed myself to sitting here as long as I have to.

The look on Angel's face, his haunting words. I couldn't move if I wanted to. If I'm honest, I can't stop thinking about how it felt to have him accept my touch and help. All things I shouldn't want but can't resist craving.

"Mr. Dalton, can I offer you another bottle of water?" Eric's office assistant breaks into my thoughts.

"Yes, please." I nod.

The door to Eric's office opens just then. Angel comes through first, looking a bit better than when we arrived. He was still shaken up on the ride here.

"I'd like to see you again this week, if you're comfortable with that," Eric says.

Angel clears his throat. "All right."

"You can make an appointment before you go." Eric looks at me with a grin. "You planning on making one as well, Beau?"

He already knows the answer to that question. "Not this time," I mutter.

My main focus is on Angel. I tug him into a hug just as I did back at the gym to settle him down enough to come here. He receives the embrace, returning it tightly. No words are needed. Just like earlier. It's a part of this connection I'm still trying to deny.

When we pull apart, Angel looks at me with a small smile. "Didn't you say something about food?"

"Sure, darlin'. Whatever you need," I reply. "I know this great outdoor bar and grill uptown."

"Thanks, Beau."

I give a tight nod, my throat raw with emotions. It's clear that this has been a lot on him from the look in his eyes and the set of his shoulders. I'm just glad I could be here for him. Placing a hand on his shoulder, I give a reassuring squeeze. Again, words are unnecessary. The appreciation in his gaze speaks volumes.

CHAPTER NINE

In the Ring

Beau

Everyone's excited that the Golden Gloves Tournaments are coming up. I have four fighters entering. We've been preparing for months. My own anticipation has been building. I remember the days when I was the one getting ready to jump in the ring and pound my way to the top.

I wanted to make a name for myself then. Now I just feel like something is missing. Coaching isn't enough. Although I'd never say that out loud to Kyle and Emma. They both would be relentless.

Neither of them can understand that I just don't belong in the ring. Not as a fighter. Not after what I've done. Wanting something and deserving it are two different things.

"Why do I always get the feeling you want to be in there?" Angel says as he walks up and hands me a bottle of water.

"Keep those hands up, Ricky," I call into the ring.

I glance at Angel quickly, taking the water from his hand. I want to avoid his question, but his eyes burn into the side of my face. He's not going to let this go. Something I've learned about him in the last few days.

Once he decides on something, he can be darn right stubborn. I say that's a gift and a curse. At the moment, I lean more toward the latter.

"Come on. I've heard about you. Those hands are lethal," he teases.

I wince. I know he doesn't mean anything by it. I can hear it in his tone. I guess whoever has been telling him about me either doesn't know about my past or just didn't tell him. Either way, his choice of words slices into me.

"Yeah, more than you know," I say tightly.

"So why aren't you boxing? You're in shape. You're still young. I can see in your eyes you want it. What's stopping you?"

"You already answered your own question," I snap.

"Hey." He touches my forearm. "Did I say something wrong? I... I'm sorry."

I sigh and shake my head. I don't mean to be short with him. He just picked a very sore topic.

"It's not something I want to get into here. I'll tell you some other time," I reply with less venom in my voice.

"Okay." He nods. "Your fighters look good. Ricky could use some work on that jab, though."

I turn to look directly at Angel. I study him more closely as he watches the fighters in the ring. Before I can dig, Andres calls for him from across the gym. Angel slaps my shoulder twice.

"See you later," he says.

I reach for his wrist to stop him. Angel looks better than a few days ago. I think taking him to see Eric was the right thing to do.

"You working tonight?"

"No, I have the next two nights off," he replies.

"Have a few beers with me after work. I'll tell you about—" I nod toward the ring, not able to say the words and not really sure why I'm making this offer.

"Yeah, I'm with it." He nods with a small smile.

I return the smile and release him. Turning back to the ring, I probe my thoughts to understand why I'm planning to open up to Angel. I already told myself we can't be more than friends.

I can tell a friend about my past.

I can, but I get the feeling that I may just crack the vault and allow my secrets to slip through as well. My shoulders sag, and I dig my fingers into the canvas beneath my palms. Nothing but hurt will come of this road I'm trotting down. I'd have better luck racing a dead horse in the Kentucky Derby.

"Get those hands up, Ricky. Watch your feet. He's leading you. Take the fight back," I call out.

Take the fight back.

Those words echo in my ears and resonate deep within. I lost my fight. I used to be known to come back, but this time I just haven't found the will.

Angel and Andres's twin laughter floats to my side of the gym. Again, I note that Angel looks better. He's fighting. A few days ago, he declared he wanted to take his own life. Now, he's smiling and fighting to stay here in the land of the living.

"Enough," I bark out.

The fighters in the ring stop, but I'm not so sure I was talking to them. Pushing off the ring, I end the session and retreat to my office. I have some things to think about before tonight.

Angel

When Beau asked me to join him for beers, I thought we would go to a bar. I was prepared for that. What I wasn't prepared for was his place. After the way things ended the last time I was here, I feel a little awkward returning.

I will admit it's a bit different this time. I'm getting to see the place with the lights fully on. Beau has a great place. It's the kind of place I wish I could afford. The loft's open floor plan and views of the city are all the things on my checklist for the perfect place. The wraparound balcony and rooftop deck with a pool are just bonuses I know I'll never be able to afford.

"The steaks will be ready in a few," Beau says as he closes the lid on the grill.

We've been on the rooftop, taking in the gorgeous view of the city. I was blown away when we walked up the iron stairs to the second-floor split-level and continued to another set of stairs that led us up here. The crisp night air is exactly what I needed to calm my nerves a bit as I sit here on a barstool and enjoy the company.

"This place is great," I say and sip my beer.

"Yeah, I bought it right before I retired." He takes the seat next to me.

"Why'd you retire so early?"

He looks out over the city, his face tight. This question is the reason I'm here. I know this to be a touchy subject, but I feel like knowing the answer will help me to know Beau. I want to know him. After the way he handled me and helped me out the other day, I want more than what we promised each other that night.

I think Beau and I could have a real connection. I haven't felt connected to anyone in so long. I need to see if I can make this work. I get that he's as reluctant as I am to enter a relationship. I just need to know why.

"I was in a serious relationship six years ago. I loved Roman as much as I loved to box. He was there when I started to figure my shit out. When I decided to go pro, he was in my corner, cheering me on.

"My career was in a different place than his. Ro needed to work on his skills. But he was arrogant. It was one of the things I loved about him. That cocksure attitude…." He takes a pull from his beer.

He makes a face as if it tastes bitter to him. I go to tell him he doesn't have to tell me anymore. It's clear that this is bringing him pain. That's the last thing I want for him, but he continues.

"Roman was all about the flash when it came to the ring. He… I was sure he would block the blow. He was skilled enough to block it. Instead he was showing off. I put more power behind it than I meant to.

"I mean… I just wanted to stun him when the hit met his block," he says, his voice choking up. "Hit his guard hard enough to make him stop fooling around. I was always so fucking serious in the ring. I hated that he clowned around, but I….

"Things ended badly, and I retired," he says in a way that shuts the subject down.

The pain rolling off him causes me to swallow, it's so heavy. I know what it's like to wear my pain, to feel trapped in my past. He may not have finished just now, but I don't think Beau and I are that different.

He needs to be free just as much as I do. Suddenly, it's like I need to speak up for us both. An offering to lead us both from our pain.

"I have days when I want to run from this shit." I tap my forehead. "I just want an escape. I've thought about taking my own life more times than I can count. Two of my buddies have since I've been home. They got out before me and never figured shit out.

"Hardcore Marines that just couldn't deal with the fucked-up shit in their heads. I try to remember them on days when it's all too much. Not just them, but their families. You know why?"

"Why?" he whispers.

"Because I may free myself, but I have a huge family that would be left hurting. We Hernández are fighters. Andres is a fighter. Being a twin, you feel your other half. I fight daily because I don't think I could sleep in peace knowing I ripped my twin apart, knowing I snatched some of the fight from my family."

"Why are you telling me this?" Beau says while staring down at his feet.

"Because I think you and I are a lot alike. *You* just stopped fighting."

He whips his head up and stares at me as if he's in awe. A ton of emotions cover his face, sorrow being one of the most prevalent.

"I don't want to live the rest of my life like this. For me, I have to believe that I have a choice to get better. I want to get better. I want to fight this. You have a choice too. Fight your demons or let them eat you alive," I say, not sure where any of this is coming from.

I just know we both need to hear this. I see the way Beau looks at that boxing ring. His muscles coil every time as if he's ready to get in there and release whatever's holding him back.

"Shit," Beau mutters, turning for the forgotten steaks.

"I love Cajun." I let out a laugh as he lifts the lid to the grill, releasing a billow of smoke.

"Yeah, I hope so." He snorts, shaking his head.

CHAPTER TEN

Night Terrors

Beau

"Those steaks were terrible," I groan, propped up against the headboard of my bed.

"Man, I ate that steak and the Chinese food you ordered. I'm not complaining," Angel says with amusement in his voice as he sits on the other side of me in the same position.

We're in my bed, but there's nothing sexual about it. We stopped here instead of going down to the lower level. Our bellies are full from our attempt at eating the steaks and polishing off some takeout from my favorite place.

"You're welcome to stay the night. You had more than a few," I offer.

"I'm a big boy. I can handle the train ride."

Angel smiles, stretching out his long legs. I follow the action with my eyes. My hands beg to reach out and touch him, but I refrain.

"Yeah, but I'm not ready for you to go, and it's getting late. Stay, if you're comfortable enough to."

"I guess since I already kicked my shoes off and you have me in your bed, I could chill for the night."

My gaze flickers over his face. He's so damn gorgeous. Those dimples popping as he smiles. I want to lean over and kiss him, but I hold back.

Friends, I'm just trying to be a friend.

"I'm plum tuckered out." I sigh.

Angel bursts into laughter. "How old are you?"

"Twenty-nine. What are you trying to say?" I ask, humor lacing my own voice.

"Nothing. When did you move here to New York?"

"When I was sixteen," I reply, remembering that time. "Not long before my seventeenth birthday."

"Man, that explains that country-ass accent." He laughs.

"You have something against my accent?"

"Nah, I like it," he says and winks. "Emma, that's your sister's name, right?"

"Yeah." I nod.

"She doesn't have as much of a drawl as you do. Man, my entire family sounds like me. Our Spanglish, the New York accents... it carries over four generations, B," he says with fondness.

"I like listening to you talk like this. You're different at the gym and the club."

"It be like that sometimes. You know, you talk one way to be professional and shit. Then when you're with fam or laid-back, chilling with friends, you can relax all that. I mean, you do it too. You just don't see it the same," he says.

"How do you figure?"

"Dude, I've heard you get real country when you're frustrated or talking to your sister. Other times, you dial it down. Same thing."

"I guess. Never thought of it that way," I say.

Now that he mentions it, Kyle does the same thing all the time. Most of my friends do. Sometimes Javier forgets we don't speak Spanish and will have an entire conversation before he catches himself. The more comfortable he gets, the more Spanish he uses in between his English.

"I don't think about it. It's not even a conscious thing anymore. If you didn't point it out, I probably wouldn't have noticed," he says.

"I like that you're comfortable with me. That I'm a friend you can chill with."

He stares at me for a long moment before shaking his head and smiling, causing those dimples to pop again. I double down on my restraint to keep from reaching over and dragging him to my lips.

"I want to be more than friends with you, but I'm going to allow you that wall you have up. I'm a lot to take on—"

"My hesitation has nothing to do with you," I say.

He searches my face but nods after a moment. I never want him to think I don't want to pursue more because of his PTSD. That's so far from the case. I want more with Angel; I just know my issues will be a problem.

"So, Mason, the little dude. That's your nephew?" he asks, lifting a brow.

"Yeah, Kyle, his biological uncle, was adopted by my parents."

"That's cool. Are you close with your parents?"

"As tight as can be, but it's just my mama now," I reply, looking down into my hands in my lap.

"Sorry to hear that."

"Heart attack. Kyle was just getting the family he deserved. A mama and daddy that cared about him. Emma and I were settling into our new lives here in New York. In the blink of an eye, it was all snatched away," I say, rubbing at my chest.

"Damn, that's rough. I hate to hear shit like that. You know, good people that have their time cut short. My father and I have had our differences, but I couldn't imagine losing him," Angel says.

Something distant takes over his expression. A longing, I would say.

"Are you out to your family?"

"Yeah, Papi lost his shit when I brought my first boyfriend home. I think it was a shock. It sort of came out of nowhere for my family. Everyone but Andres. He knew. My pops got over it, but I've always felt like he never looks at me the same. Like I disappointed him," he says somberly.

"I never told my daddy. I think my mama always knew. She has a way of seeing what no one else does. Makes me wonder if Daddy saw too," I offer without thinking.

"Would that have been a bad thing?"

I yawn and shake my head to clear the sleep away. I'm enjoying my time talking to him. I haven't been this relaxed in a long time.

"No, I don't think it would have been. Daddy was more focused on me being happy. That meant making me into the best damn fighter I could be," I say and smile wistfully.

"All the more reason to fight for what you love," Angel says in a knowing tone.

I don't reply. His words from earlier are still swimming in my head. I'm choosing to hold off on digging into these until I'm alone and can pull back the cover I have on those open wounds.

Another yawn escapes me. My lids are starting to feel heavy. I give Angel a lazy smile. "You don't have to sleep in your clothes. You can use any of my stuff you want."

"I think you're just trying to get me naked." He grins.

"Sounds good. Not a bad thought at all." I return his smile and close my lids for a brief second to relax and clear my mind.

Angel

He looks peaceful in his sleep. Even as I long to look into those gray eyes, I can't say that I'm not admiring the gorgeous sight before me. The hard plains of his face, that hard jawline. My fingers itch to graze his beard and feel that softness against my skin again.

It's such a contrast to the look of Beau. He's strong and rough around the edges. The silky hairs both soothing and abrasive against my own skin prove that nothing is as meets the eye. I know this to be true all too well.

I look around the loft and take in a deep breath. I agreed to stay, but I'm not sure I'll be able to sleep here. I just couldn't force myself to leave once he asked.

The curtains billow from the night breeze, drawing my attention to the balcony. I take one more glance at a sleeping Beau before I get up and head out for some fresh air. Immediately I feel tension release I hadn't even noticed before.

Resting on my forearms against the rail, I think about my conversation with Beau on the rooftop. I admitted things to him that I've never told anyone. I was so fucked-up just a few days ago.

At first, I didn't think talking to Eric would do anything for me. Then I walked out of that first session to find Beau still waiting. I know he said he would be there, but I didn't think I'd see him again after he dropped me off.

Beau has been a man of his word. Which is why I'm conflicted. He doesn't want a relationship. He can't give more than sex. He has said as much, but I feel this spark between us, and I want to know more about it, him, and where it will take us.

I inhale the night air and blow it back out as if I can blow out my wandering thoughts. Maybe Beau is right. We shouldn't try for more. He's the closest thing I've had to a friend in a long time. I need that more than I knew.

"No!" I startle as Beau's deep voice booms from inside, drafting out to me. "No!"

I rush back in to find him thrashing in the bed. Just as I reach the edge, he sits up bolt straight, sweat coating his face, his shirt clinging to his skin. His eyes are wild, and his hand trembles as he reaches up to run it through his thick dark hair.

"Hey," I say gently as I climb onto the edge of the bed.

He jerks his head toward me as if he's just realizing he's not alone. I reach out cautiously, placing a hand on his shoulder. He stiffens at first, but when I give a small squeeze, he sags into himself.

It's his turn to sob and my turn to be there for him. Only I don't think my sobs were this soul wrecking. This comes from somewhere so deep that has the potential to shake us both.

I wrap my arms around his shoulders, and he reaches an arm out to wrap it around my waist. He turns his face into my chest, and I hold him tighter. I don't know how much time passes before the room falls silent and we just sit holding on to each other.

I don't want to break the silence with needless words. I can't pretend to know his pain, but I sit praying he will tell me. Just when I resolve myself to be content with our silent bond, Beau begins to speak.

"It was my first real relationship... I... I killed him. It... it was a freak accident. I thought he would block the punch. I just wanted to stun him a little to force him to focus and get serious. Instead of blocking the hit, he went on showboating.

"I saw the moment it was all about to go wrong. He stepped into the punch and lost his footing. His momentum toward me and the force of the punch... it was too late to pull back.... It all shouldn't have happened." His breath hitches.

I rub a hand over his hair and kiss the top of his head. I don't realize I've been rocking until he tightens his arms around me. Something tugs in my chest, but I ignore it and listen as he starts to talk again.

"I was known for power-punching. Roman had no business in the ring playing games with a fighter like me. My promoter was an asshole. He tricked me into the fight for a bigger payout. I had the contracts to fight a different guy. I read them and agreed to the terms.

"Somehow, when my back was turned, the bastard switched the contracts. By the time I knew it, it was too late. The fight was announced, and to back out would've been career suicide." He snorts.

"That's some fucked-up shit to do," I finally say.

"It was just the beginning. He was the one waving the fan at the flames. He... outed us to the world. Not that I cared what people thought of me. I just didn't want my relationship to be what put butts in the seats.

"People actually paid just to see me beat on the man I loved. They were salivating for it. The roar of the crowd still haunts me as much as the silence as Roman laid there lifeless," he says.

"Damn," I breathe, closing my eyes as I ache for him.

The pain in his voice is so thick, it's choking. I wish I had a way to soothe him, an outlet to offer. It's just on the tip of my tongue to ask him if he has ever talked to Eric, when he speaks my thoughts.

"I started to see Eric for a while. After the nightmares began, I was so lost and broken. Eric helped me to find a way to function, and the nightmares became less frequent. I don't know why they're coming back," he says, sounding like a small boy at the end.

"Could be time to officially free yourself. Surviving isn't living," I murmur softly.

Silence greets me, but I hold on tight. I anchor us both, fighting back my own demons to be here for the man who was there for me when I needed it.

CHAPTER ELEVEN

Epiphany

Beau

"Stamina and endurance are as important as how well you throw a punch," I call out to the kids jumping rope before me. "If you can endure, you can wait your opponent out. Come on, dig in, guys."

Their little faces are covered in sweat and determination. Damian is the first to hit the floor and call it quits. He looks at me with apologetic eyes. I give a nod, proud that he even tried.

"You're only as strong as the team in your corner. You guys just lost a man. You gained his load. Thirty seconds," I say, causing groans to fill the air in chorus.

"I think you're trying to kill them," Emma says as she comes over.

"Nope, I'm building them up. They'll be able to survive through anything."

"They're eight and ten. Come on, they can't even enter the ring for another four-to-six years," she says, side glancing me.

"When they're old enough, they'll be ready. This group has started martial arts training."

"Yeah, but look at them." She pouts.

Daddy always treated her like a princess. Emma won't even run two miles. This would look like torture to her. "They'll be fine. Daddy taught me just like this," I reply.

Her face softens. She reaches to pat my shoulder. The soft smile on her face reminds me of him. Those smiles were something special, but I saw them most while doing this, training to be my best.

It had been his dream to move to New York and train fighters. He made that happen even when we as a family tried to protest. We had family and friends we didn't want to leave behind in Dallas. Looking back now, so much about my father's dream changed all of our lives.

"He would be proud of you," she says softly.

"I doubt that." I scoff and give my attention back to the kids.

"I wish you weren't so hard on yourself. Daddy would've been really proud of you. He would want you to be doing what you love again too—"

"Don't," I say tightly. "Not now. I don't want to talk about this, but especially not now."

"Fine, I understand. I just wish we could talk about it sometime. Now hear me out just a little," she says when I go to cut her off again. "I want to see you happy. As hard as you push to look okay to everyone else, I see you. I want to be here for you. Talk to me. It doesn't have to be today, but I'm here for you."

I reach to tug her in, kissing the top of her head. I know she means well. Our family has been through a lot. We're always looking out for each other.

"I'm fine," I say.

"You're surviving," she replies.

Her words hit hard as they echo Javier's and Angel's. I'm hearing this too often. Am I truly just surviving? They're all probably right. I honestly don't know whether I'm coming or going anymore.

"You and Andres have started dating, I see."

Emma purses her lips. "You're amazing at that."

"At what?"

"Avoiding what you don't want to talk about. But to answer your question… yes, we have gone on a date. We talk a lot on the phone as well."

"I want to see you happy too, Emma. I may not say much, but that's all I want for you and Kyle."

"We get it. You speak when we need it most. That's what counts," she says.

"Another thirty seconds. You're starting to drop like flies," I call out.

"Look at Mas." Emma giggles. "He's determined to make you proud."

"No, I think he's determined not to look weak." I snicker.

"Billy's giving him a run for his money. They're so cute," she whispers.

"She's not going to let him outjump her."

"Yeah, he's just as bent on outlasting her," Emma muses.

Mason and Billy push themselves. Angel walks over to join us. My sister's cheeks turn bright red. She's still embarrassed about thinking I stole her potential boyfriend.

"Hey, how are you doing, Emma?" Angel says.

"I'm good, and you?"

"Hanging in there," he says and nods at the kids. He laughs. "These two at it again?"

"Always."

I give a short laugh and look at my timer. I smile as I see they've both broken their best. "They may be battling each other, but they're making each other better," I say.

"Sometimes you just need to find the right motivation. Every now and then that turns out to be in the form of a person," Angel says.

"I like the sound of that," Emma chimes in.

"Do you have a person?" Angel directs at Emma, but his eyes remain on me.

"I don't know yet," she says, her blush returning full force.

"Time," I call out to Mason and Billy.

They both stop jumping and double over to catch their breath. Billy glares at Mason. Mason has a little grin on his face. This little guy is determined to win her over as a friend.

"Good job, all of you. Billy, Mas, you guys beat your best times. Nice work."

"Uncle Beau," Mas pants. "Are we still hanging out this weekend?"

"Sure are. Mama's making us cookies for our trip," I reply.

"Yes." He pumps his fist. "Can I bring a friend?"

"I don't see why not."

He turns to Billy with a hopeful expression. Billy glares back at him warily. I cringe inside as I watch this little train wreck about to happen. That is until Mason stuns everyone.

"Uncle Beau is taking me to ride horses this weekend. I can bring a friend. You're my friend. You coming or not?"

Emma, Angel, and I all stifle laughs behind our hands. I'm going to have to tell the little guy that's not how you win women over. Then again, Mas teaches me something.

"Horses?" Billy says, her pretty brown eyes widening.

"Yeah, you'll get to ride one if you want. There'll be lunch and Grandma's chocolate chip cookies."

Billy looks between me and Mas as she processes the information. Her small mouth creeps up in the corners. I think it's the first time I've seen her give a smile.

"Yeah, I'm going," she says, shocking me. "But we're still not friends."

With that she walks away, leaving Mason smiling after her. These two are cute and funny as heck. Mason turns to me still grinning.

"Make sure we have extra cookies, Uncle Beau," he says and disappears in the direction Billy just went.

"I can't say I'm mad at the little guy." Angel laughs when the kids are gone. "Might not have been the smoothest line I've heard, but it worked for him."

"Yeah, I totally wasn't expecting that one," Emma says. "I'll see you later. I'm going to round the kids up and head back."

"Give me a call later. I still owe you a few beers."

"You got it, bro," she says and leans in to kiss my cheek. "Maybe we can talk then."

"Maybe."

"Later," Angel calls as Emma waves at him.

I start to straighten up the area, and Angel joins me. We work in silence, but I can sense he has something on his mind. I wait him out, getting lost in my own thoughts in the meantime.

I can't get those words out of my head. I've been surviving. Doing what I have to do to get by. I haven't moved forward much in the last six years.

My biggest accomplishment—the time I had the most peace—has been while working on the apartment complex and the orphanage. My partnership with Kyle to build that place was just what I needed, a distraction.

I pause in the middle of hanging up the jump ropes, my thoughts clicking into place. The nightmares started again after I finished the project.

"Hey, Beau," Angel calls. "You okay?"

He's watching me closely. It takes a second for me to find my words. He moves closer, searching my eyes.

"Yeah, I just thought of something," I say, rubbing the back of my neck.

He takes the ropes from my hands and hangs them for me. I shove my empty palms in my pockets and rock back on my heels as my epiphany hits me harder. Over the last three years, I've run myself so hard with getting that deal done, then getting the project finished. Never once did I have time to be consumed by my past.

"Want to talk about it?" Angel asks, pulling my attention back to him.

I think his question over. Do I want to talk about this? For the first time, I think I do, but only with him. That realization blows me away as well as while giving me a ton of other thoughts to deal with. "Yeah, I wouldn't mind that."

"How about dinner at your place? I'll cook this time," Angel replies.

"Sounds good." I nod.

"All right, we'll leave in about thirty, right?"

"Yeah."

It shouldn't make my stomach so warm to know he knows what time I leave for the day. Yet I can't shake the feeling. Friendship, that's what I said we could have. This is a part of building a friendship. Talking and having dinner.

Angel

"Are you still sulking because I wouldn't let you pay for the groceries?" I murmur in amusement as I look up from the plantains I'm frying.

Beau gives a grunt and sips his beer as he sits at the island in front of me. I can't help smiling wider. With the music playing in the background, my hands busy cooking, and the mellow atmosphere, I'm the most content I've been in a long time. "It's my turn to treat," I say.

"I didn't expect you to have to buy your own cooking utensils. I could've put out for the things I didn't have here," he says.

"I'm sure you've never cooked Mofongo in your life, and you probably won't after tonight. I didn't expect you to have to pay for things you won't use."

"It was too much," he grumbles.

I pause from removing the plantains from the oil. I purse my lips and level Beau with my glare. We'll have to get a few things straight.

"I'm not poor. I make good money now at the gym and the club, in addition to my benefits. I could afford to do this," I say. "I was in the mood for shrimp and Mofongo, and I thought you'd enjoy it. I wasn't thinking about the cost."

His eyes widen and his cheeks pink. It's an adorable look on him. Much better than the grim expression he's been wearing since we left the gym.

"I didn't mean to imply that you're poor. I just didn't want…. You know what? I sound like an ass any way I put it, at this point. It smells delicious. Thanks for cooking," he says. "I can't wait to taste it."

"It's my mother's recipe. The sofrito takes it over the top," I say, grinning as I think of my moms.

"You cook a lot with your mama?"

"When I was younger." I beam at the memories. "Yeah, you couldn't get me out of the kitchen. It was where we all gathered around and hung out. It wasn't possible to live in our house and not learn to cook."

I salt the plantains and move to get the shrimp finished off while they cool. The aromas are taking me back. Those were such good times in my life. I rub at my chest as a punch of longing hits.

"My mama won't let us near her kitchen. To this day, I don't know what she puts in that chili or her special cookies. I don't think Emma knows either. For my mama, the kitchen has always been her sanctuary. We knew to steer clear."

"There were five of us in my home growing up. It was hard to stay clear of each other. Someone was always in your business." I laugh.

"I spent most my time with my daddy. He had me in boxing gloves as soon as I could hold my hands up." He grins. "If we weren't boxing, we were out with the horses. When we moved here, we spent most our time together at the gym. By then, Kyle joined the family."

"That must have been hard to share your pops with someone else so late in life. How did that work out?"

"I wasn't sure about Kyle when he first arrived, but we became best friends almost out of necessity," he says.

I glance up at him curiously. There's a story in his words. His expression confirms what I hear.

"How so?"

"Kids in school picked on him for living with a white family, and they picked on me for being country as hell." He frowns. "We started using our fists to shut them up. I had his back and he had mine. Been like that ever since."

"I think Andres and I came out the womb swinging." I laugh.

"Your brother was a great fighter."

"Yeah, he's not the only one. I saw some footage of your old fights. You were good, really good," I say, studying his face for a reaction.

His expression turns sour. I watch as he stares into his palms as if they're talking to him. So much trouble enters his eyes.

"I think I know why I'm having the nightmares again," he says.

"Is that what was on your mind earlier?" I ask cautiously as I turn the shrimp in the pan.

"Yeah, it's been so long since I've had them so often. I had been working on a side investment for about three years. The complex the kids from the orphanage live in, four phases of it were dictated to apartment buildings. The orphanage was added on later.

"I oversaw all five phases of the project. I covered every detail of every inch of that place. Some nights I'd fall on my face before I could get food into my stomach. It's not far from here, so I'd jog over some mornings to walk through before anyone would arrive.

"I put my blood, sweat, and life into that place. It's done. The project has ended. The distraction is gone," he says.

"So what now?"

"That's the thing. I don't know. You were right. I've been in survival mode for so long I don't know how to come out," he muses. "The gym... it's not a distraction. It's...."

His eyes take on a distant look. I've been crushing the plantains and fixing our plates while we talk. I add sauce to his and place the steaming plate in front of him. After finishing my plate off, I round the counter and sit beside him.

"A reminder," I offer after thinking over his words.

"What?" he asks as if he's lost.

"The gym is a reminder," I repeat.

He swallows. "Yeah. Yet I have so many memories and ties to it—" He sucks in a breath, then turns to his plate and tucks in. "This is good. I think I feel even worse about burning the steaks."

I laugh and accept his change of subject. The kitchen has grown heavier than it had been. The lighter topic is welcomed. Getting to see a ghost of a smile on Beau's lips makes it even better.

"I can take over the cooking from now on," I tease.

His smile grows, and he turns back to his food. Damn, that smile is gorgeous. I'm going to make it my mission to see it more. We eat, allowing the music to fill in the silence. When

Beau looks up from his plate, staring longingly at the pots and extras, I laugh and get up to get us both seconds.

"Thanks," he says out of the blue.

"For?" I glance up from my task.

"I don't know what to do with all of this, but it felt good to talk about it."

"Not that I'm an expert at getting my shit together, but I got some great advice and I'm repeating it. You can live in the shadow of who you were, or you can figure out who you want to become. You decide," I say.

"Yeah." He smiles. "I've heard that somewhere before. Sage advice, I might just have to revisit it."

I round the island again with our plates, passing him his. Our fingers brush and a spark travels up my arm into my chest. Our eyes lock. He had to feel it too.

It wouldn't take much to lean in and take his lips, but I want to respect his boundaries and our new friendship. Still I can't help myself. I reach up to brush the corner of his lips, catch some sauce that lingers. I stick my thumb into my mouth. I don't so much as move my eyes from reading his.

"You can do the cooking when we hang out. This is delicious," he says with a heated stare.

I smile back at him and shake my head. He's not ready. I appreciate the invitation, but he's not ready at all.

Yeah, I could get used to hanging out like this. I just need to be patient.

CHAPTER TWELVE

Brother to Brother

Beau

"Something's different," Kyle says as he looks at me from behind the desk in his new home office.

"Nothing's different."

"I remember I once called something nothing and you called me on it. Rumors fly in our circle. I heard about this guy down at the gym. I just haven't been able to come down to see about him for myself," he says, leaning forward to place his elbow on the desk.

"Nothing to see." I shrug, mirroring his action placing my elbows on my knees as I sit in front of him.

"Bullshit." Kyle laughs. "I know you too well for you to get away with that."

"I like him as a friend. I'm not dragging him into my fucked-up head and life. He has his own issues," I relent, shifting in my seat.

"Andy and I had a buttload of issues when we started. You know that better than anyone. That's not an excuse."

"I'm not making excuses. I'm stating facts. I'm not ready to be in a relationship. I'm happy you and Andy are going so strong, but I just.... Let's talk about something else," I say, annoyance rising.

One thing I love about Kyle is that he knows me well enough to back off when I ask. It's been our thing since we were younger. He'll leave you alone to be left alone. We have that in common. I relax in my seat as his face shows he gets it.

"I got your text. You want to place a bid on that complex across town?"

"This time we'll be working with standing structures, but I think we should go for it. If the inspector and our team think it's better to flatten it and start over, we'll look at our options to optimize the use of the lot," I say.

I'm excited to get into this project. It will give me something to focus on. Maybe I can get the nightmares to dial back and give me a damn break.

"Looking at the specs you sent over, it looks like a sound investment. I mean, I'm still sulking over that bid we lost, but this sounds like the next best thing," he says.

He's calculating and thinking this through. I don't realize I'm holding my breath until he gives his nod of approval. I exhale and feel more relaxed than I've felt since realizing how much I need to be working on a project outside the gym.

Kyle purses his lips and leans back in his chair. His arms fold over his chest. I stifle a groan because we're headed right back where we started.

"You're my brother, so I'm going to be straight with you. If you're not ready for a relationship, fine. I get that, but I see what's going on here. These projects have become band-aids. You're keeping yourself alive for now.

"Let me ask you a question? What happens when the blood starts to leak through the bandages? What happens when you can't handle the hemorrhaging and you're no longer surviving?" Kyle says.

His words are like a blade slicing right through me. Hold no punches: that's our motto. He just went in for the knockout, and he doesn't even know it. Here we are with that word again. *Surviving.*

"I better get Mas," I say and stand. "It's a long drive."

"You may not see it now, but these projects aren't the answer. You live for the ring. It's why you've been on life support. You won't step back into your body and live. When you get back in the ring, you'll breathe again," he calls to my back.

I freeze, turning to look him in the eyes. I want him to see my face when I speak the words. I need him to see the hurt.

"I took a man's life in that ring. I took the life of the man I loved. I don't deserve to be in that ring. If I lost the one thing I loved more than anything in the world… that's my cross to bear. That's what I deserve," I choke out.

"Fuck out of here with that," Kyle bellows and stands. "I was there. I saw two fighters in that ring. I watched one act like a child, and he tripped. In a freak accident he lost his life. You killed no one, and you damn sure didn't die in that ring with Roman."

"So then why does it feel like I did?" I shout back.

"Because losing someone you love hurts like a motherfucker, and for some reason, brother, this life is intent on taking people we love away," Kyle replies, sounding more like a small boy than the man standing before me.

"Which is why I can't let anyone else in," I whisper back.

"But we were talking about you getting back in the ring," Kyle says.

I blink a few times before I realize what I've just said. Pushing a hand into my hair, I tug tightly. Just then Mas pushes his way into the office with Andy following behind.

"You guys okay?" Mason says with concern on his small face.

"Yeah, buddy. Your uncle Beau just needs a minute. Why don't you and Andy go get Billy. By the time you guys are back, he'll be ready to go," Kyle says.

Mason stands watching me for a few seconds. I force a smile and reach to rub a hand over his head. He's getting so tall. Instead of walking out, he wraps his arms around me for a hug.

"Thanks. That's just what I needed," I say.

He beams up at me and nods before turning to leave with Andy. Kyle watching me. I blow out a breath. "He makes me want to try to find my way back. A part of me doesn't like what that could mean," I admit.

"Then take it a step at a time. I see you, Beau."

"Yeah, that's the fucking problem," I mumble.

I stare at Kyle as his words ring in my ear. I know he's right. I also know I'm just as stubborn as he is. I turn to leave, but my phone is burning a hole in my pocket.

It's time to make some decisions.

CHAPTER THIRTEEN

Making a Move

Angel

"Thanks for the call," I say as we sit on a picnic bench, watching Mason and Billy run around.

"I'm glad you could come with us," he replies.

I watch Beau's profile, noting the tension in his face. Something has been on his mind since he and the kids picked me up from the gym. At first I wasn't sure I should've come along after all. Now, I can see it's not me. It's something bigger. "Want to talk about it?"

"I want to see if we.... Maybe we can...." His jaw works.

I bump his shoulder with mine, causing him to look me in the eyes. Within all that trouble in those grays, I see… longing. I think I can understand that. "I was thinking about trying a movie this week. No guarantees I'll be able to sit through it, but

I've started something new. I try something that used to come naturally to me at least once a week, if I can. You coming or not?" I tease, making light of the mood.

Beau cracks a smile, hearing his nephew's words repeated to him. It's a breathtaking smile that draws my eyes to his lips.

"I'm coming," he laughs.

"Good."

"Yo, Beau." Billy's voice pulls our attention as she runs over breathlessly.

"What's up, darlin'?" he replies.

"I need to go the bathroom," she whispers.

"I pointed the restrooms out earlier. Do you remember?"

She turns to look in the direction of the restrooms, then back at Beau. I noticed she hasn't gone once since we've been here. Mason has gone a few times. It's warm out. We've been feeding them plenty of water to stay hydrated.

From the fidgeting she's doing, I'd say Billy has to go pretty bad now. Her eyes are pleading for Beau to understand something. I've been around my nieces and nephew enough to have some understanding.

"She's scared, bro. You're going to have to go with her. Stand outside the door." I lean to whisper in Beau's ear. "She trusts you."

Beau looks surprised, but he catches on. He stands and murmurs something to Billy. She looks relieved and falls in step with Beau as they walk toward the restrooms. Billy looks back over her shoulder at me and gives a small smile.

She's a cute kid. I ball my fist wondering who hurt her. My nieces and nephew are around her age.

"Hey, Mr. Angel," Mason says as he runs over. "Did you like the horses?"

"They're cool, but I don't think I'm ready to ride one. I'll leave all of that to your uncle."

"It's fun. You should try next time. Uncle Beau could teach you. He's a good teacher," he says.

"Did he teach you?"

"A little. I was scared the first few times too."

"Nah, I'm not scared. Horses just aren't my thing."

"If you say so," he says with a knowing smile.

I pull him into a headlock and give him a knuckle sandwich. His giggles fill the air, and it's a calming sound. I never thought about having my own kids, but today has been fun.

When Beau and Billy return, Billy takes a seat next to Mason. She had been standoffish with him as usual when we arrived. Although she seems to be warming up to the kid.

"You guys ready to head home?" Beau asks.

"Ah, man, already?" Mason whines.

Billy looks a little crestfallen as well. It's a long drive back. We should head out soon.

"We'll do this again soon. Promise," Beau says.

"I can come too?" Billy asks softly.

"Anytime you want, darlin'."

"I'd like that," she chimes with the biggest smile I've ever seen on her face.

I feel like I'm watching a rainbow reveal itself. Billy is half Latina from what Andres told me. She could easily pass for my own little girl. Mine to protect and make smile just like that.

Another goal to fight for, Angel. A family.

Beau

I pull up in front of Kyle's building at the complex. It's been a long day. I wanted Angel to come along to the horse ranch after talking to Kyle. I felt like I needed an anchor. As much as I want to fight it, Angel is already a part of my life.

I didn't fully recover from my conversation with Kyle this morning, but having Angel join us at the ranch did bring me some peace. Enough for me to admit to myself I want to date him or at least try. Trying is more than I've done in a long time.

"That was cool, wasn't what I expected, but cool," Angel says.

"Some people take time to warm up to the horses," I reply.

"I might be one of those. I'll admit that."

"The time to relax and think draws you in. Next time maybe it should just be the two of us. I can teach you to ride. You might like it more than you think."

"I'll count on that," he says, a grin on his lips.

I scoff. "I bet."

He turns to look into the quiet back seat. "Look at them. They're knocked out," he whispers.

I turn to find Mason and Billy slumped into each other, fast asleep. I look at their little hands linked together. I smile and laugh to myself.

"Looks like he may have won her over after all," I whisper back.

"Sometimes you just have to be patient."

I turn, coming face-to-face with Angel. We're so close it would only take an inch to press our lips together. His whiskey-colored eyes shine from the street light breaking through the windshield.

My phone buzzing breaks the trance. Reaching for the device, I see it's a message from Kyle asking if we've arrived so he can come downstairs for the kids. I'm not ready for Angel to meet Kyle.

I know my brother. If he meets Angel, he'll ride me harder about dating him. I want to do this my way. I shoot back a quick text, letting Kyle know I'm already on my way up.

"Let me get them inside. You mind staying with the car?"

"No problem. You need help?"

"Maybe just to get them out," I say, pursing my lips.

I don't want to wake them. They're probably worn out from all the running around and horseback riding. Angel climbs out, unfastening Billy and plucking her from the car while I get Mas out.

When I round the car, Angel places Billy on my free shoulder. I balance the two small bodies in my hold easily. He gives me a sexy grin.

"Kids look good on you" he says.

"You think?"

"Yeah. Attractive, real attractive."

CHAPTER FOURTEEN

Small Offerings

Angel

"Yo, Angel."

I turn to find Billy staring up at me with a frown on her little face. I'm amused that she can tell the difference between Andres and me. Most people are still having a hard time if we're not in our work areas.

Right now, I'm in Andres's area, looking at some charts he asked me to bring to his place after work. It would have been easy for her to mistake me for my brother. This kid intrigues me. "Hey, Billy, what's up?"

"Where's your twin?" she demands.

"His little girl was sick. He had to stay home with her today," I reply.

"He has a kid?"

"Yup, my niece is about your age."

"You got kids?" she asks, tilting her head to the side.

"Not yet."

"Where's Beau?"

"Not here yet."

"*Vamos, hombre*," she says. "*Qué diablos?*"

I roll my lips. This kid is a tiny adult, I swear. She's as direct in Spanish as in English. Obviously, she doesn't appreciate Beau and Andres not being here.

"*Tú hablas español?*"

"*Sí.*"

"Okay, I see you, Billy," I tease.

"Yeah, not that many people at Savanna's House speak Spanish."

The scowl she's been wearing deepens. She looks around the gym as if trying to figure something out. She turns back to me with her lips twisted to the side. "You're from Brooklyn, right?"

"Born and raised." I nod.

"All right," she replies thoughtfully. "Mason isn't here either. He had to do wedding stuff or something."

"Wedding stuff?" I ask in confusion.

"Yeah, the two guys that keep us safe and stuff. They're getting married. Mas asked me to be a guest, but I don't know," she says, placing her hands on her hips.

"That sounds cool. Why don't you want to go?"

"One, I'd need a dress." She counts off on her fingers, making a face like the idea of a dress is something questionable. "Two, it's going to be fancy and stuff. Three, that's a lot of people. Mason will be busy with his family...."

I fill in the blanks. Not for the first time, I notice Billy has trust issues. It breaks my heart that such a small girl already has so much distrust in the world.

I squat before her to get eye level. "What if I helped you out with the dress?" I offer. "We can ask my niece, Aryanna, for her help. She loves to shop."

"Andres's daughter?"

"Yeah."

"I don't have any money," she says softly.

"It will be my treat. We'll get shoes and everything. That's if you want to be Mason's guest," I say.

She looks at me warily. Again I feel an ache in my chest as I watch her eye me with so much caution. However, it's her words that nearly tear me in two.

"What do you want?"

"Not a thing," I reassure her softly. "Nothing at all. If you want, you can go with Emma instead. I'll still pay."

She chews on her lip for a minute. Something lights up in her eyes. In this moment I wish I had a little girl of my own to look back at me with such hope.

"I want you to take me with your niece, but only if I decide to go to the wedding. I don't want you wasting your money. I have one more request, though. You can buy the dress if I can be your assistant in your classes."

"You want to be my assistant in my self-defense classes?"

"Yeah, I won't get in the way. I just want to watch," she says. "I can help out, earn my dress, and watch."

She wants to learn. I read between the lines, and that's what I'm getting. She wants to protect herself. I won't deny her this.

"All right, kid, you can be my assistant. We'll make sure all of this is cool with Beau, first, but you have a deal."

"Deal."

She holds her small hand out, and I wrap it in mine. If I didn't think it would freak her out, I'd hug her. I vow to make it my business to find out more about Billy. She may not know it, but she just earned a new protector.

"All right, kid. I'll talk to Beau as soon as he gets in."

"Okay," she says.

She turns and looks around the gym again. She goes to stand by the boxing ring to watch a couple of fighters spar. I'm done for the day, but instead of heading to Andres's for a bit like I planned, I stick around to wait for Beau. We're supposed to catch that movie tonight.

I head over to the bleachers and have a seat to observe the fight in the ring. It doesn't take long before Billy quickly finds her way over and sits in the bleacher just below me. I grin as I see I've gained a new friend.

I'm lost in thought when Beau walks in dressed in a three-piece suit. The navy-colored suit fits him to a T, making his long body look like a piece of art. His hair is blown out, keeping it out of his face. The pompadour style suits him perfectly.

He looks like he should be in a boardroom or on a magazine cover. Images of peeling him out of that suit fill my head. He looks around the gym, his eyes landing on me.

"Yo, you going to talk to him now?" Billy says.

I turn and give her a smile. "Yeah, I'll talk to him now."

"Good, let's go."

I snort and shake my head as she heads down the bleachers in Beau's direction. She doesn't even look back to see if I follow. Beau meets us at the bottom of the bleachers, a curious look on his face. I roll my lips to hide my amusement. This should be interesting.

"Hey, darlin'," Beau says to Billy.

"Hey, we need to ask you something," she says.

"O... kay."

"Billy here wants to be my assistant. We made an agreement. She needs a dress in case she decides to be Mason's guest for the wedding. I'm going to treat her to it, and in exchange she's going to help me out and watch the classes." I make sure to shift my tone for Beau to catch when I say the last part. His eyes light with understanding. He turns to Billy, his gaze sharp.

"You good with that, Beau? I mean. I'm not sure I'm going to the wedding or anything. Mason invited me, but I don't know those people, so I might not go anyway, but...."

"It's fine, Billy. I'll be at the wedding. Maybe Angel can come too. You can be my guests, and I'll make sure you guys can sit together with the family," Beau says.

I lift my brows at him. I wasn't expecting that. I'm not sure how to react. I'm with Billy's earlier statement. That's a lot of people. I don't know what kind of venue it is.

"I'll go if he goes," Billy says, pulling me from my spiraling thoughts.

Her words are filled with the trust she's showing me. I'm honored and thrown at the same time. This is the same kid who ignores people if she doesn't trust them. I've watched her do it all the time. Andres has been her person since I've started working here. For whatever reason, she's now extending the courtesy to me.

Looking down into her expectant, hopeful eyes, I want like hell to go. I don't know if I'll handle it well, but I already know I'm going for her. I'll just figure it out. "When's the wedding?" I ask.

"We have two and a half weeks," Beau says and rolls his eyes. Then says in explanation, "Our sisters are driving us crazy."

"Yeah, I got lucky when my sister got married. I was out of the country until the week of the wedding," I say.

"So you'll go?" Billy asks.

"Looks like we'll be going shopping, kid," I reply.

"Thanks," she says with a sage nod.

"No problem. I hope you're ready to work. I'll see you in the next class."

"I'll be here. Don't worry," she says. "Emma's here. Time to go. You'll take care of getting permission for me to go shopping, right?"

"I got you covered," Beau says. "I'll take care of it."

"Thanks, guys."

With that she darts off, looking the happiest I've seen since I've been working here. My heart warms knowing I had something to do with that. I turn to Beau when he clears his throat.

"Looks like you've made a friend," he says.

"I think so. I wish I knew more about her life, I have to admit."

"Trust me," he says as a dark look comes over his face. "Not something you want to know. We all read the kids' intake files to stay in the loop. I'll just say hers caused me to destroy two heavy bags in one night."

"That bad?" I ask, my brows furrowed.

"Of all of the kids, I want her to find a great permanent home the most. Although I don't think she'll trust anyone to take her. Kyle has been adamant that no child leaves unless they want to." He takes a pause and frowns. "That one's not leaving. I know it in my gut."

"You guys make her feel safe."

"That's the goal."

A thoughtful look crosses his face. The orphanage kids that come here mean a lot to him. I've picked up on that before.

It says a lot about him. It's one of the things I like about him most. Beau has a big heart.

"You seem to be pretty dressed up for our movie," I say.

He groans and runs his hand down his beard. "Shit, our date."

"We can go another night," I offer.

"No, no. I just came from a meeting. I planned to go home and change. Things ran over, and I needed to pick something up from my office. What time is the movie again?"

"Not until seven. You have plenty of time," I reply.

"Perfect," he says, reaching to squeeze my forearm. "We can leave for the movie from my place."

With a smile he turns and heads for his office. He doesn't have a clue that his simple touch has left me standing here with my heart racing. I shake my head and grin. He just called this a date.

CHAPTER FIFTEEN

Undeniable

Beau

"Hey," I call, drawing Angel from his thoughts.

I don't know what made me bring him back to my place. I just drove. Our movie turned out to be more eventful than we were hoping for, and not in a good way. Now we're sitting in the parking garage of my building. The tension rolling off Angel fills the entire car.

"I tried, right," he says.

I reach to cup his face. I hate seeing him like this. I brush my thumb across his stubble-roughened cheek.

"You did more than try. You're amazing. I thought you were going to call it quits as soon as you started to feel uncomfortable—"

"Uncomfortable." He snorts. "You mean as soon as I started to lose my shit."

"However you put it. You braved your way through the movie. That shit took heart and so much more. I have the hand you squeezed the shit out of to prove it." I grin.

"Sorry about that," he says and gives a small laugh.

"Never be sorry for needing me," I say before thinking better of it.

Something changes in his eyes. They darken as they search mine. Slowly I drag my finger across his lips. His tongue peeks out on the second pass.

"I want to thank you for doing this with me. For being there for me," he says huskily.

"You're welcome. Anytime."

"I should probably head home," he says.

"You could or… you could stay."

"Is that what you want? Be sure. I'm not a casual kind of guy. Because I wanted you, I was willing to make that one exception. Now I want more. I'm not going to lie. It can't be one night," he says.

"You coming up or not?" I say with a grin.

"Nah, that line ain't gonna cut it tonight, Beau. I respect you. You've done a lot for me. Your friendship means too much to me to step all over it for just one night. Are you ready for more than just a date?"

I lean in and take his lips in response. It's a demanding kiss that stakes a claim. I show him who he belongs to. After spending two hours in a theater watching him brave his demons, I can't find a single excuse for why I shouldn't take this leap.

However, I back off and break the kiss because I don't want to finish this here. I nip his lower lip in promise. The fire in his eyes mirrors what I feel on the inside.

"I think we've been past that a long time ago, don't you? Just in case I wasn't clear just now, I want more. Not just one night. Not just one date. Stay," I say against his lips.

"I'll stay, but do you mind if we chill on the rooftop for a bit? I'm still pulling it together."

"Anything you need. I actually could use a swim to cool off."

He leans in to nip my lip, this time taking as I give. When we groan in unison, we both break away.

"Yup, that swim sounds about right." Angel smiles.

Angel

I lean back on my palms and look up at the stars as my legs move lazily in the water of the rooftop pool. The night air is just what I need to get my head right. Twenty minutes into the movie, my back was soaked with sweat, and I had the chills. I couldn't keep my leg from bouncing, and I had a death grip on Beau's hand.

None of that had anything to do with the rom-com we watched. Still, Beau had stayed. I owed it to myself. I made a promise to me that I would push through, but he didn't have to. Oh God, he didn't stay for that whack-ass movie on the screen. Beau even had to admit it was terrible, and he is a self-proclaimed rom-com lover.

"Need another beer?" Beau moves to stand beside my legs as he ends a lap in the pool.

I lower my head to look at him. His hair is wet, and his chiseled upper body is on full display. I reach to retrace the path of a bead of water on his pec.

"Nah, I'm good. Come here."

He shifts to stand between my legs, our eyes locking as I cup his jaw. My hand slides to the back of his neck, and I lean in. Our lips connect, and we ignite the rooftop with the connection that unleashes between us. I groan into the kiss, coaxing his mouth open with my tongue. We start that battle of tongues, teeth, and lips that I'm beginning to learn will be our thing.

I like knowing that. It calls to something in me. I want to bend him to my will as much as I want to give in to his. I've never felt like that with anyone else. It excites and frustrates me because I don't know which I want more.

I growl into his mouth when his arms go around my back, and he lifts me from the poolside onto his waist. It's as if he's making the decision for me. My back hits the pool wall, but we don't stop the dance of our mouths.

Beau begins to grind while I claw down his back, pulling a shiver from him. Looking into his eyes, I bite his lip and pull. He hisses, and I release my hold to give the flesh a soothing lick.

"I want you so bad," he says huskily.

"You better take what you want before I do," I taunt.

"I'm a patient man, remember. You can't rush the best parts of life."

I lower my legs and flip our positions, his back to the pool wall, while I press into him. After hooking my fingers in his boxer briefs, I push them down.

I make sure to make eye contact when I lift Beau to sit on the side of the pool. His face tightens with lust. I know the feeling. Weeks of pent-up sexual tension begins to spill over.

Wrapping a hand around his length, I lick my lips. I plan to finish what I started last time. Holding his gaze, I grab his thighs and bring him closer to the edge. When I lower my head and flick out my tongue, his hips lift.

"Easy, Papi. I haven't even started."

I take in the crown and swirl my tongue. The loud groan that comes from the back of his throat is so deep and delicious, I start to salivate for more of him. When his fingers lock into my hair, what little restraint I had been using goes out of the window.

"Fuck," he hisses.

I pump him with my hand as my head rolls and bobs. My mouth has made him nice and slick for my hand to pass over his silky skin, but that's not good enough for me. Lifting my head all the way off to spit on him, I do it a second time before stroking him from root to tip.

"You like that? Tell me how you like that dick sucked," I say, looking into his half-hooded eyes.

"Swallow it whole, baby. I want your ass choking on it," he says in a tone that has me so hard, I think am going to bust right through my boxer briefs.

He has no idea what he just asked for. I deep-throat him and hollow my cheeks on the way back up. Yeah, I'm cocky as fuck about my head game, but I back that shit up. The look on Beau's face says it all.

That's right. I own this dick now.

He releases my hair from its band and fists a handful. I continue to suck the soul from his body, becoming his puppet master before his very own eyes. When he pops from my mouth, his mouth opens as if he's going to call me back to sucking, but I silence that noise. I lick his balls and suck them into my mouth while pumping him. His head drops back, and he curses in that heavy-ass drawl.

His country ass is sexy as fuck. The way his muscles cord, the flush in his cheeks, it's all turning me on more.

"Fuck, I'm coming," he groans as he grips the side of the pool.

His hips lift, pumping into my face. I love that he still smells like his body wash, mixed in with his natural scent even after swimming. His grip tightens on my hair, and that first hot rope of his seed coats the back of my throat.

I suck him clean, lifting my head to lick my lips. Beau drags me to him and crushes his lips to mine. My hand goes into his hair as he deepens the kiss.

I'm thoroughly dazed when he starts a trail of kisses from my jaw to my neck. My skin is on fire. His hands kneading my back only intensifies the feel of his lips' and tongue's exploration.

"My turn," he breathes in my ear.

Beau

I push back some and gesture with the crook of my finger for him to get out of the pool. He deserves a reward for giving me the best blow job of my life. There's still a tingle at the base of my spine.

I watch as he leaps out of the pool, water cascading from his body. He stands to his full height, pushing his boxers from his hips. They hit the ground with a wet plop.

He's in front of me with his hard cock aiming right for my face. I place a hand on his thigh to guide him to straddle me. I'm going to take my time and make this last.

I lick his inner thigh and nip the soft brown skin. "Widen your legs, baby," I command.

He steps wider, and I dip in to tease the other side, slow kisses and licks up his thigh. His cock bobs and twitches, begging for my attention. I don't give in. I go back to the other leg for a repeat.

"Beau," he says tightly.

"Patience," I breathe against his balls and flick them with my tongue.

"You're killing me."

"Not yet." I chuckle darkly.

Giving him a small reprieve, I lick the underside of his shaft, kissing his tip when I get to it. His jaw tightens as I watch him through my lashes. I tease him with another lick, and he groans.

"You're so damn beautiful," I say as I wrap my hand around him.

It's the truth. Everything about him is gorgeous. His strong thighs, his thick, long cock, that dark hair, his eyes, those lashes, and for the love of all that's holy, those dimples—all of it marks perfection.

"Beau," he strains out as I move to his thigh and freeze there, allowing my facial hair and breath to tease him.

"I've got you, darlin'," I murmur just before pulling him into my mouth.

And just like that, he goes from gorgeous to stunning. His head falls back and a vein pops in his neck. The sight alone spurs me on. My own groans mix with his as I suck and pump him.

"Damn, Papi. Fuck yeah," he croons. "Fuck yeah."

My fingers dig into his hip. My hand pumping him moves to cup his balls. I massage them while guiding him in and out of my mouth. Angel cups the back of my head and starts to take over.

It's that power play again. I relish watching how much that excites him. I only resist a bit to watch the light that comes to his eyes when we fight for dominance. If not for that, I'd yield simply because his cock has my mouth watering for more.

I smile around him when he releases a loud curse as I swirl my tongue around him. I have him. It won't be much longer before he releases into my waiting mouth. He swells against my tongue.

"I'm so close," he says tightly.

I grab his ass harder and guide him into my face, taking the control back. His legs start to shake and buckle, but I hold him up.

"Shit, Beau, fuck," he roars when he finally lets go.

I cradle his waist as his knees give. Gently I bring him into my lap. I kiss the side of his neck and face. I'm already growing hard again. He palms my face, and we lock lips.

We kiss lazily until we both find our legs again. I lead him inside to my bed, but I can sense that something has shifted between us. The urgency has burned out.

I pull the sheets back and slip into bed. When Angel follows me in, I cup his face and kiss him softly. I think we've made a big enough step forward for tonight.

Neither of us is going anywhere. Once I'm in, I'm in. When it comes to Angel, I'm all in.

CHAPTER SIXTEEN

Small Steps

Beau

"Where are we going?" Angel asks as we walk a few blocks from my apartment.

"New York is filled with these hidden gems all over the city. Private nooks of paradise. You'd be surprised what you'll walk right by and never know it's there," I say.

"This is true. A lot of hidden restaurants too. Places passed down by generations with some banging-ass food. We should head out to Brooklyn one of these days," he says. "Wait, you didn't answer my question."

I bump his shoulder. "Because I was trying to distract you." I laugh. "Be patient."

"Man, you got me around all these white people looking at me like I'm about to snatch their purse and shit. I have a right to know where we're going," he teases.

I've been trying to ignore that. I've noticed a few white women change direction or put more distance between themselves and us. It's something I'll never get used to. It used to happen all the time when Kyle and I would hang out as teenagers, growing into men.

Kyle tells me to get over it. It's his life as a black man. I think that's bullshit. My daddy never tolerated that shit, and neither will I. I call that shit out when I see it. However, I've been trying to enjoy this night and make it special.

"Funny part is, I'm the one dressed in black construction boots, a black hoodie with a big-ass black bookbag on my back," I grumble.

"It was a joke," Angel says, touching my arm.

Angel is still dressed in a suit from working Club Refuge tonight. He looks like he could be coming from a hard day in the office. Another woman with a dog looks at him and crosses the street. I grit my teeth and shake my head.

"Wrapped in truth."

"So is life, B. I can't peel my skin back and pretend to be someone I'm not. So I live my life knowing other people's opinions don't make me or break me," he says and shrugs.

"That's bullshit and you know it. You served this country like any other red-blooded American hero. Yet we could walk to the end of this corner and the police will throw your ass up against a wall and cuff you for walking while being brown. Meanwhile I could have an eight ball in my pocket, strip butt-ass naked, and spit at them, and it will take damn near twice as long for them to put me in cuffs," I say bitterly.

"You say that like you have experience," he says.

"Kyle's my brother, remember? Most my friends are from other ethnicities. I've seen a lot more than I'd like to admit. I don't live in a bubble pretending it's not a reality."

"Okay, I hear you. But what you know about eight balls?" he says with mirth.

"Man, I have stories. I watched some great fighters fall to drugs."

"Yeah, some good soldiers got hooked on all types of shit just to get by. When you start to see and do too much, it can fuck with your head," he says. "Some need the escape just to cope day to day."

"Man, I don't even want to imagine," I reply and wave for him to follow me into the small alleyway. "Come on."

I grin when he gives me a strange look. I head through the small passageway. With the key to the gate, I unlock it and push the fence open. Angel follows me in.

"I'm locking the gate. We have the only key to get in. Which I'm giving to you. If you need to leave, you do what you need to do. I just wanted to try this. I don't know if it will work," I say and hand him the key.

We walk farther in, and I turn to see his reaction. His brows are drawn, but I can see the tension that started the moment we entered the alley ease. I release the breath I didn't know I was holding.

"A garden?"

The small alleyway opens to a huge open garden between two of the smaller buildings in the city that allow for the sun to spill in and a third structure. The third building is the largest and highest at the back of the garden.

The center of the space has a bed of green grass big enough to toss around a football with a few friends. Around the perimeters are beds of roses, lilacs, and sunflowers that bloom in season. Murals cover the walls of the two smaller buildings, adding to the rustic city charm.

"Not just any garden. Just wait," I say with a huge smile. My excitement returns. I can't wait for him to see this. I almost forgot about this place. Angel is actually what reminded me of it. "It's good to have friends in hidden places," I say as I spread a blanket in the center of the grass.

I reach into my backpack for the snacks I packed and spread them out. I glance up at Angel as he looks around us, an amused expression on his face. Next I pull the device from my bag that will make this all clear for him.

"Oh, shit," Angel breathes as everything falls into place.

On the back wall of the garden, the opening credits to *Purple Rain* appear. He once told me it's his favorite movie. The black paint on the back of the building serves as the perfect screen.

"Want to watch a movie with me?" I say, holding my hand out for him to join me on the blanket.

Angel looks down at me in awe. He nods and takes my hand to sit beside me. I toss him the pack of M&M'S and grab the Sour Patch Kids for myself.

"Beau?"

"Yeah." I turn from the movie to look at him. His eyes are misty. He swallows hard.

"So I don't forget to tell you. This shit…. Thanks," he chokes out.

"Anytime." I nod. "If there's ever something you want to see, no matter what it is, I have a guy that knows a guy. We can get anything you want. That is until you're ready to go back to the theater."

"I think I like this better," he says.

I'd do this every night for the smile he's giving me now. I tug off my hoodie to get settled in. Angel loosens his tie and shrugs out of his jacket.

"Come here," I say.

He eyes the space between my thighs with a wicked smile on his full lips. We haven't gotten physical beyond kissing here and there since that night at the pool. I think we both subconsciously decided to tone things down.

The desire that builds between us can be all-consuming. I may have given into wanting to try this relationship, but I don't want to burn things out before they can start properly. I reach for the front of his shirt and tug him forward.

With a laugh, he comes to me and settles with his back to my front. I relish the warmth of his body against mine. We both settle in to watch the movie for the next hour and fifty-one minutes.

Angel

"That movie will always be my shit," I say as I stretch.

Beau hit this on the head. Even in the confines of this hidden getaway, I'm able to relax and watch the movie as the open night air kisses my skin. The city noise is somehow canceled out by the surround sound system built into the garden's walls or wherever they're mounted. This place is an amazing sanctuary.

"I'm not going to lie. It is a classic," Beau says.

I look over my shoulder. "Did you ever doubt me?"

He gives me a sexy smile as his eyes roll over me. "Never."

I go to turn to face him, but Beau has other ideas. He reaches for my shoulders and starts to massage. I don't protest. It's been a long day.

This surprise date was so unexpected. I thought we were going to order in and chill. When I arrived to find Beau with the backpack in his hands, I was curious, but I followed along.

Our relationship is built on a huge amount of trust. I knew whatever he had planned would consider my needs, but I really hadn't thought it would be such a thoughtful gesture. Shit like this has me falling for him faster than I thought possible.

"How are things at the club?"

"Pretty good. I'm not going to take the traveling gig Javi offered me. I don't think I'm ready for something like that. It would've been good money, but I'm not there yet," I reply.

"I can understand that. Javi's schedule can get crazy. I don't know how he does it."

"I was thinking the same thing. That guy is always on. Even when he hasn't been at the club for days, he knows everything that's going on with everyone," I say and shake my head. "He has my respect for real."

I've learned that my other boss likes to keep tabs on everything. He knows everything about everyone. One of the guys at the club just had a baby. Within the hour Javi had flowers, balloons, and gifts at the hospital. It was one of those times when he wasn't even in town to know something like that.

It's stuff like that that makes the guys working for him loyal. Everyone has so much respect for him at the club. It makes for a cool vibe.

"You sound like you like it there," Beau says.

"Yeah, I do."

"Good. Javi will look out for you in other ways if you don't want that promotion. It's just who he is," he says.

"I appreciate it. I'm trying to figure out my next moves, though. You know. What I want to do with my life once I can get a handle on it," I think out loud.

"What did you want to do before you enlisted?"

I take a moment to think about that. It seems like a lifetime ago. I was certainly a different person, driven by much different things. I laugh as I'm honest with myself. "You want to know the truth?"

"Always."

"Andres and I always talked about being fighters. MMA was his thing, but Papi had his eye on a boxing championship belt for me. I could've done it too." I smile at the thought now, in retrospect.

Back then I ran as fast as I could from the idea. I wonder what my life would be like if I would've followed that path instead. I might have met Beau in the ring.

"You were a boxer?" Beau pauses, his voice sounding haunted, causing me to turn to face him. His eyes search mine. My brows furrow.

"I boxed for a bit. I was in the Golden Gloves back in the day," I say cautiously. "You okay?"

"Yeah, I just didn't know you were a fighter."

I study him for a minute, and it clicks into place. I turn my body fully to face him. Placing my fingers beneath his chin, I lift his head until he meets my gaze.

"I don't think I'll ever get back in the ring. Being a soldier took a toll on my body. I don't think I could move around the ring the same. I've thought of coaching, but not fighting," I say.

He nods. Still that haunted look remains. He's either fearing for my life in the ring or haunted by dating another fighter. I'm not sure which, but I get the feeling it's one or the other.

I'm good at reading him, which is the reason I won't ask to see if I'm right and figure out which of my assumptions is the truth. After reaching for his palms, I bring them into my lap. With my pointer finger, I start to trace the lines in his hands.

"Everything about us lies in the palm of our hands. These lines tell so many stories. These hands have a great story to tell. The question is... will you tell it?" I say.

Beau clamps his hands shut and turns to busy himself with placing things back in his backpack. I don't want the date to end like this. We were having a great time.

"Beau."

He turns to me and I kiss him.

He's stiff at first, but as I push my way into his mouth with my tongue, he comes to life. I go to push him back against the blanket, but he switches it up on me. My back hits the ground as he hovers over me.

I don't mind now that I have his attention. I savor the taste of candy and Beau. My hands slide beneath his T-shirt.

"Shit," Beau grumbles as his phone starts to ring. "I have to answer that."

"No worries," I pant.

Beau rolls his eyes as he listens and grunts at the caller on the other end. It must be Emma with more wedding drama. He's been getting a lot of calls like this the last few days.

"Fine, fine, I'm coming." He sighs.

It was still the best date ever. I'll never forget you did this for me, Beau.

CHAPTER SEVENTEEN

Perfect Dress

Angel

"That's the one," Beau and I say in unison as Billy steps out of the dressing room. She looks like a little princess in the little blue dress. It's perfect for an eight-year-old little girl. Not too grown, like a few of the dresses the woman tried to show us in the other store.

The puffy skirts soften everything about Billy. The smile on her face says a million words. It's brightening the dressing room all around her.

It's important to me that she gets what makes her happy. I've only ever seen her in jeans and T-shirts. Neither Beau nor I wanted to bring her here and force her into a dress that wouldn't be comfortable for her.

Yet, the look on her face. This is it. It's Billy.

"I love that one," Aryanna says. "You should wear your hair down."

I've never seen Billy's hair not in that top knot braid style. It's always up and out of her way. She reaches up to touch her hair as she sways in the mirror, looking at her reflection.

"It's pretty," she says with that beaming smile.

"So is this the one?" I ask.

"Yeah, I like it." She turns to look at me. "I just don't know if it's right for the wedding. I've never been to one."

"You'll be the prettiest one there," Beau says gently. "It's perfect, darlin'. I think you should get it."

"Really?" she says with big wide eyes.

"I wouldn't lie to you," Beau says.

Billy's face shifts as she takes in Beau's words. She moves to us cautiously, looking up between us both. The decision made, she wraps an arm around each of our waists and hugs us at the same time.

When she releases us, the blush on her little brown cheeks makes her face glow. I smooth a hand over her hair and smile at her. This kid has been building her own home in my heart.

"Thank you," she whispers and turns back for the dressing room.

I wipe at the corners of my eyes and clear my throat. Beau's eyes are misted over as well. I guess I'm not the only one she's getting to. I wave over the clerk.

"That dress and the shoes please," I tell her.

Beau reaches in his pocket and pulls out his wallet. I glare at him and fold my arms over my chest. He knows good and damn well I promised Billy this was my treat. "What do you think you're doing?"

"I'm paying for her things," he says.

"No you're not. We're not getting into this one again. It was my offer. Put your wallet away."

"I wan—"

"Beau, you're here as a staff member from the home. This is something I'm doing for her," I say.

"Fine."

He frowns, but after side glancing my niece, he slips it back into his pocket. I shake my head and pull my wallet out to go pay. Billy comes to join me at the counter once again dressed in her worn jeans and T-shirt.

I can't help wondering why she's in such worn-out clothes. I've noticed that the other orphanage kids tend to dress in nicer things. Not wanting to embarrass her, I bank the thought for later to ask Beau about.

"Here you go, little miss," the clerk says, handing Billy the dress bag.

"Thank you," she beams.

"Your daughter is so polite and well mannered. You're doing a great job," the clerk says to me.

I go to correct her, but the small hand that creeps into mine cuts the words off. I look down at Billy's big brown eyes on me, a hopeful smile on her lips.

"She's a great kid," I say instead.

Beau

"You did a great thing for her today," I say as I climb back into the truck after dropping Billy and Aryanna off.

"I'd do it again if I could," he says. "Can I ask you something?"

"Anytime."

"Billy doesn't seem to dress as nicely as some of the other kids. Why is that?"

I laugh and look him in the eyes. "You really don't understand what took place today. Billy won't take the clothes we try to give her. She wears what she came with."

"Wow," he says, falling back in his seat.

"She likes and trusts you."

"That's... wow."

Kyle and Andy said the same thing when I told them about Billy accepting the dress. They were excited about her finding something for the wedding. Everyone knows how much Mason wants his little friend to join him.

Angel sits with a thoughtful express on his handsome face. I lean over to kiss his temple before I start the car. Things have been going well. We've been taking things at our own pace and it feels right. "Are you coming over tonight?" I ask.

"I don't know. I've been keeping you up with my pacing."

"No you haven't," I reply. Yes, I've noticed that halfway through the night he wakes to pace outside. When I asked him about it, he said that it happens. I wonder if it happens as often when he's alone at the gym.

I'm sort of a light sleeper, but it doesn't bother me when he gets up in the middle of the night. I usually fall right back to sleep. I've gotten used to it.

"Yes, I have. You pop up every time I get up to go out and pace the balcony."

"Would it be better if I come stay with you?"

"You would do that?" he asks.

"Why not?"

"You have that amazing apartment. Why would you want to sleep at the gym with me?"

I reach over to place my hand on his thigh. I glance over to find him frowning. I give a light squeeze to his leg. "You're my boyfriend, Angel. I want to spend the night with you," I reply.

A brief silence fills the car. I chance another look at him as I stop at a light. He has a small smile on his lips as he stares at me.

"We can go to your place," he says.

I lean and kiss his nose quickly before the light turns. My own reasons for having him over are selfish. I haven't been having the nightmares with him in my bed at night.

I rethink my own selfishness and consider his needs. I do want him to stay the night with me but not at the expense of his own comfort. I purse my lips in frustration with myself. "You know, I shouldn't have pressured you on this. If you feel you'll get more sleep at your place…?" I say after thinking it through.

"It's a hit or miss thing. I can sleep peaceful for a week or two and then not at all for a month. I'm staying with my man tonight. It's cool," he says.

That gorgeous smile is aimed at me when I peek at him, his dimples peeking out. I swallow hard when it hits me that I'm really in a relationship and I'm allowing my feelings to get involved.

You know what? That's a lie. I haven't allowed anything. I just like to think I have. In truth, Angel has pushed his way in and claimed something I didn't know I still owned.

"I wanted to ask you something," I say.

"Shoot."

"Have you ever thought about having kids of your own?"

"Yeah, I have. I come from a big family that comes from a big family. My moms would love nothing more than more grandchildren," he replies.

"So you can see them in your future?" I say. "I love Mason. When Kyle got custody of him, it made me think about having that someday, you know?"

"Yeah, I hear you. I was there when Andres's daughter was born. I swear it was one of those times when I felt like I could feel what my twin felt.

"I want to know that feeling for myself. But knowing that I'm gay and broke as fuck, I never really invested a lot of time into when or how I'd make that happen. Now I have all kinds of things going on. I don't know if that's an option," he murmurs.

He's looking down into his palms. His concerns have been my own. I want what Kyle and Andy have. The relationship, a kid. Heck, if I could have two or three, I'd be happy as a pig in shit.

"I believe it will present itself at the right time. My mama always says when you tell the Universe your heart's desire it fiddles with your life until you're turned in the direction of your heart's request," I say.

"Well, I guess I better start speaking up." Angel gives a dry laugh.

"You already have. Your heart speaks before your mouth. We live life being turned and not noticing it until we arrive," I say.

"Beau, are you being a philosopher on me?"

"No, darlin'. I'm just a man with a wise mama." I chuckle.

Angel shifts and I can feel those eyes on me. I turn to him and see the wheels turning. I place my focus back to the road just as he speaks.

"I want to meet her."

"You will at the wedding. She's threatening me with bodily harm. If I don't bring you to the wedding now, you may not find my body." I laugh.

"I like her already."

CHAPTER EIGHTEEN

Wedding Bells

Beau

This has been a beautiful wedding. Andy, Emma, and Tara did an amazing job. A private beachfront wedding that took everyone's breath away. I couldn't be more happy for my brother. If anyone deserves happiness like this, it's Kyle.

My friends are standing around me, drawing a huge smile to my lips. We've come a long way, the seven of us. We've been standing at the bar taking this chance to do as we always do. Our time to catch up. We're all here so we have to have this drink before the night's over.

"To Kyle," Javier says as we raise our glasses for our customary toast.

"Salud," we say in unison.

"Well I'll be," Jordan says. "Is that Billy?"

Everyone's attention turns to the dance floor. She looks gorgeous. Emma had a stylist come in to do her hair. It's falling down her back in large ringlets. She has the biggest smile on her face as she and Mason run around Angel on the dance floor.

"Who got her in a dress?" Javier says.

"Angel," I reply.

"You don't say." Javi grins. "I like Angel for you both. I've never seen that little girl smile that much. I knew there was something special about him."

"She's not the only one smiling. I haven't seen a smile reach your eyes like this in years," Daniel says.

I look around at the six men I consider my brothers. Men I've come to know and love. Friends I know I can always count on to have my back. "He's…. Well, the total opposite of what I'm used to. He has that sense of humor I love, but there's something else I can't put my finger on. It's just easy. We fit."

"Don't hurt that he's fine as hell," Chris says. "You know how to pick 'em."

"Yeah, he is killing that suit," Ray says.

"I personally think he took the cake with the man bun and the shape up." Kyle snickers as he takes in my pink cheeks. He steps away from the bar to place a hand on my shoulder. "But we all need to stop checking Beau's man out before his fists start flying."

"I was just about to point that out." Daniel laughs, patting me on the back.

"Billy looks like she could be you guys' little girl," Jordan muses. "Would love to see that girl have a good home."

"I think you are placing the cart before the barrel," I say. "Angel and I are just getting started. We have a lot to get through before we can even think about adopting that little girl."

"I'm only putting it out there. As much as I want to see her find a home, I'd hate to see her go. I've been toying with adopting her myself, but she's still so wary of everyone," Jordan says.

We all turn to look at Jordan. He's the playboy bachelor of the group. I can't even imagine him settling down and adopting a kid.

"Um," Kyle says in response to Jordan as he narrows his gaze.

Yup, Kyle's not the only one that's on to a change in Jordan. I've noticed he's been making comments that have given me pause. Hey, we're all getting older and changing. Kyle and I are the youngest. I guess it would be time that Jordan starts to think about what's next.

"She's wary of everyone except for your boyfriend." Chris nods back to the dance floor, bringing the subject back to Billy.

She now has her head thrown back in laughter as she stands on Angel's feet, while he dances her around the dance floor. I take out my phone quick to capture the moment before it's too late. As I peer down at the image, it's perfect.

"Excuse me, fellas. I see something I want to be a part of," I say, shoving my phone back into my pocket and heading for my Angel and the little angel who's wrapping him around her finger.

I walk across the dance floor to them with a huge smile on my face. Angel looks up in my direction when I'm about two feet away. I close the distance quickly as his eyes draw me in.

"Hey, do you two mind if I join in?" I say.

"Beau," Billy sings. "This is so much fun. Come on."

She waves me closer, taking one of my hands. Removing a foot from one of Angel's, she places it on mine. Angel grasps my other hand and we're all dancing together to Maroon 5's "Girls Like You."

"Can I ask you guys something?" Billy says a few moments into to the dance.

"Go on," I reply.

"You already know," Angel says.

Billy beams at him. I've noticed that when Angel and Billy have their small conversations, Angel falls into his most relaxed speech. He seems to be building a rapport with her.

"Does this mean Mas has two daddies now?"

"Technically, Kyle is Mason's uncle. Mason lost his mama when he was about four, but Kyle is more like his daddy now, I guess. So when you put it that way, I think you're about right. He does have two daddies now," I reply.

Billy's fingers flex around mine. I get the feeling they might have done the same with Angel's from the way his hand firms around mine. Her eyes bounce between the two of us.

"It's not my business or anything," she says more softly. "But... I was sort of wondering. Are you two like boyfriends or something? Not that I think that's bad like the stupid boys back home."

"Yes, we're together," Angel tells her.

Her eyes light up as she looks between us. Her grip tightens. I feel my throat clog with emotions.

"When can we go horseback riding again?" she asks.

"When would you like?"

Her face scrunches up in thought. Angel grins down at her. My heart palpitates as I think of this being my family someday.

"I don't want to be a pain or anything. You let me know when you can," she says, turning on her tough-girl act again.

"I'll check my schedule and let you know," I say, winking down at her.

Suddenly, the sound of a dish crashing to the floor rings out. It happens so fast, Angel pulls away from us, almost tipping Billy onto her behind. I'm quick enough to catch her and shove her behind my body.

Angel's head whips from side to side, his eyes distant and lost. He's gone. If I don't do something fast, this wedding day is going to be remembered for the wrong damn thing.

Against all my better judgment and knowledge, I do something I know I shouldn't. In a quick move, I pin his arms behind his back. He goes to headbutt me, but before his head gains full momentum, I grasp his face in my free hand and put my lips to his ear.

"Angel, baby, focus. Focus on me." I sway his body as the song playing says the same words.

I caress his jaw with my thumb, making this look as sensual as I can to the outside world. If anyone's looking close enough, they'll see the tension in both our bodies. Still, I work to make this look like a simple dance between lovers.

"Baby, I need you to focus," I repeat as he gives a struggle. "Angel, come back to me."

I go with what my mind tells me. I kiss his temple, coaxing him back to me. Mason appears, placing a hand on Billy's shoulder and leading her a few steps away, protecting her like a good little man. I'm aware that all of my friends, including Darwin and Andy, have surrounded us.

They're not making a scene of this. They've all begun to dance around us, covering and positioning themselves to step in if needed. I'm not surprised. I'm grateful. They're all aware of Angel's situation; they will do what they can to help.

"Come on, baby, focus," I whisper, ghosting my nose behind his ear. When he stops struggling, I look into his clouded-over eyes. "It's me. Focus on me, right here."

Slowly I release his arms and run my hand up and down his back. I continue to present an intense dance between lovers to everyone else. However, the look in Angel's eyes and the racing of his heart against mine tell a different tale.

That is until his eyes clear and a look of... appreciation, fear, and gratitude fills his eyes. I nod at him so he understands I have him. I continue to sway him as tears fill his eyes. I shake my head at him.

"I'm here. I've got you. It's fine," I whisper against his lips.

His arms go around me, holding me tightly to him. I flick my tongue over his lips, again coaxing him to relax. I move my mouth back to his ear.

"Only thing that matters right now is that you're here with me," I say, slipping my hand beneath his suit jacket. "Did I tell you how good you look tonight? I've been wanting to peel you out of this suit since I saw you in it."

"Beau, this isn't going to work. I shouldn't be here," he chokes out.

I nip his earlobe, then lick the flesh behind his ear. "Bullshit. You're mine now. You're right where you belong. In my arms. I told you, focus on me, on us. You're stuck with me, baby. We're in this together."

"Billy," he gasps.

"She's fine. Me and you," I whisper, tracing the shell of his ear with my tongue to distract him. "You and me. Let's stay here. Let everything else go for now."

I bury my face in his neck and inhale. My lips brush his skin, and the tension in his body finally fully relaxes. My hand roaming beneath his jacket rubs soothing circles. I lift my head and lock gazes with him.

"That's it. Come take a walk with me," I say.

He nods, and we turn for the beach. Billy watches us, as she stands with Mama, Emma, and Mason. My family.

She's safe.

Angel

I can't believe I almost ruined the wedding. I could've hurt Billy. I'm ready to go home. I loosen my tie and kick off my shoes.

Beau removes his as well. Leaving them behind, we start down the beach, walking against the shoreline. I'm still coiled tightly inside.

"Can I tell you something?" Beau says.

"Yeah."

"Eric diagnosed me with PTSD a year after the... the incident. While I know mine isn't nearly as severe as yours, it affects things I wish it didn't. Like me being able to step into the ring," he says.

Realization hits. While Beau trains his fighters from the outside of the ring, he *never* enters. I've never noticed until now.

"Wait, but you offered to stay with me at the gym the other night. You know I've been sleeping on a pallet in the ring, right?"

"Yeah, I know."

"You were willing to sleep there with me, though?"

"I hadn't thought about it until later that night, after you left bed. I realized I would've tried. I would've done my best for you," he says.

"For me?"

"For you," he says, giving me that heated stare.

Yet, there's something more than lust. Something I've been trying not to dwell on. I don't want to get my hopes up. I know where my feelings for him have gone. My skin is still buzzing from his touch on the dance floor. When I focused on him, all I could register was his touch. My thoughts were scattered, but I had a full sense of Beau.

"Will you try to get in the ring for me if I ask?" I don't know what makes me ask; the words just tumble out. As they do the desire to see him try rises. I've been watching videos of his old fights. Beau belongs in the ring.

"If you want me to stay the night with you. I'll try," he says after a beat.

"Nah, that's not what I meant," I reply.

He stops and turns to me. His gray eyes turn hard as they search my face. I don't back down.

"Now what are we talking about here?" he says, his drawl heavy.

"Will you step in the ring? One step at a time, right? Try something that used to come naturally to you. Step in the ring."

"This isn't the same thing," he says tightly.

"Yeah, it actually is. A few months ago, I wouldn't have come to this wedding. Not for you, not for Billy. But I want my life back, so I'm fighting with everything I have to try. A simple request, a little step at a time."

"It's not the same. You didn't kil—"

"I didn't kill someone?" I snort bitterly. "Nah, baby. I didn't accidently kill someone. I killed hundreds with intent. For my country, I have more blood on my hands than you can imagine."

"Shit, Angel. I didn't mean to say that." He blows out. Frustration twists his features. His words don't anger me. I'm just as frustrated as he is. I want him to see where I'm coming from in requesting this.

"Do you think I like living like this? I stay the night with you, but I can't stay the night in your bed. I'm always out on that fucking balcony trying to breathe," I say, the pain and torture clear in my voice. "But I do it. I do it because I want this. I want this so much even though I'm scared to death I'm going to fuck it up."

"Angel—"

"No, all I'm trying to say is this shit *is* hard. Fighting to have a life. I'm not trying to downplay your shit, Beau. But try… for me. If I can see you try… I… I'll know I'm not in this alone."

He closes the small distance between us, pulling me into him. His hand comes up to cup my jaw. He gives a small nod.

"I can't promise you anything." He pauses to swallow hard. "I'll try. You're not in this alone. I'll try."

"And I'll be there when you do. I promise you that."

He gives me another nod. His eyes soften. I lean and kiss him lightly, my arms going around him as we start a slow-burning kiss. He tastes of brandy and vanilla from the wedding cake.

The kiss deepens, and we both moan. I push his suit jacket from his shoulders to the sand. Mine follows. I'm tugging at his shirt to get it out of his pants as he releases the buttons of mine.

"We can get to the room from here," he says against my lips.

"We better move fast before we don't make it."

"Agreed, or the alcove. It's closer," he breathes.

We'd gone for a run this morning before things got crazy. We both noticed the alcove off from the view of the rest of the properties and the beach. Almost like it's there to lure lovers in. "Tempting, but I've embarrassed us enough for tonight."

Beau grabs the back of my neck, forcing me to look at him. His face takes on a serious look. "You didn't embarrass anyone. Those are my brothers back there. They have our backs no matter what. When we make you family, we take care of you," he says.

My heart swells. I miss having a brotherhood like the one I see between Beau and his friends. Not that Andres isn't there for me. It's just something I can't explain. A comradery that builds while you fight through things together. I can see that Beau and his friends have been through those types of battles together.

"Thank you. For what you did back there," I say.

He traces a finger from my temple to my jaw. "I don't think there's anything I wouldn't do for you," he says.

I grab the front of his shirt and tug him to me. "Are you sure?" I say against his lips.

"Pretty damn certain."

"Give yourself to me. Let me take you someplace no one else ever will."

"Too much talking, Angel. Let's go," he says, with a grin on his full lips.

I bend to snatch up our coats and drag Beau with me back down the beach. We all rented rooms for the night. Emma offered to keep Billy with her in her suite. Before I can say a word, Beau has his phone out, shooting off a text.

"Emma should be able to handle Billy. Things were about to wrap up soon," he says as we reach our rental.

I'm still annoyed he won't let me chip in for this place. While most of the guests staying over are in the main hotel, Beau rented the spacious condo suite because of me. The space is wide open, and there's a deck in the back.

I toss our jackets onto one of the wicker chairs by the front door. Beau spins me to face him, pressing my back to the nearest wall. His hands are on my skin beneath my shirt. Our lips lock on each other's once again.

This kiss is harder. That war begins and a smile comes to my lips. I work to get his buttons free. I have to fight the urge to rip them open.

"Your lips taste so good." He groans.

"I've something else I want you to taste."

I want my hands on him. Memories of him sucking my dick has me so hard, I can't think. I get the last button open and push the shirt from his shoulders, tossing it to the floor.

I wrap my hand around his throat and give a gently squeeze. Surprise lights his eyes, but not for long. Lust quickly replaces the stunned expression. I seize his lips, nipping, licking, and sucking.

He meets my passion as his hands bury into my hair. I start to walk him back toward the master suite. With my free hand, I reach for his belt and start to work it free.

I slam his back into the wall right outside the bedroom door. I drag my lips from his, moving to his neck that I release from my grasp. I take my time to nip and suck there. His moans and groans grow with each inch of his skin I cover with my heated mouth.

"You have all of my attention, Papi," I say against his skin.

"What should I do with it?" he croons.

"I don't know, baby. What do you think you can do with it? Or better yet, do you think you can keep it?" I challenge. I push his pants down his hips. His dick springs free and his thick thighs come into view. I grin. Even his stance says he's ready to take control of this. I don't know if he realizes how much of that swag he gives off. That shit is sexy.

His fingers tighten in my hair, tugging me to his lips. Yet he doesn't kiss me. Instead, he tugs my head backward and nips his way down my throat. I groan when his teeth sink into my skin. Not breaking the surface, but a warning of his dominance.

I can play these mind games with him all night. Learning how to find balance in our relationship will be a challenge, but it's one I'm ready for. That is if we're not consumed by the fire of the journey to get there. Instead, I release my own belt and pants. I push them down my hips with my boxers, while he feasts on my neck and collarbone.

"Am I keeping it, darlin'?" he whispers in my ear.

"Yes, you still have it. Do I have yours?"

"Damn sure do," he says, taking my lips.

I reach between us and wrap my hand around him. My strokes are nice and easy to start. I want this to build slow. This time when we explode, I want it to be clear that we're fighting for each other. Him agreeing to step in the ring is huge. I know it is. I want to show him what that means to me.

"I'm not going to last if you keep that up," he grunts.

"Don't worry, we have all night. *Créeme*," I reply.

"What?"

I give a breathless laugh. "Trust me, Beau. I said, trust me, Papi."

I release his dick and grab his wrists, pinning them above his head. I hold his gaze as I press into him. Our erections trap between our bodies. He's hot and hard against my belly, and I'm pulsing with need against him.

I use one hand to hold his together. With the other I explore his torso. The feel of his warm skin beneath my palm brings a calm to my entire being. My hand travels back up his ribs, and I place it over his heart.

"I've learned that everything in life has a cost. What I want from you is priceless, but I know you're the one I want it from because I've already given the same to you," I say as the word bubble up inside me.

"Ask."

"Give me your heart, Beau. *Te amo.* You already have mine."

He breaks the hold I have on his arms. In the next breath, he has me lifted onto his waist. The shit shocks and throws me. His holding my weight in the pool was one thing. When he starts to walk into the bedroom with me on his waist, I'm stunned. I'm at least two-twenty.

I mean, Beau's sexy-ass body is fit. I guess I'm finding out what real power lies within it. My hands are in his hair as we devour each other's mouths.

My back hits the cool sheets, and Beau's weight presses down on me. I groan, loving the feeling. He plants his hands on either side of my head, grinding into me as he skillfully sips from my lips. I wrap a hand round the back of his neck, taking over to guide his mouth over mine. He smiles against my lips.

Beau breaks the kiss to look down at me with such intensity. I run my hand down his chest to his waist. He stills.

"I can't give you something you already own," he says huskily. "It's broken and battered, but it's yours. I don't remember when you stole it, but you snuck in somehow without me knowing."

I flip us, slamming his back onto the mattress. We grin at each other. I dip to nip his chin. "Are you saying you love me, Beau?"

"*Te amo*," his country ass says, and it's the sexiest thing he has ever said to me.

"I love you too," I say and start to kiss my way down his body.

I pause to dip my tongue into his belly button. When I drag it back out, I make circles through the trail of hair leading down to his pulsing erection. He always smells so damn good.

"Come here, Angel," he says gruffly.

"Nah-uh." I shake my head.

He bites his lip and nods. "I said come here, put your cock in my face."

Seeing his intention, I grin and shift my body over him. I lower my head to take him in at the same time his mouth slides over my dick. I groan around him, but I continue in my task. I take him in until my nose hits his balls.

"Oh, fuck," Beau grunts as I pop from his mouth.

I deep-throat him a few more times before working him with my hand and mouth. It takes him a moment to recover and join in again. However, as usual Beau isn't to be outdone. He releases my dick from his mouth to lick from my balls to my ass. Parting my cheeks with his big hands, he starts to eat my ass.

My eyes roll in my head and I falter in my own mission for a moment. Moaning, I rub my face and mouth all over his soaked dick. I take him back in and focus on getting him there as he drives me insane. He starts to rub at my opening, and I shiver.

He begins to swell in my mouth. I have him close. Reaching behind his balls, I press two fingers into the flesh there and rub. He bursts his hot seed right into my mouth on cue.

"Holy fuck," he bellows.

I laugh and shift from hovering over him. I flip him onto his stomach and straddle his hips. While he comes back down, I kiss and massage his back. I lick my way down his spine, stopping at the base.

"Don't give up on me now, Papi. I'm just getting started," I call out.

Beau

I grunt into the sheets, and Angel laughs against the sensitive spot at the base of my spine. He doesn't even know my lower back is one of my hot zones. It shouldn't be possible that I'm starting to harden again.

I'm spent, and we haven't even started. I've never come so hard in my life. I thought that the last time Angel went down on me, but this time was twice as intense.

I'm just starting to calm my heart and breathe when he begins to lap at my crack. He pries me open for him with his long fingers. His tongue leads the way to my puckered hole. I groan and grip the sheets. His tight grip on my ass has me grinding my teeth.

"Relax," Angel whispers.

He releases me, and the bed shifts under his weight. I look over my shoulder to find him reaching into his overnight bag. He retrieves lube and condoms.

"I think you planned to take advantage of my Southern hospitalities this weekend, Angel," I tease.

"Don't go blushing on me now. I saw the box of condoms in your bag." He laughs.

"Have no idea what you're talking about."

"Sure, you don't." He gives me a pointed look and grin, moving back for the bed.

Placing the items on the nightstand, he climbs onto the bed. Angel goes to straddle my hips again, but I turn onto my back and drag his body down on top of mine. My hands are in his hair again as I take his lips in a slow drugging kiss.

His hands caress my sides, moving up to cup my face. I turn to pull his fingers into my mouth and suck on them. Those whiskey-brown eyes watch me with so much want.

"Make them nice and wet for me, Papi," he says, his voice raw with lust.

I twirl my tongue around them, soaking each digit, one by one. My jaw tightens, and I groan when he pulls them free and sticks them into his own mouth. I watch as he moves his hand down between us and starts to massage my asshole. He takes his time preparing me slowly with his fingers.

After reaching for Angel, I bring him back to my lips. I reach between us to stroke him, but after two strokes, he knocks my hand away. I think of taking the lead, but just like on the dance floor, I go with what I feel Angel needs. Sensing that this is how tonight has to be.

"I won't always need things this way. Tonight—"

"I didn't ask for an explanation, so stop explaining," I cut him off.

He smiles, reaching for a condom from the nightstand. I watch him as he tears it open with his mouth. He rolls it on without looking away from me. I reach for the lube packet and hand it to him.

His eyes soften. The action shows my surrender to him. A surrender I'll never give to another. A surrender I've never offered to anyone else. Not even the man I once thought was the love of my life.

"I love you," Angel says.

"Show me how much."

He makes quick work of the lube before covering my body with his. Heart to heart, eye to eye, he pushes in just a bit. I relax as much as I can.

"Slow, *mi amor*. I won't hurt you. Let me in," he says, taking my lips.

He guides himself in with one hand, lacing the fingers of the other with mine at the side of my head. I dig the nails of my free hand into his back. He pushes deeper, and my hold tightens.

"Ah, Beau." He groans.

He reaches for my other hand, and I lock my legs around his hips as he eases out again. He sets a slow pace that bites and sends shock waves through me at the same time. He searches my eyes as he pumps in and out of me.

"Don't stop," I say when concern enters his eyes.

"You feel so good," he breathes.

"You do too. So good."

"Stroke your dick for me," he commands, releasing my right hand.

He lifts onto his palm, and I reach between us and start to stroke. His eyes are locked on me as I stroke my cock and mine are on him. Sweat start to drip from his face onto my chest, and his pace picks up as my grunts and groans increase.

"Fuck, you're about to come again. I can see it," he says. "I'm going to come with you."

I stroke harder as his movements become choppy. He takes my mouth, but I don't stop stroking, and he doesn't stop rolling his hips into my ass. We call each other's names as we release in sync.

When he collapses onto my body, I absorb his weight like a blanket that I've cherished all my life. I never want to let him go. I begin to absently run my fingers up and down his back.

"You were just what I needed right when I needed it," he says as if reading my thoughts.

"I was just thinking the same exact thing."

CHAPTER NINETEEN

Broken Peace

Beau

"I can't say that I've been this at peace in a long time," Angel says as he sits between my thighs in the tub.

I push his wet hair from his neck and kiss his soft skin. I inhale, allowing my own peace to wash over me. The warm water and soft music from his phone add to the aura surrounding us.

"I know what you mean. I was thinking the same thing."

The water splashes as Angel shifts his body, reaching to palm the back of my neck. I close my eyes as he starts to massage and knead my skin. I kiss his neck over and over, getting lost in the silence, within the peace.

It's a place where no sound exists. Just us and our peace. Nothing can touch us here.

This has been what my life has been missing. If I could make this last forever, I would. I'd capture it for us both and share it with the one person I know needs it as much as I do.

"It's funny how much your life can change in five months," Angel says softly.

My brows furrow. "It seems like it's been so much longer than that."

"It does, but it hasn't. Exactly one hundred and fifty-five days ago, I started living in your gym," he says.

"You know exactly how many days?"

"Marine life. We live in days. Everything was counted in days for me," he says.

I think on that. I don't think I want to know how many days have passed since I became a walking zombie. I run a hand into the front of his hair and tip his head back. I brush his forehead with my lips.

"I'm going to start work on the new project soon. More changes will come," I murmur.

"We'll figure it out," he yawns.

"We will," I reply. "Angel?"

"Yeah."

"Move in with me."

I hold my breath as a new silence fills the room. My shoulders feel like a weight rests on them. It's too late to snatch the words back, but that wouldn't be me. I said it; I meant it.

"Honestly, I've been at your place most nights over the last two weeks. It already feels like I live there," he says.

"I—" I frown as my phone rings in the other room. It's my ring tone for Emma. Knowing she has Billy, I jump up. My mind races as I step from the tub. "That's Emma's ringtone," I call over my shoulder as I rush off without a glance back.

I find my phone on the nightstand and answer. My heart sinks as Billy's cries ring out in the background.

"What's going on?" I demand.

"She had a nightmare. She won't settle down. She's asking for you," Emma rushes out.

"Me?"

"Yeah," Emma says as if she's talking to an idiot.

"I'm on my way," I say.

"Everything all right?" Angel asks as he appears with a towel round his waist.

"It's Billy," I say. "She had a nightmare."

He rips the towel away and rushes to get dressed in sweats and a T-shirt. I have on shorts and a zip-up as I shove my feet into my sneakers.

"Let's go," Angel says, moving for the door.

Angel

We enter Emma's suite to Billy's sobs. When Beau and I enter the bedroom she's in, she jumps up and runs across the mattress into Beau's arms. The look of awe on his face would cause me to laugh if I weren't so concerned for the little one in his arms.

"*¿Qué pasa, carino? Dile a Ángel qué tienes?*" I croon in Spanish, asking her for the source of her tears.

"He was in my dreams again. I couldn't fight back. The fire was coming for me," she says on a shuddering breath. She turns her sad eyes to me as she sniffles. After a moment's thought, she leaps from Beau's hold into my arms. Beau reaches to rub her back soothingly.

"*Nunca dejaré que nadie te vuelva a lastimar,*" I say into her hair. I make the vow to protect her and mean it with everything I am. There's not a chance in hell I'll ever let anyone hurt her again.

"*¿Me lo prometes?*"

"*Te lo prometo con cada aliento que tengo.*" It's a promise I plan to keep.

"Are you going to be okay?" Beau asks, his face tight with worry.

She turns to look at him. "Yeah, I am now," she whispers.

"Looks like this calls for a slumber party," I say, kicking off my shoes.

I move to climb into the bed. I place Billy beside me, and she wiggles into my side. I pick up the remote and turn on the TV. After reaching for the covers, I pull them up over our legs. Beau looks at me like I've lost my mind.

"Beau, you're not made of glass. Do you mind moving?" I say.

Billy turns the covers back. "Come on, you're in the way," she says and rolls her eyes.

Beau shakes his head, but he moves to the side of the bed and steps out of his shoes. Emma stands in the doorway with shock written all over her face. Her features soften into a wide smile, when Billy shifts to lean her head on Beau.

"Plenty of room," Beau says to Emma.

"No, I think it's already picture perfect. I'll sit this one out," she replies.

CHAPTER TWENTY

Motherly Wisdom

Beau

"You boys arrived just in time," my mama says as we enter the kitchen.

It smells amazing in here. I look around and see she's gone all out. Homemade biscuits, a roast, green beans, and her seafood chowder. If my nose is telling me the truth, cookies and cherry pie are in the oven.

"You didn't have to do all of this, Mama," I say.

"Oh, please," she waves me off. "You two are huge. I had to make sure I had enough for the both of you."

"She expecting ten more of us?" Angel whispers.

I elbow him, and he tries to stifle his laugh. Rolling my eyes, I move to give my mama a kiss on the cheek. She returns it, wiping her lipstick away after.

"Nice to see you again, Angel," she says with a mischievous smile.

"Behave," I whisper in her ear.

"I'm going to keep telling you. You're not my daddy, Beau James Dalton."

I snort and grab a green bean to pop in my mouth. As always she's outdone herself. I love my mama's cooking.

"I thought you were a gorgeous man in a suit. You are just as breathtaking in jeans and a T-shirt," she says to Angel. "My son has good taste."

My stomach drops. And this is why I've been dreading this dinner. This woman will embarrass me as if it's her job to do so.

I've never been so nervous to come to my mama's house in my life. With everything going on at the wedding, she didn't get much time to spend with Angel. She's been calling me for weeks now asking us to come by.

We've both just been extremely busy. I have the tournament coming up and the new project fixing that run-down complex. I've been working nonstop. I barely get time to spend with Angel myself. Javi has been asking him to put in more hours for private events, and Angel has taken on a lot of my tasks at the gym to help me out.

Most nights we both fall face-first into the mattress. Angel has even been sleeping more. Exhaustion will do that to you.

"Good looks run in your family as well," Angel says, turning on the charm.

"A smooth talker too." Mama actually blushes.

The sound of running feet comes from the front of the house. Within seconds Mason, Billy, and Aryanna push their way into the kitchen. I look at my mama, but she looks away guiltily.

"It smells good in here," Kyle croons as he and Andy walk in holding hands.

A smiling Emma brings up the rear with Andres. I fold my arms over my chest and glare at my mama. She swore up and down it would just be the three of us for dinner. Not that I don't love my family, but it's tiring to have to interact with so many people.

"This was the first weekend both Angel and I had off at the same time. We would've stayed home if I'd known you were planning a party," I say.

"You too good to spend time with your family?" Kyle says, coming over to punch me in the arm.

"I'm too tired," I grumble.

"I'm not going to argue there," he says.

"Yo, Beau, what's up?" Billy says as she stops in front of me, munching on a cookie my mama just finished handing out to the kids.

"You'll spoil your dinner eating that," I say.

She looks at the cookie, then back at me. "Worth the sacrifice. Someone has to do it." She shrugs.

Everyone laughs except for me. I glare at Billy, causing her to stuff the rest of the cookie in her mouth. She smiles around a mouthful of the confection, and I can't help cracking a smile. I reach to pinch her nose between my fingers.

"No more until after dinner, smarty pants," I say.

"I'm not making any promises. Your moms is the truth with the baked stuff. I came here for the food," she says.

"God, she's adorable," my mother snickers.

"She's a brat," Angel teases.

Billy places a hand to her chest in mock horror. "And here I thought you guys loved me."

"*Te amo amiguita*," Angel says. "I just know you're a brat."

"Not feeling the love," Billy huffs and takes off after Mason and Aryanna who have gone into the living room.

I smile after her. Billy has truly relaxed into her surroundings lately. At least at the gym and around my family.

"We never got to have cookies before dinner," I pout at my mama.

"Aren't you too old to be whining?" Mama levels her eyes on me.

"It's better than brooding. I'll take it," Emma chirps.

"Point well taken," Mama says.

I glare at Emma as she grins back at me. I take offense to her words. I'm not a brooder. "I don't brood."

"Yeah, you do," Angel snorts around the cookie he just stuffed in his mouth.

Mama pats his arm and beams at him. I turn my glare to them all ganging up on me. I look around, and everyone nods in agreement.

"Whatever," I mumble.

"Thank you for the invitation, Mrs. Dalton," Andres croons.

"None of that," Mama waves. "You boys call me Daphne."

"Yes, ma'am," the twins say in unison.

Watching Angel stand next to his brother, I still can't get over how much they look like each other. Yet I would still know the difference. Angel sees me staring at the two of them and winks.

"You look happy." Mama comes to hand me one of her famous cookies from the fresh batch she just pulled from the oven.

I smile wide. She knows I love them when they're piping hot and all gooey. I think over her statement as I chew. "I am," I say in between bites.

"More good things are coming your way, just you wait," she says, reaching to squeeze my hand.

"Let me go," Mason cries out.

"Oh my God," Aryanna's voice says simultaneously.

The only person I don't hear say a word is Billy. We all head for the living room where the two voices came from. When I step across the threshold, I find Aryanna with her hands over her mouth and a look of surprise on her face.

Next I find Billy and Mason on the floor. Billy has Mas in a chokehold as Mas tries to break free. At first I'm stunned and confused at what I'm looking at. I don't know what to make of this scene.

"Take it back," Billy says.

"Let go," Mason gasps.

"Billy," Angel and Andres bark in unison. "Let go."

She looks up with a scowl but releases her hold. Mason sucks in air as he rubs his neck. Billy stands with her little fists balled.

"What's going on in here?" Kyle demands.

"He just asked if I wanted to go horseback riding with them," Aryanna says.

Her face is crestfallen and confused. I look at Billy, feeling my own confusion. I've never seen her become violent like this before. "And you put him in a sleeper hold?" I say incredulously.

"Yeah," Billy says to her shoes.

"*Por qué?*" Angel asks.

"It's our thing," she whispers. "He shouldn't have invited her."

"I thought we were friends," Aryanna says as tears start to spill.

"We are," Billy says as her own lips start to tremble. "But that's special. I'm sorry."

I sigh and rub my forehead. Is this what I have to look forward to if I have kids? Good Lord. Angel and I may have to rethink that talk.

I walk over to squat in front of Billy. My heart bleeds when those brown eyes look up at me. I couldn't be pissed at her if I tried. I cup her little chin in my hand.

"First, no matter who comes with us to the ranch, it will always be our thing. No one can replace you. Sharing is a good thing. The more people, the more fun.

"Second, you can come to the gym to help Angel, but you're banned from your lessons for a month," I say, and her shoulders sag.

"Listen to me, Billy. You can't go around using what we teach you to harm people. Self-defense and competition are one thing. Choking your friends because they do something you don't like is not acceptable."

"Okay," she says.

"You owe Mas an apology."

"I'm sorry, Mason," she says.

"It's okay, I wasn't thinking. I just thought you would like to have a girl come with us sometimes," Mason says.

Billy's face really twists up, and she bursts into tears. I think Mason's thoughtfulness hit her in the heart as much as it does me. He was only thinking of her.

I pull her into a hug, until her sobs slow. She pulls away, wiping her face. My heart fills with so many emotions when she walks over to Mason and pulls him into a hug and whispers something to him. He nods and hugs her back, rocking her as she sobs a little more.

I don't think there's a dry eye in the house. I stand, and Angel moves to my side and squeezes my shoulder. Mama catches my eye and tilts her head for me to follow her. She points to Angel, signaling from him to come along.

Angel

We step into Daphne's den, and she closes the door behind us. I feel like a kid being called into the principal's office for something I didn't do. She turns on both of us and levels us with a stare.

"I wanted to talk to you boys about that little girl before everyone arrived. I watched her with you two at the wedding, and that—" Daphne points toward the living room, her voice hitching. "—is proof I'm right."

"Right about what, Mama?" Beau rubs his temples.

"She belongs to you two."

"Wait, we're just getting started. There's no way we can drag that little girl into our lives," he whisper-yells.

"Have you forgotten that you were twenty-five the last time I took a spoon to you? I'll tan your hide."

I snort a laugh but cut it off quick. Pursing my lips, I cover my mouth with my hand. Beau folds his arms and frowns at me.

"You do realize she's talking to the both of us?" he says.

"I do."

He narrows his eyes. I sigh and drop my hand. I know I should be taking this seriously. Daphne just has a way with words and Beau.

"Beau, the way you just handled that situation not only shows how much you care about her, it shows that you're what she needs. I've been to that home you boys built. I've watched her. She doesn't act the same there as she does when she's with you," Daphne says.

"I volunteer as much as I can at the complex, and Billy is one of the kids that comes to the gym," Beau starts.

"But she needs more than that," she cuts him off.

"We barely had time to come here. How does a little girl fit into that?"

"You make her fit," Daphne says firmly.

Beau throws his arms in the air. He tugs at his hair and starts to pace. The frustration on his face ages him in the moment.

"Daphne, I think Beau has a point. We're not quite ready to take on a little girl. I have issues. We don't have room for her at the loft—"

"Yes, you do," Daphne cuts me off. "He owns the damn building. The other two apartments on that floor are vacant. He's been talking about blowing them out and expanding since he bought the damn place. With my son's imagination for designing property, he can make her a darn Barbie house of her own on the other side of the apartment."

Daphne's frustration starts to spill over. I begin to see how much thought she has put into this. My wheels start to turn as I hear her out.

"Mama," Beau says, bracing himself against the back of a wingback chair.

"Beau," she replies. "I'm not saying you boys need to take her home tonight. I'm just telling you, that little girl is yours. It's time to buck up and get things in order for her."

"Who says we'll even still be together after I tear my apartment apart to make a home for her?"

I stiffen and rock back on my heels. Beau turns toward me and grimaces. I hold my hands up and shake my head.

"You're right. Who knows," I say tightly.

"Angel—"

"It's fine."

It's not, but it's too late to take the words back. He places his hands behind his head and throws his head back. Daphne moves over to me and places a hand on my arm.

"My son has a habit of sticking his foot in his mouth." She looks between us. "You two don't see the way you look at each other. I noticed what happened at the wedding. You may have fooled people that didn't know you two.

"I don't know you well yet, but I know my son, and I noticed," she says to me, then turns to her son. "What you did was dangerous, Beau. Don't try something like that again. You could've been hurt."

"I'm sorry," I say.

"For what, sugar?" she says turning back to me. "You have nothing to be sorry for. My point is, I watched the love in what Beau did. I saw the look on your face when you focused your attention on him.

"I think you two are capable of anything. Including slaying that little girl's demons and yours. I know you, Beau James. If I don't say something now you'll drag your feet on this because you'll tell yourself all the reasons not to do it," she says.

I wrap an arm around her shoulder, still feeling the sting of Beau's words. "We'll talk about it," I assure her.

Beau tries to catch my eyes, but I avoid looking at him. Daphne pats one cheek and kisses the other. "That's all I ask. You boys will do the right thing."

CHAPTER TWENTY-ONE

Things You Love

Beau

There's a gap a mile long between me and Angel. That stupid comment has been haunting me for a month. Just as fast as we've fallen for each other, we're falling apart.

I don't know what to do to fix this. He says we're fine, but he's been distant. I'm just so damn frustrated.

"Yo, Beau."

I look up at my office door. Billy's standing there with her arms crossed. "Hey, darlin'. What's up?"

"It's been a month," she says.

I furrow my brows, and my head clouds with a ton of thoughts. It hits me what she's referring to after a moment. She's right; it's been a month since I banned her.

"It has."

"Can I get back to my lessons?"

I put my pen down and sit back in my seat. I regard the little girl before me. I thought she would choose to stop coming to the gym once I banned her from training. She's been committed.

"Come in and sit for a minute," I tell her.

She moves to one of the seats before my desk and climbs into it. This isn't the little girl who has cried in my arms twice now. This is tough Billy.

"I wanted you to know I'm proud of you. You handled your punishment like a big girl and you stuck to your responsibilities," I say.

"Life gets tough. You do what you have to do. I'm no quitter," she says.

Her words hit me like a brick to the chest. Here she is barely nine years old. Her life has been pure shit for seven and a half years, but she's still fighting her way forward.

Billy reminds me so much of Angel. They fight for what they believe in. They never give up when it gets hard.

"Hey, that's you," she gasps, looking at a poster on my wall. "So it's true? You used to fight?"

The awe in her voice tugs at something in me. I look at the poster. My dad had passed three years before that. I had vowed to make it to the top in honor of his name. It's why I became so serious about the sport.

"Yeah, that's me. I used to box," I reply.

"Why'd you stop?"

I swallow. I don't want to lie to her, but I don't want to see that pride and awe disappear from her eyes. There's no way I'm telling her that I killed a man in the ring. "I had to step away," I say.

"I bet you were great. I wish I could've seen you fight. I'm going to be a fighter when I grow up. Andres says I'm fast, I just have a bad temper. I'm working on that," she says with a sage nod.

"A level head always makes for a great fighter. That's what my daddy use to tell me."

"Your dad used to watch you fight?"

"He was my first trainer." I can't help but smile. My daddy was the best trainer I had. After he died, I used to think about what he would tell me if he were still in my corner.

I miss him so much. I wish I still had his advice in my life. There's so much I want to ask him about.

"Did you stop fighting because he's not here anymore?"

"No, it was something else."

"Did you stop loving it?"

Her eyes search my face as she pries for an answer. I give a tight smile and shake my head. Her brows furrow.

"I still love the sport very much."

"Oh. I bet your dad was proud of you. I wish I had a dad to be proud of me," she says. Her face grows sad, and she looks down into her lap. "I'll just have to make myself proud. I'm never going to give up on fighting. I love it. I'll never give up on something I love. Not like people do me."

This kid has me bleeding out in here. I stand and round my desk. Squatting before her, I lift her head.

"You're right not to give up on what you love. It's a wise decision. You're right, life gets tough sometimes, but sometimes amazing things happen too. One day you're going to look up and realize you have so many people that love you. So many people that will never give up on you," I say.

"Yeah, I hope so," she says with so much longing.

"Go on out and tell Andres I said you can start training again."

Her brown face lights like the sun. She leaps at me to wrap her arms around my neck. I hug her back tightly, giving a silent thanks to her for showing me the errors that have stilted my life.

When I release her, she jumps from her seat and rushes for the door. I return to my seat, staring blindly at the paperwork before me. So many thoughts are running through my head.

"Yo, Beau."

I look up.

"I'd like to ride the horses again if we can," she says as she peeks back into my office.

Ah fuck. We've been so busy, I never scheduled time to take her. I chide myself for dropping the ball.

"You have a birthday coming, don't you?"

"Yeah."

"It's a date, darlin'," I promise.

She beams another smile and disappears from sight, but not my mind. I get nothing done for the rest of the day as Billy's words echo in my head.

I'm not a quitter… I'll never give up on something I love.

CHAPTER TWENTY-TWO

In the Ring Again

Angel

"I've been standing here for about an hour," he says over his shoulder.

I stand with my hands in the pockets of my slacks, staring at Beau as he stares at the ring. The lights in the gym are all off except for the ones over it. He's dressed in shorts and boxing boots. He still has the fit body of a boxer. He looks like he belongs inside that ring. "What's stopping you?"

"It's the moment of truth. Once I step in that ring I'll know the truth. I'll no longer be retired by choice. If I can't handle it... I'll know... it'll be done," he says.

"Or you could step in and feel like you've finally gone home," I say.

"But which will it be?"

I stroll closer to him and stop by his side. Sweat lines his temple, and his hand is shaking. I can taste his fear in the air.

"What are you really afraid of?"

Beau turns to look at me. His gray eyes are so troubled, his face flushed. I feel for him. Yet I know he needs to do this.

"If it's over, I've lost him for good," he says.

I close my eyes and nod. He doesn't need to say any more. I finally understand. When I open my eyes to look him in his, it all becomes clear.

"I lost three people in that ring that night. Roman, myself, and my daddy. This was what I knew made him proud," he says and lifts his palms. "I used what he taught me to kill someone. I shamed him and our name."

I cup the back of his head and place my forehead to his. We're eye to eye, nose to nose. I need him to hear me on this one. When I know I have his full attention, I lay it on him.

"I've seen the tape from that fight. It was a God honest accident. Your daddy would've been proud of how professionally you handled that fight. What would be a shame to your name and your father is to never reach the potential you've had inside you all this time.

"You were an amazing fighter. With the right corner, you could take boxing by storm. You have no business being retired. You're a smart fighter, and you have amazing speed and power for a boxer your size. Not many heavyweights can move like you.

"But for tonight, let's set you free. Step in the ring. Find your way home, Beau. It's time," I say and release him.

"I was frustrated with my mama that day. I love you, Angel. I'm not going anywhere," he says.

I kiss his cheek and take a step back. "We're fine. We can talk later. I'll be right here."

He nods and starts to bounce on his feet and shake out his hands. Turning for the ring, he rolls his neck, then his shoulders, and starts forward like a soldier headed into battle.

Please let him survive.

Beau

My heart is pounding as I approach the ring. I wipe the sweat from my forehead before climbing up onto the platform and through the ropes. Rubbing my chest, I stave off the panic attack threatening to rise up and consume me.

After moving to the center of the ring, I turn in a circle to look around it. I stop and stare down at the canvas. Waiting… waiting for Roman's body to appear. After staring for I don't know how long with nothing happening, I drop to my knees and sob.

"Fuck," I bellow.

So many emotions hit me at once. I place my palms on the canvas and let its energy seep to my bones. I rest my forehead between my hands and let it wash through me that I'm in the ring.

Something drops beside my head. When I turn I find my gloves lying beside me and sneakered feet. Angel is staring down at me. He has changed out of his suit and now has on gym shorts and a T-shirt.

"Let's get you taped up. Then we can figure out how much work we have on our hands," he says.

"We?"

"'Dres and I ain't shit for getting in a ring, but we'll whip your ass into shape." He smiles.

"Now, wait a minute, Angel. What happened to a step at a time?" I frown. "I'm just stepping in the ring."

"Why wait for tomorrow for what you can do today?" He winks. "Come on, gorgeous. I'll make you dinner after and massage your feet."

"I want rice and beans and fresh sofrito," I grumble.

"No problem. Your new diet starts tomorrow."

I can't help but grin. The Marine comes to the surface. I wouldn't have wanted to do this with anyone else. I'm glad he arrived when he did.

I lift to my full height and lock eyes with Angel. In that moment, I make a decision. I'm not running from the things and people I love.

It's time to do more than survive. It's time to live.

CHAPTER TWENTY-THREE

A Plan for Billy

Beau

"How do you feel?" Angel asks.

I groan as he works out a knot in my shoulder. I'm between his legs on the floor while he sits on the couch. My belly is full and my body aches from the beating I put on it tonight. "I'm not eighteen anymore. That's for sure."

"You're using muscles you haven't used in years, even though you work out. It's not the same," he says.

"This is true, I know, but damn," I scoff.

"We'll start with a 5:00 a.m. run instead of six. I want to increase your miles."

"So we're going to ignore the elephant in the room, then?"

Angel's hands still. I lean forward and turn to look back at him. His face is as impassive as it's been for the last month.

"Darlin', I can't read your mind. I need to know how we fix this tension. Running in these circles ain't getting us much of nowhere," I say to his silence.

"I get that you were frustrated. I know this is all new. I… you were the one to ask me to move in with you. This has been the first sense of security I've had in mad a long time. To hear your flippant words about that ending—"

"I was an asshole for that. My family has a way of getting things in their head and then pushing until you fall in line. The only reason they backed off about me fighting again was because of how fucked-up I'd been. But they still pushed more often than not." I pause as I feel my frustration with myself rise.

My jaw works, and I pick at nothing in the palm of my hand. I've been feeling like a jerk about that since that day. I reacted. I didn't think. "Her words hit home," I say. "I would love to give Billy a family and a place to call her own. While Mama was talking, I could see that room for her in my head."

"We'd be great dads for her," Angel says.

I look up at him to search his face for humor. I find nothing but sincerity. I blow out a breath. "Would we?"

Angel furrows his brows and runs a hand through his hair. He slides forward in his seat. Thoughts race across his face before he speaks them. "I thought it then, I know it now. The more time I spend with her… I feel in my heart like we would. Spending the day with her at the wedding… she just wants to be loved and to have people she can trust to care for her. I know I'd give my life to do that for her."

He pauses, his eyes searching my face. It shows through how much this means to him. I lean in to hear him out, drawn in by the look in his eyes.

"Listen, when Javi offered me that job to travel, my first thought was... I'm not ready to be responsible for another life again. Then Billy came along and all I want to do is protect her," he says with so much life in his gaze.

I can see this is something he really wants. I know I'll never deny Angel anything he asks of me. Becoming Billy's family will be no different. "You think we should adopt her?"

"I would love to. I think we have a long way to go to get ourselves ready to do that, but I wouldn't mind working toward it," he says.

"You sure about this?"

"Here's what I'm saying. Someone could come along any day and see how special she is. She'd be lost to us forever. What if we make a plan? You know, a time table to at least move in the direction of being what she needs," he says.

"All right, baby. I hear you. I just want to run something by you. I redo this place, I'm going to have to close off some areas. Our bedroom would need to be walled," I say cautiously.

His eyes span the apartment. He releases a breath and pulls a hand down his face. A war happens in his eyes.

"I'm sure we can get creative. Your moms says you're good at that," he replies.

"Fair enough. I'll have some plans drawn up. This place will be a mess during construction, but we can stay at the gym. Meanwhile, we'll volunteer more at the Savanna's House. That way we can spend more time with Billy at the orphanage and can see if she continues to open up to us," I muse aloud.

"So we're going to do this?" Angel asks with a sparkle in his eyes.

"Yeah, let's start planning." I smile.

Angel

My heart is full. We've decided not to tell Billy our plans until they're final. It's going to be so hard to keep all of this from her. My little assistant has grown on me something fierce.

Her infectious smile that has become more present, her smart mouth and quick wit, Billy keeps my life full of laughter. She has made a place in my heart for herself. I look forward to her visits to the gym.

"You're really happy about this." Beau's voice pulls me from my thoughts.

I focus on him seated across from me in the bathtub. I moan as he continues to rub my foot in his hands. His massaging is what has me so relaxed, my mind drifted. I appreciate him returning the favor. "Yeah, I am."

"She came into my office today… Billy. She's actually what pushed me to attempt stepping into the ring tonight," he says.

"Really?" I tilt my head as I take in the thoughtful look on his face. That must have been some visit. I hadn't mentioned him getting back in the ring since the wedding, but I was waiting.

"Yeah, she's wise beyond her years. She wants to go horseback riding again."

"Her birthday is coming."

He smiles. "Always reading my mind, baby."

I grin at him as my brain starts to form ideas of things we can do for Billy. She has been on her best behavior after choking Mason out. I think she deserves something nice. "Do you think Emma would help us plan something?"

"Mama and Emma will be all over it." He laughs.

"I'm with a few batches of your mom's cookies," I reply, patting my stomach.

Beau's features take on a thoughtful look. His eyes bounce over my face. I brace myself for him to change his mind about everything we've talked about.

"I want to meet your family. Do you think you're ready for that?" he says instead, shocking me.

"Mommy has asked me about you. I try to call her at least once a week to let her know I'm okay. I'll give her a call in the morning. It's… my parents' home is a bit tight. I can't stay there long without feeling boxed in and trapped," I say.

"There's this amazing restaurant downtown. They have a sunroom that's available year round. It gives the illusion of being outdoors and open. I know the owner, I can make reservations for us to book the room," he offers.

"Who don't you know?" I tease. "Nah, but seriously, I think that would be cool. My moms will hate that she's not cooking for you, but I think getting to spend time with me will make up for that."

"You got it, darlin'. Just let me know when and I'll take care of the rest," he says.

We fall into a comfortable silence. I reach for my waiting beer and drain it. After the workout in the gym, this has turned into the perfect night. I put down the empty bottle and relax with my eyes closed and an arm hanging over the side of the tub.

Beau releases my foot and the water slashing as he shifts. My lips turn up into a smile as I feel his heat against my chest and his breath fanning against my neck. I tilt my head to the side to give him better access as he pushes my hair aside.

"You've been telling me we're fine for a month," he says and kisses the skin behind my ear. "I think it's time you prove it."

"I'm starting to think you just want me for my body, cowboy."

"And your cooking. Don't forget your cooking," he says between kisses. "I just learned about the back rubs. You're stuck with me for life now."

"Am I?"

He backs away. His intense gray gaze says so much. Beau can be short on words at times, but his eyes will tell you a full story if you're willing to read them.

"If we're going to do this, we're going to do this. Sharing last names and all," he says.

"Was that a proposal?" I tease.

His face remains serious. He leans in and captures my lips in a tender kiss so uncharacteristic of us. It's a kiss that says a thousand words.

"Yes," he says when he pulls away.

"Okay. All right, so we're doing this, doing this," I say.

"All or nothing."

I shove my hand into the top of his hair and tug him to me. Our lips meet in a kiss that packs way more heat this time. I drag him into my lungs like inhaling smoke that consumes all and chokes off anything in its way. Breathing him in like the breath I need to survive my next seconds.

He breaks away, his eyes filled with enough steam to set the bathroom on fire. I place my fingers before his mouth, and he sucks them in. When I pull them free from his lips, I reach for his erection.

"Come suck my cock," he says huskily.

I grin. He's staking claim of the lead out the gate. From the look in his eyes, I won't protest too much. It looks like we're both going to be on the winning end of the passion ready to be unleashed.

He rises before me, his erection pointing at my face. I lean in and take him into my mouth. His hand fists in my hair, biting into my scalp, causing me to groan around him.

"Yes," he hisses out. "Let me feel that pretty mouth, my Angel."

I take him in halfway before releasing him to spit on the tip and work my hand over him. Our eyes lock, and I keep my gaze on his as I cover him again. This time I take him all the way down my throat.

His groans of pleasure vibrate through me. The water surrounding us starts to splash as he rides my face, bucking and rocking his hips. The water may have cooled, but our heated bodies need the cool moisture to keep us from being consumed by our own flares.

"That's my Angel." He grunts. "So good."

I release him, looking up through my lashes as I stroke him and ask, "You going to come for me?"

"Keep sucking me like that I will," he says.

I accept the challenge. I go back to sucking with more vigor. His hand in my hair tightens and starts to guide me. His hold only loosens when I start to work my head over him from side to side.

"Mmm," I moan when his salty, sweet flavor gives me a small preview.

"Fuck, yes, that's it," he pants.

It doesn't take long for me to push him over. My fingers dig into his thighs, and I deep-throat him a few times. When I hollow my cheeks and swirl my tongue around him, he loses it with a roar that fills the bathroom and washes through my body.

He releases my hair and grasps the back of my neck. Bending, Beau shoves his tongue into my mouth, taking and demanding. I take back and demand as well.

"Stand up and turn around," he commands.

He backs away just enough to give me room to do so. My palms plant against the wall, and I look over my shoulder to see him drop to his knees. More water splashes, but Beau ignores everything but me.

He slaps my ass before kissing and licking the sting. He parts me open for his hungry mouth and goes to work. Reaching between my legs, he massages my balls, kneading them with care as his mouth works magic.

My head dips between my shoulders, and I reach for my dick to start stroking it. He slaps my ass again. I look back at him once more.

"Don't touch yourself. That's my job tonight," he says.

I grin at him, biting my lip. He's so damn sexy like this. I give in to his request just to see where this will go.

He lifts to his full height, reaching for the coconut oil we keep in here. After pouring some in his palm, he begins to stroke himself. He pours more oil down my back, ceasing his stroking to massage the moisture into my skin.

His hand slips between my cheeks, and he starts to massage. The feel of his warm chest against my back has me leaning back into him. His free hand wraps my throat.

"If only you knew how much I love you," he whispers in my ear.

Before I can reply, he's easing into me. I bite down on my lip, bowing my back as I take him. He starts easy, but soon all thoughts of gentle go out of the window. His hand flexes every few strokes, adding to the mix of sensations he's inflicting on my body.

His hand on my hip digs in, dragging me back into him. I've learned that Beau likes to fuck hard when he's full of emotions he can't or won't express. I'll take it.

Our grunts and groans mix in their own conversation that fills the air. Beau slows long enough to plant a foot on the edge of the tub. My fists clench against the wall as he uses the leverage to push deeper and pound my ass harder.

"*Coño*, so good. Fuck, yes." I groan. "So, so good. Damn, Beau."

"You like that?" he says in my ear. "You feel how hard you make me?"

"Yes, Papi, don't stop."

My teeth chatter as he rocks into me. I know when he's close. He shifts his hand from my throat to my shoulder, then down to my dick. His hand is slick from a mix of my sweat and the oil, helping him slide over my flesh. My eyes roll back. He stills his hips for a moment, stroking me until I begin to swell in his palm. He begins to thrust again, and soon we come bellowing our release together.

His kisses against my shoulder are much more tender than the fucking we just did. His arms wrap my waist tightly as he slips from my body.

"Sorry," he says.

"For?"

"I really thought I was going to lose you. I think… I just lost my head," he replies.

"Not complaining." I laugh. "Lose your head whenever you like."

He grunts. "Say that in a few hours," he says, licking my shoulder before nipping it.

CHAPTER TWENTY-FOUR

Family Engaged

Beau

"Here goes nothing," Angel breathes, leaning across the console to kiss my cheek.

"One way or another we're all going to be family soon," I reply. "There's my family. Let's catch up with them."

We step out of the car, pulling Andy's attention first. He says something to Kyle, and everyone halts for us to catch up to them. I may have spent the day trying to settle Angel's nerves, but mine aren't too much better.

"You two look stunning together," Mama says as she kisses each of our cheeks.

"You're looking lovely as always," Angel says with his dimpled smile in place.

"Flattery will get you everywhere, sugar," Mama says, patting his cheek.

I embrace Emma and give Mason a high five. Andy is next to hug both Angel and me. Kyle and I give each other a one-armed hug and pat on the back.

"Four times in one week. I might be getting tired of seeing you." Kyle laughs.

"You took the words right out of my mouth," I toss back.

We've approved the plans for the apartment and started to pack up my place. Andy and Kyle have been coming over to help us get things done quicker. It's surreal how fast things are moving. I mean, I watched Kyle date Andy for almost two years before they got engaged. Angel and I are taking a much different approach.

We've both fallen hard and fast. We still have a lot to work out, but we have the same vision for our future. I think in the end we want it all sooner rather than later.

"You sure you want your family to meet this dude?" Kyle says to Angel.

"If he can make it through this, I'll marry him tomorrow," Angel replies, patting me on the back.

Today I'm meeting the Hernández family. I know deep down in my core my daddy raised me as old-fashioned as it gets. He'd be pissed if I didn't sit down with Angel's daddy and ask for his son's hand, since I'm the one that did the proposing.

"I'm still waiting to hear how you proposed," Kyle says.

My cheeks heat and I glare at him. Kyle's proposal to Andy was much more romantic than mine. I honestly don't think Angel's the type for all of that shit. I mean it was great. I was proud of my brother, but that just ain't me.

Suddenly concerned with if I did things the right way, I turn to look at Angel. I search his face, but he's smiling with a twinkle in his eyes. I release a relieved breath.

"That's a story I don't think we'll ever share," Angel replies as he beams at me. "Some things should just remain private."

"Was it at least romantic?" Kyle snorts.

"It was Beau," Angel says.

"Nope, not romantic at all. Um, I'll fix that," Kyle croons.

I narrow my eyes as he steps into the restaurant behind Mama and Emma. I don't like the sound of that. I told him already I don't need his help.

There was a time I'd get Kyle to help me out in the romance department, but it's been so long since I've leaned on him as a wingman. He better not do anything that embarrasses me tonight.

"I think it's my turn to tell you to relax," Angel leans to whisper in my ear.

I turn to him and give a tight smile. My heart is currently in my throat as we move to the outdoor area where the rest of our party is already waiting. We're not late. Angel told me that his mother forced everyone to arrive early as to not embarrass her. Andres has been texting Angel to complain for the last two hours as he rushed to meet her demands.

"Here we go," I say as we step into the area reserved for our party.

It took us almost a month to be able to get our families together all at once. There's been no shortage of excitement in our lives between this dinner, Billy's surprise party, getting my lawyer on starting the process to adopt Billy within the next year, me training to come out of retirement, and getting out of the apartment so construction can start. I feel like I'm going to bounce right out of my boots as we enter the sunroom.

"*Hola,* peoples, the party has arrived," Angel croons.

All heads turn to look at us. I look around at all of the smiling faces, which causes the one not smiling to grab my attention. He's not scowling, but not smiling either.

I don't really know what to make of it. He looks like I imagine Angel and Andres will look when they're older. Not that he looks past his midforties, which from what Angel told me, I know he is.

"You must be Beau." A little woman with black curly hair stands, rushing to me with open arms.

"Yes, ma'am, that would be me," I reply.

"Angel has told me so much about you and what you do for the little ones at your gym and the orphanage," she says with a beaming smile.

"This is my moms, Paula," Angel says.

"*Sí,* where are my manners? I'm so excited to meet you. I haven't heard Angel so happy in so long," she says excitedly. "Come, come. Meet the rest of the family."

"This is my sister, Martina, and her husband, Devin. These three are their kids, Natisha, Rosia, and Justin," Angel introduces.

"Nice to meet you," Devin says, reaching to shake my hand. "You look familiar."

"Oh my God, I told you he's a professional boxer, ay," Martina says. "Nice to meet you. Ignore my husband. He be bugging."

"It's fine. I don't box anymore, so I'm sure that's not where he knows me from," I reply.

Devin snaps his fingers. "No, that's exactly it. You were in that Golden Gloves tournament back in the days. The white boy that came in and fucked shit up. I remember now."

Martina slaps him in the shoulder. "Watch your mouth. Stop embarrassing my brother," she chides, glaring out the corners of her eyes at her husband.

"He's fine."

"So you box or you don't? *Mi hijo* says you're training. Which is it?" The older man has come to stand beside Paula. He moved so stealthily, I didn't see him get up from the table.

"Papi, this is Beau. Beau, this is my father, Alejandro," Angel says proudly.

"Nice to meet you, sir," I say, holding out my hand.

"Well, which is it?" he says, leaving my hand hanging.

"I'm retired, but I've been training to fight again," I reply.

"Umm," he grunts, grabbing my hand as I begin to drop it. "Retired. You're just a baby. You don't retire from boxing. It retires you."

"Alejandro, don't you start. *Cállate*, we don't want to spend the night talking about boxing. *Por favor*, my nerves," Angel's mother says.

"Um, fine, we can talk about when we're going to eat. I'm hungry," he replies. "Do you know she wouldn't let me eat all day, *m'ijo?*"

"Is that why you look so grumpy?" Angel chortles, moving to pull his dad into a hug.

"It's more than a look," Andres says. "This is what I've been dealing with."

"Let's get some food on the table, then," I say.

"*Gracias*, I just might like you." Alejandro nods and pats his belly.

We all laugh. I make quick introductions between my family and Angel's, and we sit to eat. It's a good thing I booked the room. This is one lively bunch. Heated discussions about boxing, plenty of teasing and laughter, and everyone begins to play musical chairs at one point. This one or that one moving here or there to join a different conversation.

I've spent the night relishing in the smile on Angel's face that I want to see there for life. Knowing how much he wishes he could visit longer with his family in their homes, it warms my heart to see the joy on his face. I make a vow that I'll figure out how to do this for him again.

"Come," Alejandro says to me and Angel after everyone has eaten and dessert has been served.

We stand and follow him to a table in the back corner. Angel grabs my hand and squeezes it. I lace my fingers with his and return the squeeze.

"When I was younger, that would've guaranteed you trouble," Alejandro says pointedly, looking at our intertwined hands. "I grew up in the Bronx. I watched some shit happen in my time. Things I never wanted to see my boy go through. *Siéntate, siéntate.*"

Angel and I take the seats across from him as he encourages. Angel pulls our locked hands into his lap. I feel like he needs me as an anchor as much as I need him.

"I love my son. I don't think he understands how much. When he brought his first boyfriend home, I was shocked, angry, but most of all afraid for him. I'm old. I've seen things. I've been fed stereotypes.

"I apologize, *m'ijo*. I should've told you that I wasn't ashamed of you. I feared for what life would bring you because of your choices. Again, I've grew up on stereotypes. I say choices, but this is who you are, not a choice," he says to Angel.

"I waited to tell you because I didn't want to break your heart."

"Break my heart? You didn't break my heart. Angel, when I was fifteen, I watched my transgender neighbor and her boyfriend dragged up the street. Those guys beat them with bats. Your great uncle, Caesar. I watched him disappear into *nada*.

"AIDS ate him until he was nothing. Everything I knew from a boy made me fear for you, my son. Not for who you loved."

"Papi, all I ever wanted was to make you proud," Angel replies.

"And you have. It hurt me to find out you enlisted. I thought you would go on to box or do something with your cooking. War alters a man—" He swallows as his eyes mist. "—as it did you."

"But you talked of your days as a Marine with such pride," Angel says.

"Yes, but I'm not without my own scars from my time. I didn't want that for you. I was too stubborn to see what my fear and stupidity was doing to you. However, when it comes to my children, I educate myself to be a part of their lives.

"I still fear the cruel people of this world, but you are the son of an Afro-Latino man. I already live in fear of the reality outside my front door. Yet I don't ask you to change your skin.

"*Coño*, I had this thought out. You know, how I would say this," he says, drawing a hand down his face.

Angel grins. "What are you trying to say, Papi? Just spit it out."

"I did research on safe sex and how AIDs is really transmitted. I've gone to the gay pride parade for the last five years. I wear a shirt with your name on it. I keep a candle lit for your safety at the cathedral.

"I do all this because you are my son and your happiness means the world to me. You can't stand to sit in my home for more than five seconds. That pains me. I want more time with you, but I understand. The pills I've been taking since you were a boy… that's how I've come to cope with my return to civilian life," he says.

"I didn't know that. I always thought they were for your blood pressure or something," Angel says.

"Shit is expensive, *joder*. But I'm one of the lucky ones. It works," he says and looks at Angel sadly.

"All this time. I thought that look was because you were disappointed in me," Angel says.

"What look?"

Angel sits back and takes a minute. I squeeze his hand for support. He frowns.

"I don't know. It's this look you give me," he says.

"You and Andres are my sons. Do you know some days it takes me way too long to figure out which one of you is which? It frustrates me. I think it has something to do with the meds or it could be from getting knocked around in the ring. If I give you a look, I'm probably pissed because I don't know which one you are," he says and shrugs.

"Yo, you're serious?" Angel says incredulously.

Alejandro shrugs his shoulder again.

I turn my focus to Angel's profile. Seconds tick by; a frown marks his face as he processes this. Suddenly recognition lights his features. Angel bursts into laughter.

"I can totally see that," he says through his laughter. "You don't call us by our names."

Alejandro cracks the biggest smile I've seen him give tonight. Angel's smile shows through in his dad's. It makes Alejandro look younger.

"You learn to make life work for you. You both answer to *m'ijo*. I'm sorry if the confusion in my head has made you feel like I love you any less than I do," he says more solemnly.

"I should've talked to you about how I felt," Angel murmurs.

"I think you're good for my son," Alejandro says, turning to me. "He has remained here with us for almost three hours now. He looks happy, and he has been calling his mother more. You're a good boxer too."

"How do you know that?" Angel asks.

"I know how to use YouTube. I told you, when it comes to my children, I educate myself," he says.

"You've seen me fight then." I grin.

"I have."

For the first time tonight, I fully relax. I understand the man sitting before me. He reminds me of myself and Angel rolled into one.

"I want to marry your son and start our own family. It's important to me that I have your blessing," I say.

He looks between us. I feel like all of the air is sucked from the room as I wait for him to speak. That smile lights his face again.

"What makes Angel happy makes me happy. You both have my blessing. I want to meet this Billy. My wife says Angel can't stop talking about her," he says.

"She is something." I snort.

"She's lucky. I can see she will have a life full of love."

Angel

"How are you holding up?" Andres's voice pulls me from my thoughts.

I turn to my brother and smile. I stepped out of the restaurant to get some air and truly let my father's words settle in. I have so many thoughts floating through my mind. I've made so many decisions based on my perception of things.

"Have you ever felt like you want to press rewind?" I ask.

"All the time. I would've done so much different with Tati. I can see all the shit we did wrong, the day it was truly over, and the moment we fell out of love," he replies.

"Yeah, I know what you mean. After talking to Papi, I know the day I changed my life forever. I can see it so clearly, and now that I have his side of things I see how wrong I was."

"But I can't say I regret any of it, you know. I love my daughter. My mistakes with Tati have taught me how to love the next," he says.

Andres and Tati were bad for each other. Their divorce wasn't a surprise to anyone but Andres. I wish I could've saved him the heartache.

"Does that mean we're about to marry into the same family? Should we plan a double wedding?" I tease.

"Nah, we're not that far yet, but I care about Emma. I can see getting there," he says with a grin.

"Don't fuck this up. I don't want to have to kick my husband's ass for fucking you up."

"What? I'll kick Beau's ass," he says.

"Why is my ass being threatened?"

We turn to see Beau closing in on us. So much for my alone time to think to myself. Although I don't mind the company at all. My twin and my soul mate. I couldn't be in better company.

"Don't worry. He's all mouth," I say.

"Um, okay. Your mama wants you both. She's ready to say good night. The kids are getting restless," Beau says.

I nod, and the three of us start back into the restaurant. When we get to the entrance that leads to the private area, something is off. Everyone's standing in a semicircle facing the door.

Beau groans beside me, causing me to look at him. His cheeks are pink and he's shaking his head. He reaches for my hand and holds it tight. I'm lost until singing fills the private dining room area.

I turn to find Kyle crooning "All My Life" by K-Ci and JoJo. It takes a second to click. So this was what he meant about fixing things.

Beau pulls me to stand in front of him as he wraps his arms around me from behind and starts to sway me. Kyle has an amazing voice, and his choice of song is perfect. I have waited all of my life for someone like Beau.

"I'm going to kill him," Beau breathes in my ear.

"Why? It's the perfect song," I say.

"Yeah, but that's not the problem."

Kyle continues to sing, but my focus turns to Beau. He is now bright red. He releases me and digs into his pocket.

"I didn't know if I'd do any of this. I had planned to just give you the ring." He turns to glare at Kyle. "My brother didn't feel that was right."

"You drop to your knee, I'm walking out," I warn.

I'm serious too. The song is cool. I appreciate the gesture.

Beau's eyes widen and his cheeks grow brighter. Before I can apologize and let him follow through with whatever he had planned, a smile breaks across his face. He takes the ring from its box, grabs the front of my shirt, and tugs me to him.

Placing his forehead to mine, he grabs my hand and lifts it. "I don't have a bunch of pretty words, but that doesn't make me love you any less. When I asked, you said yes. Now that I have your daddy's blessing, this is just to show you I meant it. I love you," he says, pushing the ring onto my finger.

"I love you too," I say and kiss him.

Our families begin to applaud around us. It's the perfect moment. Not what most would call romantic, but it's me, and it's Beau. I was fine with our private moment three weeks ago. Yet, I'll admit, when I turn the look of pride and happiness in my parents' eyes... this is more than I could've asked for.

CHAPTER TWENTY-FIVE

Special Moments

Beau

"I'm going to get me a horse one day," Billy says as we head for the stables.

I look at Angel with wide eyes, and he purses his lips as mirth lights his eyes. Everyone has put so much into planning this day for her. We wanted it to be perfect. Her comment sends me straight into a panic.

At thirty, I never thought I'd be planning to be someone's father. Finding the perfect gift for Billy seemed like the world's biggest task to me. I want this to be the best birthday she's had yet.

"That would be so cool. Then we could ride together all the time," Mason says.

I hold my breath as we get to the stable door, and I reach for the handle. Pulling it open, I allow Billy to enter first. She starts inside, skidding to stop as everyone yells surprise.

"This is for me?" she looks up at me and whispers.

"Yes, darlin'. It's your birthday party," I say.

She looks around at all of the people here for her. Balloons and streamers are everywhere. The place looks perfect for a little nine-year-old girl.

However, the moment that makes my own heart stop is when the crowd parts, and Emma comes forward leading a horse beside her. The horse has a bow around its neck, and its mane is braided with a bow at the end. Billy's face runs through a number of emotions, settling on excitement and awe.

"Is that mine?"

"Yes," Angel replies.

"You got me a horse?"

"He's a beautiful stallion and he's all yours," I say.

She takes a step forward, then turns back to look up at me. The gears are going. I should expect her words, but they still send a sharp pain to my heart.

"I'll work hard for him. I'll come to the gym more days and clean up, and—"

I squat to get eye level with her. "Sugar, that horse is yours. You don't owe me a thing for it. It's your birthday gift. Angel and I wanted you to have it. When we give you something, it's because we want to see a smile on your face. You never have to give us anything in return," I say.

She throws her arms around my neck and squeezes me so tight, if she were stronger she might cut my air off. I wrap her little body in my arms and squeeze back. I fight back the tears.

"Thank you, Beau. This is the best birthday ever," she whispers.

"You're welcome."

I guess we got it right.

Angel

"You boys did an awesome job," Daphne says as I walk up with more ice from inside the main house.

She and my moms have been cleaning up the picnic tables Beau had set up inside the barn for the party, after serving all the kids ice cream and cake. I set the ice down and start to cover the drinks I brought out earlier. Everyone has run through the first two tubs we had out.

"I'm so proud of you, *m'ijo*," my mother adds. "She's adorable. I pray things work out. I can't wait to spoil her."

"I don't know how we're going to keep it from her. I've wanted to tell her all day," I murmur.

Daphne pats my cheek the way she always does. "It's best this way. She's had so many disappointments, we don't want to get her little hopes up."

"I know that's why we're waiting, but this is tough. I just want to see her happy, you know?"

Daphne smiles. "You raised a wonderful young man, Paula."

"Thank you. You did wonderfully yourself. Billy has been driving Beau crazy wanting to ride and feed that horse every five seconds. Poor horse," my mother snickers.

"We'll have to find time to bring her here more often," I think aloud.

"Everyone will pitch in. It's been a long time since I've had a little one to go riding with. I'll bring her as much as I can. I used to ride competitively as a girl. I bet she'd love that," Daphne muses.

"I bet she would. That kid has a huge competitive streak."

"Then she's already your daughter, *mi hijo*." My mother chortles.

"I told them she's the perfect child for them," Daphne says. *She is.*

I look across the barn to see Billy laughing with Mason and Aryanna. You would never know there was ever an issue between the three. I'd been worried about inviting others to Billy's special place, but it seems to be working out.

"I'm worried. I hope we're right for her. I read that kids adapt to things easier and faster than adults," I muse aloud. "We'll have to be patient with her and allow her to adjust on her own time, but she's more likely to adjust because of her age.

"Mommy, I was hoping you or Martina will teach me how to do her hair. I only know how to pull it up in a band like mine, but I want to be able to do more. She's not as big a tomboy as everyone thinks. She likes girly stuff," I ramble.

When I turn back to my mother and Daphne, they're looking at me like I have two heads. I think over what I've just said to see if I said something wrong. I'm still not sure what the looks are about until my mother speaks up.

"*Mi hijo*, you're going to make a great father. You're reading books, you want to learn to do her hair, you pay attention to what she's interested in. You're more than right for her," she says.

"My husband loved his kids, but he wouldn't even look at one of the baby books I had when I was pregnant with Beau or

Emma," Daphne adds. "You're already shaping up to be a great daddy."

"We have to get her first," I say.

"You will, *m'hijo*. It will all work out."

Will it work out?

I've been extra anxious in the last few weeks. I'm sleeping less and pacing more. I worry about how Billy will adapt, but I also worry about how I'll handle all of these changes.

"Your mama is right; it will," Daphne says, handing me a chocolate chip cookie.

"I hope so."

CHAPTER TWENTY-SIX

Interrupted

Angel

I can't believe we did it. I look at Beau in his suit and can't stop smiling. I wanted to keep it simple, and he was all for that. City Hall was fine with both of us. The only reason we're having this dinner is because Mommy and Daphne wanted us to have a celebration.

"I'm honored y'all could be here with us," Beau says, completing his short toast.

Always straight and to the point. I love that about him. Some days I'm not up for a lot of talking. I don't ever have to worry about Beau pushing me to do so.

That's what makes us work. Being with Beau is easy. He makes it easy to love him.

"I guess that means it's my turn," I say while standing next to my husband. Beau returns my smile, placing his hand on my back. "Today has been amazing. We have yet to tell Billy; we're waiting until it's official. However, we wanted you all to be the first to know that we've started the process to adopt. We'll be taking our first parenting classes next week.

"This is all happening so fast. It's surreal. Within two months we've started a renovation, gotten married, and now we'll be parents in the next six months to a y—"

"They're coming in hot. I need backup," Hanes shouts.

"Cover me, Bachman. I'm heading in," I say as I try to get eyes on Hanes.

Explosions are going off all around us. I just need to get to that truck and help them get out of there. If I can make it….

"I have zero visibility. Fuck. Just give me a second, Hernández."

I make a quick decision. I have to move. I can't leave them out there. No one's dying on my watch. Not today.

"They don't have a minute," I grit out.

"Hernández, Hernández, get your stubborn ass down," Bachman calls after me. "Fuck."

Beau

"It's okay. It's all right," I croon. "You're right here with me. Stay right here with me."

"Lo siento," Angel sobs for the millionth time. "I'm so sorry."

I never knew my heart could hurt so much. This day should be a happy one. It's official. We're married.

When Angel suggested something small, I was more than fine with it. It was just us, our parents, and our siblings. Everyone met at City Hall, and within a few hours we were married.

This small reception was more for our mothers and friends. I'll admit once we arrived, I was happy to see my friends here to support me. However, what made this day amazing was the stop we made before heading here to the restaurant.

Our lawyer had everything ready for us to sign. We're starting the process to become parents. Six months to a year from now, we could be bringing Billy home.

"It's okay," I whisper in his ear. "It's going to be okay."

Everything was perfect. I did everything I could to make this day special, booked out a tucked-away restaurant in midtown. The place is surrounded in glass, giving us a view of the street. I made sure the champagne wasn't opened around Angel in case the sound became a trigger.

I did everything right. I controlled everything I could. I thought of everything to make this day perfect.

"Can you get my son-in-law a glass of water?" Mama says.

"Yes, ma'am. Right away." The hostess rushes out.

I rock Angel in my arms as we sit on the floor in the middle of the restaurant. I ignore the moisture seeping through the seat of my slacks from the spilled beverages. Mama moves cautiously over the broken glass.

The hostess hands her a glass of water, and she hands it to me. I hold it up to Angel's mouth, and he takes it with shaky hands. I kiss his forehead as he empties the glass.

"I'm sorry," he says again as he hands Mama the glass.

"You stop telling us you're sorry, sugar," she says softly. "That transformer blew and scared us all. Thankfully the generator came on so Beau could help you."

A transformer. A fucking transformer blew right outside the restaurant in the middle of Angel giving his toast. He flipped the table, soaking Mama, his mama, and Emma with water and wine as the glasses crashed around them. He was ready for battle, calling out to a team not here.

At least not for the rest of us. For Angel, it was all real. There was danger and he reacted.

This one was bad. It's been about twenty minutes since that damn thing blew. I don't know how long we've been sitting here since I got him to come back to me.

"I'm ruining everything. We're not going to get Billy. I'm too fucked-up," he whispers.

"Now you listen here," I say. "This isn't going to stop anything. You're going to continue to see Eric, and if we have to, we'll go together. This isn't going to change a thing."

"He's right, *m'ijo*," Alejandro says, squatting to get eye level with his son. "You're strong. You will beat this. You will learn to cope. I believe in you. I will help. I've learned to adapt. It takes more than the meds. I work at it. So can you."

"No one was hurt. Besides, aren't broken dishes supposed to be good luck?" Emma says, trying to lighten the mood.

"I ruined dinner," Angel sobs.

"It needed seasoning." Alejandro shrugs and pats Angel's shoulder.

Brushing his hair back from his face, I kiss the top of his head. We're all doing our best to make sure Angel feels our love as he grasps ahold of himself again. Everyone's concern and love fills the restaurant as we remain seated on the floor.

"We can go to the complex and order in," Andy offers.

"I will cook," Paula chimes in.

"I can too. We'll have y'all bellies full in no time. I've been wanting to cook in that big fancy kitchen anyway. I'll bake all those babies some cookies while I'm at it," Mama says.

I tuck a strain of hair behind Angel's ear. He turns to me with tortured eyes. I clench my teeth against the helplessness I feel. I want to make this go away for him. I want to make it better.

"It's up to you, darlin'. If you want to just go home, we can. If you want to have dinner with the family, that's good too," I say.

He swallows and licks his lips. Angel's forehead creases as he weighs the options. I kiss his nose, wanting to ease the tension within him.

"I don't think I can," he says brokenly. "Maybe another time. I just want to go home. I'm sorry, everyone."

"Nothing to be sorry about, Angel," Jordan says. "We're family. You and Beau decide to try this again, you just call. We'll be there."

Thank you, I mouth to one of my best friends as Angel relaxes a bit in my arms. I take comfort in knowing I have so many people in my life that are understanding.

"All right, I'll be the first to take my leave and let the couple have a moment. You're all welcome to join me at Refuge for a drink or ten if you like," Javier calls.

Again, I'm grateful for my friends. I watch as the men I think of as brothers all give me nods of encouragement as they start to leave. I know they'll call to check in.

As the rest of the family starts to gather their things, I turn my attention back to my shaken husband in my arms. I get us both to our feet. My arms go around him to tug him into my chest.

"This isn't a setback, baby. We're going to have our family," I whisper in his ear. "We'll get through this together."

CHAPTER TWENTY-SEVEN

Ghosts of the Past

Beau

This is a shit show if I've ever seen one. I should've known it would be. It's been over six years, and my name has been in the papers for everything from who they think my sister is dating to the latest rising star I may or may not be training.

I don't know what made me think my coming out of retirement wouldn't explode into a media frenzy. I guess the fact that my first fight out of retirement will be with Gordon Norwack hasn't helped the situation. Norwack is at the top of the food chain. He's also arrogant and wants a shot at sending me back into retirement.

"Thanks for coming out. I'm officially announcing my return from retirement. I'll be fighting Gordon Norwack in a heavyweight bout six months from now."

This conference room is nearly suffocating with their thirst to find a juicy story in all of this. I just want to get to the fight, but I know this is inevitable. I'm sitting here at this table with all these cameras in my face like an offering. I've thrown myself to the wolves.

"Beau James, is it true that no one else wanted to take a fight with you?" a reporter calls.

"It wasn't easy finding an opponent," I say into the mic.

That's an understatement. We've been looking for a fight worth entertaining for almost five months. I haven't stopped training in hopes that we'd find someone willing to step in the ring with me, an opponent who takes this sport as seriously as I do. Norwack has been the only real taker worth considering.

"Do you think you're ready for a fighter like Norwack?"

"I'm ready to get back in the ring. Myself and my team are dedicated to showing up ready to take home a win," I reply.

"Do you see yourself winning?"

I hate it when they ask the same damn question, just another way. I clench my teeth and my jaw flexes. My father-in-law nods at me.

The Hernández family has stepped in as my corner. Getting me ready to fight again has become a family thing. Although, I know this is Alejandro's way of getting to spend time with Angel as well as helping Angel learn to cope with his PTSD.

"I see myself stepping in the ring and doing what's necessary," I say.

"Beau James, you walked away from boxing after a devastating fight. Do you feel like that unfortunate incident will play a factor in how you approach this fight?"

My teeth are going to break from the tight hold I have on them. I knew they would go there. Doesn't make it grate my nerves any less.

"I've always approached each fight as an individual competition. I don't take in one ring the experiences of another. Every fight is different," I reply.

"I'm sure killing your lover in the ring will play a factor in your performance," someone in the back says.

I fall back in my seat as if I've been dealt a blow. Heat surge to my ears. I clench my fists in front of me.

"This interview is about the upcoming fight between Beau James Dalton and Gordon Norwack. We're not going to rehash a fight from seven years ago," Andres says as he sits to my right.

Honestly, I'm done. I have nothing else to say. I want to get up and walk out to find my husband. We all decided that this room full of flashing lights and clamoring voices wasn't for him.

"Beau James, what's next? Is this just one fight or are you here to stay?"

"I can show you better than I can tell you. Stay tuned, folks, y'all have yourselves a good day," I say and stand.

"Beau James, Beau James…."

I don't look back. I said what I said. Truth is, that fight with Roman *is* haunting me in the ring. It's just something that I'm working through.

Angel

I'm pacing the dressing room of the studio as I watch the interview on the screen. I'm frustrated that I couldn't be out there with Beau. I hate the questions that they're asking him.

"*Cabrón. Pasa a la siguiente pregunta, estúpido,*" I snarl at the screen. "How many times are you going to ask him the same stupid shit?"

My fists tighten as this garbage continues to go off the rails. Andres steps in exactly where I would have. I grumble under my breath, pissed as fuck as I see the look on Beau's face. He looks like he wants to spit nails.

I already know he's about to end this bullshit. It's written all over him. When Beau gets up out of his seat and walks out, I start for the door to meet him.

"My bad," I say as I run into some dude when I step out of the dressing room. My anxiety has me unfocused. I start a slow count in my head to clear it. It's something Eric has me trying out.

"That was on me," the guy says.

Now that my focus is homed in, I don't like him. There's something greasy about him. It causes me to pause and take a good look at him. He was headed for Beau's dressing room.

"Can I help you?"

"I'm just here to see an old friend," he says.

"Well, this is Beau Dalton's dressing room. I think you're in the wrong place."

"No, I've got it right. Thanks, though."

I narrow my eyes. I really don't like this guy. I'm ready to press his ass and find out what the hell he wants. My body is coiled with aggravation as I sense the bad vibes coming off him.

"We have a problem here?" Beau's voice booms as he appears, moving up the hallway toward us.

This guy in front of me turns on a sleazy smile and shifts toward Beau. My husband stops in his tracks. His face changes, and his body becomes tense and ready to strike. I move quickly to place myself between this motherfucker and Beau.

I'm just in time to wrap my arms around Beau to keep his fists from flying. I've never seen him like this. His eyes are wild, and rage is rolling off him. My father and brother rush to help me restrain him.

"Calm down, Beau," I say. "You hit this guy and you can kiss this fight and your career goodbye."

"Listen to your friend, Beau James," the guy says.

I round on the little bastard and get in his face. My father and Andres have Beau. I'm so close as I tower over this guy, I'm sure he can taste my breath. "I don't know who the fuck you are, but you don't want to fuck with me. I don't have shit to worry about. I'll fuck you up and won't give two fucks. You want to try me?"

The slimy asshole has enough good sense to take a few steps back. He looks me up and down, sizing me up, and rightfully errs on the side of caution. Beau may not be able to place a hand on him, but mine are itching to land on this dude.

"You have a lot of fucking nerve showing your face here," Beau barks.

"I thought time would've smooth things over between us. You know what happened in that ring wasn't my fault," he says.

"You knew I didn't want to fight him. You switched the damn fights. You manipulated the whole fucking situation," Beau snarls, his accent thickening. "He wasn't ready to fight a fighter like me. It was always about the money for you. It never mattered how many lives or whose life you fucked up. You're a piece of shit."

"So I guess that's a no on us rekindling our work relationship," he says.

"Steve, if you don't get the fuck out of my face, I'm gonna to say fuck boxing and I'm gonna beat the shit out of you," Beau says in a deathly calm that sends a shiver through me.

"And I'll let him," I say.

Steve raises his hands in the air in surrender and moves around me. Andres and Papi glare at him as if they want to kick his ass too. I'm still debating on whether or not I should.

"Good luck, Beau James. You're going to need it," Steve calls over his shoulder. "You'll regret not having this talk with me."

I start for him, but Papi releases his hold on Beau to restrain me. I glare after the asshole, thinking of all the ways I can break him into pieces. Beau wraps an arm around my waist, tugging me into him.

"He's not worth it," he says into my hair. "Just another ghost from the past. Fuck him."

Nah, I don't do threats. This dude is going to get checked.

CHAPTER TWENTY-EIGHT

Excluded Feelings

Angel

Everything around us seems to be moving at warp speed. Beau's fight is still a few months away. We have three more months before the apartment is finished. That's grinding on my nerves. It's holding things up with the adoption.

We've completed the parenting courses, we've moved to the home study evaluation, but our home isn't ready for inspection. Beau has told me to be patient. The work he's having done requires skill and time. Nothing can be rushed.

Yet there are days like this. Days when I wish we had the right to take Billy home with us. She's been in a mood all day. Something is off, and I don't know what it is. It's been eating at my nerves.

"Hey, Billy," I say as I walk over to the table she's sitting at with her dinner.

"What's up, Angel?" she says.

"I was going to ask you the same thing? Mind if I sit?"

"You're good." She shrugs.

"Why the long face?"

She lifts those brown eyes to me, and I see a world of hurt. I want nothing more than to wrap her up in a hug and tell her it's going to get better. To make a promise that it will.

"A couple of families came in today. They were all looking for girls. They didn't even look at me," she says, reaching to brush a hand over her hair and tug at her shirt.

I noticed a few weeks ago that we're going to have to talk her into allowing someone to purchase her new clothes. She's outgrowing her things on top of them being worn out. However, she's still a cute little girl. I don't see why a family wouldn't be drawn to her.

I don't know what to say. This has to be hard on all of the kids. Pickings are slim to begin with. From what I've learned about this place, Kyle and the others are extremely selective about opening the doors to families that want to adopt. The safety of these children is taken very seriously.

"Can I tell you a secret?" I lean in and whisper.

She eyes me warily for a moment but nods.

"You're the best kid here. You're smart, you've got mad skills on the court, your skills on the mat are getting you talked about at the gym, you're funny, and you're a good friend. Mason and Aryanna talk about you all the time," I say.

"If I'm so great, why can't I go home with you? You and Beau got married, right? Don't you need a kid?" she says with all seriousness.

I have to clamp my mouth shut to keep from telling her that we're coming. As soon as we can, we're taking her home for our three-month supervised period. Our lawyer informed us that because we know Billy and volunteer at the orphanage we'll get a pass on the getting-to-know-her stage. We already know the kid we want.

"See what I mean," she whispers when I don't say anything.

"Hey, adoption isn't as easy as walking in here and saying we want to take Billy home. There are steps that have to be taken. Most of all, you have to be fit to be a parent to begin with," I try to explain.

"Why wouldn't you guys be fit? Because you're gay? My *abuela* was bi. She had a girlfriend and a boyfriend. They let her keep me," she says.

Again, I'm speechless for a second. I blow out a breath and decide to tell her as much of the truth as I can. I don't want her thinking we don't want her.

"You remember me telling you that I was a Marine, right?"

"Yeah, I remember."

"Well, my head got a little messed up while I was away. Sometimes... I'm not able to handle things the way others can. I'm putting my life back together so I can have a full family," I say.

I watch her think over my words. The wheels turning to a point I swear I can hear them. She places an elbow on the table and cups her cheek.

"You mean like what happened at the wedding?" she says softly.

I purse my lips and nod. I had hoped that she didn't notice what had happened that night. I'm so grateful she didn't get hurt.

"So you would want me if your head wasn't messed up?"

"Billy, in the perfect world, you would've come home with me a long time ago," I reply.

Her brown eyes are still sad, but I see a little bit of a smile return to them. I wish I could inject more hope, but I know it's not wise. We have to stick to the plan so Billy doesn't get hurt. If for some reason things turn south and we can't adopt her, that would devastate me and Beau, but it would crush her more.

"You know something?" she says.

"What's that?"

"I didn't like the way any of those families looked anyway. I'm better off here with the dads," she says.

I laugh. "The dads?"

"Yeah, that's what everyone's starting to call Kyle and Andy," she says.

"Ah, okay."

"I might not be the lucky kid, but I hope you get your head fixed. You'd be a great dad," she says with a look of longing in her eyes.

My heart swells. I curse the three months we still have to wait for our home to be done. I'll be talking to Beau again to make sure there isn't a way we can bring that timeline in sooner.

I'm not even allowed to go on site. Not that I would want to anyway. Construction and I don't blend. I learned that after returning home and trying my hand at it. That didn't go well at all.

"Angel?" Billy calls, pulling me from my thoughts.

"Yeah?"

She pushes her plate away and starts to fidget with her fingers. Whatever she wants to say, I can see she's warring for words. So unlike Billy.

"Most of the boys hate balling with me because I'm small and I still kick their as... their butts. I know it's time for you to go home, but will you play a game with me? I just want to shoot some hoops for a little bit," she says.

"Man, I'll do one better than that. Let me make a call," I say and grin.

Beau

"Yo, Billy." I call out her name like she does mine all of the time.

She turns from talking to Angel, and her eyes go wide. I walk in the gym with Kyle, Ray, and Chris. Mason and Andy are bringing up the rear. They didn't want to miss this.

"Yo, Beau," Billy says with a beaming smile on her face.

When Angel called me with Billy's request to play a game of basketball, I was all over it. Mas has mentioned that the other boys don't like to play with Billy anymore. Rumor is, she crossed over a few of the boys, and they've been too embarrassed to play her now.

Well, they'll be jealous after tonight. I had planned to go home, shower, and fall into bed, but now my mission is to make Billy smile. Angel also told me about their talk today. It hurt my heart that the little darlin' is feeling excluded. The families, the games, all ways that Billy has been feeling just plain left out.

I aim to fix that. All of the kids know Kyle used to play in the NBA, and Ray and Chris still do, but I don't think any of them have gotten to play with all three at once. Not like Billy will this evening. Jordan has a big game we all plan to attend together tomorrow night. Every once in a blue moon we manage to make something like this work out. It's the reason everyone happens to be in town tonight.

"So I heard my best student wanted to play some hoops," I say once we reach her.

"You guys are here to play with me?" she says in awe. "No way."

"We sure are," Chris says, giving her his megawatt smile.

"Somebody pinch me," she says.

I punch her side and tickle her. Billy has opened up to me and Angel getting closer to her in the last few months. She'd probably punch someone else in the nuts for this kind of contact.

"Beau, wait, wait, I can't breathe," she giggles.

"All right, fine. Let's break into teams. How about you and Mas be captains?" I suggest.

"Yes," the two say in unison, high-fiving each other.

I've watched these two build their own bond. Mason has been rewarded for his patience. I didn't think it would ever happen, but Billy let him in and they're the best of friends.

"You're going down, Tyson," Billy taunts.

"You need to pick your teams first," I say.

"I'm taking Lionel," she says, pointing to Chris.

Mason twists his lips and thrusts his arm across his body as if to say, *ah man*. His eyes light up as he looks up at his uncle, the championship-winning MVP. Losing Chris to Billy is soon forgotten.

"I'm taking Uncle Kyle," he says.

"Oh boy, that was my next one," Billy pouts.

She taps her chin as she looks at her choices, as if strategizing on the best picks. Her gaze bounces over Angel and me. Then to Ray.

"I'm taking Beau," she says.

Mason snags Ray up quickly, but Billy isn't fazed. She takes Angel, leaving Mason with Andy. With our teams in place, we huddle together for a pep talk. The excitement in Billy's eyes is priceless.

The gym starts to fill up with the after-dinner crowd, coming to check out this game. The other kids murmur as Billy and Mason get ready for the jump ball to get things started. We have a full game in swing in no time. I think Billy is showing off for the guys, but damn if she's not balling.

This was one of the first things we all learned about Billy when she came here. She likes to play, and she's good at it. From what I read in Billy's file, her biological father was headed up from the G League before he was murdered while going to get Billy milk from the store.

Billy's life just turned for the worse from there. One unfortunate event after the next until she arrived here. Billy didn't come to us through Child Services like many of the others. A police officer friend of Andy's brother begged Kyle to take her in. He'd known Billy from his very own neighborhood. He'd saved her from a nasty foster situation.

"She can shoot," Ray says with a huge grin. "That cross is sweet too."

"Man, I haven't had this much fun in a long time," Chris says. "Mason, you better watch out. She's going to own them ankles."

Just then Billy crosses Mas, landing him on his ass. She passes the ball to Angel, and he goes for a layup. It goes in, and our extremely larger crowd cheers.

"Oh yeah," Billy woots and does a little duck-looking dance.

"What's that?" I laugh.

"It's my victory dance. Come on, do with me," she says.

"Yeah, Beau, do it with her," Kyle says.

Angel slaps him five while laughing. I glare at the both of them. However, when I see the expectant look on Billy's face, I let her teach me the dance. Soon—even though his team just lost—Mason, Billy, and I are doing a dance that looks cute while they do it. Yet I'm sure I just lost any cool points I had. That is, until Billy wraps herself around my leg and looks up at me like I can do no wrong. As if in her eyes, I'm the greatest person in the world.

"We make a great team. Don't you think," she says.

"I sure do, darlin'. I sure do."

CHAPTER TWENTY-NINE

Shattered

Beau

"That's what I'm talking about," I shout, standing up out of my seat as Jordan sinks another goal. The box suite erupts with cheers as my friends and husband chant with me. This is one good damn game. Jordan is putting on a show out there.

"Our boy is on fire tonight," Daniel croons.

Chris rushes over from the buffet with a wing hanging out of his mouth. "Damn, as soon as I turn my back," he says around a mouthful of food.

"Really, babe?" Joey says as he glares at Chris.

"What?" Chris says.

Joey rolls his blue eyes and turns back to the game. I laugh to myself. Joey and Chris are complete opposites and hilarious to be around.

"What?" Chris repeats. "You bugging? This food is banging. I can't believe I missed that shoot, though. Damn."

Joey turns to Chris and rolls his eyes again, holding a napkin up for Chris to wipe his chin. Instead of taking the napkin, Chris pecks Joey on the cheek, getting sauce on his face. I shake my head at them.

"That's exactly why I haven't moved a muscle," Angel says beside me. "I'm not even a big hockey fan, but he's killing it."

I smile at Angel. I wasn't sure he'd be up to this, but he's been glued to his seat and doing well. He has also grabbed my hand a few times when his anxiety did take over. I think being in the box and the excitement of watching Jordan have anchored him in the moment for the most part.

"Oh, come on," Kyle shouts as Jordan draws a penalty. "That ref's been on some bullshit all night."

I purse my lips and shake my head. After leaning to kiss Angel on the temple, I take this chance to go get something to eat and a fresh beer. Javier follows with a look on his face that I know too well, and I don't like it. I prepare myself for what's coming.

He pulls out an envelope and hands it to me. I take it, giving him a questioning brow. He gestures his head for me to just open it.

Blowing out a breath, I tear into it and start to read. My blood begins to boil, and I can only see red. I keep scanning, trying to decipher what I'm looking at. "What the hell is this?"

"Me covering your ass. There was a clause in your old contract. Steve has a right to claim financial interest in your future fights, and he's trying to exercise that right," Javier says.

"Are you shitting me?"

"This is very real, my friend, but I'm taking care of it. I just wanted you to be aware," he says.

I fold the papers back into the envelope and shove them in my back pocket. I want to take a closer look at them later when my head clears. I should've known Steve was up to some bullshit the day he showed his face. "Javi, I don't want you getting involved in my mess." I sigh.

"What is my motto, *hermano?*"

"I am my brother's keeper," I say. "Yeah, yeah, but—"

"There's no but. I only brought it to your attention because I didn't want you blindsided before I got it under control, *sí*. He is barking up some big trees with big talk. No one likes him," Javi says with the look of something sour on his tongue.

"Thanks, Javi."

"*De nada,*" he says. "I'll take care of this. How are things coming with the apartment?"

"It's a lot to take on. The permits are what's taking too long. The structural changes are extensive and affecting the integrity of the existing structure. We have to reinforce everything to make sure it's all sound and up to code."

The designs to make our home both kid and Angel friendly have been a challenge. I needed to strike the perfect balance for them both. I've consulted childproofing companies, interior designers, and so many more to make the place perfect for the two most important people in my life.

"Sounds intense."

"We've had three different engineers in on this. It has to be right," I reply.

"If you need me to make a few calls on those permits or anything else, say the word."

I've been meaning to ask him for a favor. It pops into my head as I look over at Angel. I smile and turn to Javi, feeling the blush in my cheeks. "Actually, there's something you can help me with. I want to learn to speak more Spanish," I whisper. "Angel and Billy already do. I want to learn for them."

"*Sí*, I can help. Although I will warn you. I don't always speak the same Spanish they do. I'm Puerto Rican and Cuban. I mix the two different dialects sometimes. I'll do my best to keep it straight for you, though."

I give a chuckle. "I wouldn't know the difference either way. I know the little I've learned from being around you. Anything you teach me will be appreciated."

"I've got you, my friend. *Pronto hablarás español, mi amigo.*"

I pat him on the shoulder and nod. His promise that I'll be speaking Spanish soon gives me something new to hope for. I understand more than I can articulate in the beautiful language. It comes with being Javi's friend. He often bounces between the two languages.

As usual, I know Javi is always there when I need him. All of my friends are. We look out for each other.

We pile our plates and head back to our seats. Jordan is back on the ice by the time I sit down. I place a fresh beer in front of Angel and a plate of food between us to share.

"Thanks," Angel says.

"No problem," I say, leaning in to peck him on the lips.

Ray clears his throat and we turn to him. He has an amused look on his face. He looks at Kyle and Andy, then back at myself and Angel. "I have a question for the four of you," he says.

"Oh boy," Kyle says and folds his arms over his chest. "Let's have it. What's going on in that big-ass head of yours?"

"You two do know that Mason and Billy will be kissing cousins," he says.

"What?" I drawl.

"Mason has it bad for Billy. It's only a matter of years before he figures out what those feelings are. Technically they'll be cousins," he says.

"*Coño*, we haven't even signed the dotted line and you're bringing up boys." Angel groans.

"There will be no boys," I bite out.

Everyone around me starts to snicker. They can laugh. I'm serious.

"You're right. There will be no *boys*. There will be just one, Mas," Daniel says.

"Man, they're nine. We have plenty of time before we have to worry about that," Kyle says from his leather lounge seat behind us.

"I don't know," Andy chimes in beside Kyle. "I'm kind of with Ray and Daniel. I also don't think Mason is in it alone. I caught Billy tripping one of the other girls that tried to take up too much of Mas's attention."

"*Dios*," Angel says beside me. "I like Mason. I can't pull a shotgun on him to warn him off."

Laughter fills the box suite. *Boys*. I'll have things like that to worry about in the future. Billy is a beautiful little girl. I'm sure Angel and I will have shotguns at the ready with matching T-shirt that say, *I have a beautiful daughter, I also have a gun, a shovel, and an alibi.*

Yup, I'll be that father. I don't even know how to feel about Mason being the boy that rings the bell for our baby's first date. *Our baby.* I'm getting anxious for the day I can say those words out loud.

"We'll just have to make sure they know they're family," I grumble.

"I'm with that. Billy scares me. She'll have my poor boy by the balls." Kyle laughs.

"Already does," Andy, Ray, and Daniel say in unison.

"Change the subject," I mutter.

Suddenly the entire arena falls eerily silent, and the game comes to a screeching halt. My heart jumps in my throat as I watch one of my best friends lying on the ice, rolling in agony. I close my eyes when I take in his oddly twisted leg.

"Ah, fuck," Daniel breathes.

Being the closest to Jordan, I can feel Daniel's pain for our brother coming off him. Hockey is Jordan's life. This is not good at all.

I'm in shock at first. Angel places a hand on my shoulder and squeezes. I appreciate his comfort.

"We need to get down there," Daniel says.

Nothing else needs to be said. We all head out. Wherever they take Jordan, we'll be there for support. We're his family.

Angel

I'm exhausted and so is Beau. I learned tonight just how close Beau and the six of his friends are. At some point during the time we were at the hospital, Darwin appeared, looking disheveled and worried. I've come to understand he's like the father of the group. I totally get how that works now that I've seen them interact with one another.

"Are you all right?" I ask Beau as we stumble sleepily into our place.

We've been staying in the apartment over the gym. I manage to sleep in the bed up here and not in the ring downstairs. It's getting easier to sleep longer through the night with my husband. Hardly ever a full night's rest, but more hours than I used to get.

"I don't know. Jordan is… he'll hide how he feels from everyone. I know this hit him harder than he's letting on," he says.

"I can only imagine. He's a great player. It's crazy how fast the night took a turn."

We enter the bedroom area and start to strip. I want to shower, but I don't know if I can keep my eyes open long enough to get one in at this point. Everyone waited for them to set Jordan's cast and get him in a room for the night before taking off.

"It's a bad break. I just hope he can get back out there," Beau says, running a hand through his hair.

"Let's get some rest. We can go back to check on him in the morning," I say.

"I can't. I have to be at the site to sign off on a few things. I'll be able to go in the afternoon maybe." He sighs.

"I'll go. At least one of us can show our face and be there for him," I offer, climbing into bed.

Beau gets in and pulls me into his arms. He starts to run a hand through my hair, and I can feel myself fading. I yawn.

"Thank you," Beau says, causing me to lift my lids.

Turning to look up at him, I murmur, "For what?"

He takes my lips, igniting a fire neither one of us has the strength to douse tonight. I give a lazy smile when he breaks the connection. He's handsome even when he's exhausted and on the verge of passing out.

"Being you. I needed you more than you know tonight. We've all lived some tough lives. When one of us falls, we all feel it. I was grateful to have your strength. I appreciated that more than you know," he says.

"You don't ever have to thank me for being there. I see what the guys mean to you. I'll always be there for them just like I know you would come through for my brother or sister if they ever needed."

"Sometimes you have to make sure the ones you love know why you love them and how much," he says, settling his head back on the pillow.

"I love you too."

His arms tighten around me, and the last thing I remember is the sound of his snores. I smile in my half-asleep state. If I don't get any sleep tonight, it won't be because of my head.

CHAPTER THIRTY

Sacrifice

Beau

"Looking good, Beau," Billy calls into the ring. I grin but stay focused. She has joined my training team on her days at the gym. Angel gives her a chair to stand on so she can see into the ring and call out her encouragement and tips. I've come to look forward to it. She's learning a lot about the sport. It reminds me of how I learned, and the time I spent with my daddy.

"Switch to southpaw," Angel calls.

We've been going back and forth. Not many are aware that I can fight orthodox and southpaw. We've been working both stances to change things up on Gordon.

"I don't like this timid fighting," Alejandro calls from the side of the ring, his hands pressed to the canvas. "Take a break."

I drop my arms and roll my eyes. My father-in-law has been riding me the hardest in these last few sparring sessions. He's right. I'm not putting any real force behind my punches, and I've slowed my pace considerably.

Kyle spits out his mouth guard, while looking at me as if he can see through me. I'm used to that look. I know it well. He's been my sparring partner for the last three weeks. Angel and I thought it would be good to have a fighter in here with me who knows me well.

"You know he's right," Kyle says.

I look away. Kyle knows me *too* well. Daddy was thrilled to find out Kyle was as good with his hands in a boxing ring as he was with a basketball. We've been in the ring together since we were teenagers. He knows I'm holding back.

"We all know he's right," Emma calls from her seat in the bleachers.

"So everyone is going to gang up on me," I grumble.

"The offer still stands," Darwin calls from the bleachers with a straight face.

I know he's annoyed with me. Darwin has been trying to get me to talk to Eric. I know that's why his visits to the gym have become more frequent. Darwin introduced us all to Eric when he first came into our lives. "I don't need a shrink."

It's a lie. If I keep telling myself these lies, I might believe them. I need to put my ass in Eric's chair immediately, but I panic just thinking about it.

For now, Pandora's box is sealed. If I open it this close to the fight with Norwack, I don't know what I'll get. I know my head is already restraining me, but I'm afraid that this will become all-consuming if I unlock that latch.

Nope, ain't gonna do it.

"I think it's a good idea," Angel says.

I glare at my husband. We've had this talk repeatedly, and I've told him no each time. Shaking my head at him, I turn to walk and lean on the ropes facing my friends and family that have started to gravitate to the gym these days in support.

Emma, Mama, Darwin, Andy, and Mason have all been sitting to watch me and Kyle spar. I'm grateful for their support, but I'm starting to feel the judgment coming from them. I already know the problem.

"Gordon is going to lead you around the ring fighting like this," Andres says.

"I won't be fighting like this. Kyle isn't Gordon. I'm not going to go full steam on him," I say.

"Not going to or won't?" Kyle says, coming to stand beside me.

I ignore him. It took a lot for me to allow him in this ring with me. Even knowing it was a good idea to have him as my sparring partner. Angel had made the suggestion about a month or two ago after Kyle had offered.

"My worry is that you'll fight like this with Gordon in the ring," Angel says.

"Maybe not," Mama chimes in. "He looked like the Beau James I know when those cameras were here last week."

"This is true," Andy says.

"Yeah, I did notice that," Emma says.

"There were reasons for that," Angel says with a knowing smile.

I return the smile as I remember last week. Yeah, I was on a high. I'd been totally focused too as the cameras were here to get footage for the commercials and special that will air before the fight.

"Oh, come on, there are little people here," Emma says, palming her forehead.

"That's not what we mean," Angel says, shaking his head at my sister.

As always Javi came through. He pulled a few strings with a high-profile member of Club Refuge. Once the apartment is finished next week, we'll be bringing Billy home. Javi's connection happens to be a judge. He agreed to finalize the adoption in two months, instead of us having to wait the three months plus time for the courts to get us on docket and give us a date.

We'll be skipping right over all of that to make things official just in time for Billy's birthday. We spent last week in awe before we started to panic about all the things we still needed to do. We weren't expecting to skip over so much so soon.

Emma's face softens as she catches on. Mama's cheeks turn red; she's just been bursting at the seams to call Billy her granddaughter for the first time. Soon, everyone around me except for Billy has a grin on their face as we think of the secret we're keeping.

"Well, how do we get you to keep that same energy, short of the little miracle?" Andres speaks up. "If you're in your head, that's a problem."

My smile slips and I start to work my jaw. I can't keep fighting my team when they're right. Yet I'm stubborn to a fault.

"Why not talk to this Eric dude?" Billy says, as she comes to stand at my side.

I look down at her as she asks the question as if it has a simple answer. I tug my gloves off in frustration, not knowing how to tell a child that I'm plain scared shitless of my own shadow when it comes to being in the ring.

I want this fight more than anything. I've been telling myself it will be different on fight night. I'll be present. I'll be ready. Yet I don't know if that will be the truth. I'm falling deep into this rabbit hole, and I have an audience watching it happen.

"It's not that simple," I say to Billy.

"Why not? Make it that simple. You want to win. Shouldn't you do what it takes?" she replies.

"Shouldn't you be doing your homework?"

She levels me with a look, placing her hands on her hips. I swear she must think she's my mama. Nine going on thirty-five, she is.

"First of all, I did my homework. For the week, mind you. Second, I'm just trying to help. Don't get stink with me, you big grump. Don't you tell us to listen to our trainers? You should listen to yours. But hey, it's not my butt that's gonna get kicked," she says.

Snickers and stifled laughs ring out around us. Worst part is, she's damn right. I go to tell her so, but she rolls her little eyes and storms off out of the ring.

"Did a nine-year-old just hand me my ass in this ring?" I say, watching her storm away.

"Yes, she did," my mama snickers.

"If you don't get your head right, she won't be the only one handing you your ass," Alejandro says.

I look at my father-in-law and sigh. This fight is two and a half months away. I started out strong. It's the only reason Angel was okay with me signing on for this fight. I just need to get back to where my head was after stepping in the ring for the first time again.

Yeah, that's all I need.

Angel

"Anybody seen Billy?" I call out in concern.

I haven't seen her since she told Beau off and stormed away. We've all been so focused on Beau in the ring, I don't know if anyone has checked on her. I hadn't noticed until Emma said she was heading out. Billy came down with her today to help Beau. It's not one of the usual days for the Savanna's House kids to be here.

"Not me," Rustle says as he walks past me.

Moving past the self-defense class room, something catches my eye. When I look closer through the glass, little sneakers sit by the door. I turn back for the entrance and step inside. I pick up the sneakers.

My heart aches. They're falling apart at the soles. Emma bought these last year for Billy's birthday, and it took the kid almost three months before she actually would wear them. I think that was only because her last pair had become too small.

Emma had purposely bought her a bigger size, knowing she had been outgrowing her old pair. We're taking this kid shopping. I can't allow her to walk around like this anymore. She can be stubborn if she wants, but this is going to stop here.

"You don't have to look at them like that." Billy's voice comes out of nowhere.

She's huddled in the corner, with her knees to her chest. I gently place the shoes back down so they don't fall apart. After walking over to where she's sitting, I take a seat on the floor beside her.

"Andy's going to let me start a lemonade stand. I'm going to earn some money for new clothes," she says, lifting her chin.

"I respect that. You wanting to make your own money and take care of yourself. Andres and I used to sell candy in the neighborhood at your age," I say.

"You did?" she says as if I just told her we took over the world.

"Yeah, but I want to tell you something."

She sighs, turning to face me. I take in her outfit. It's another gift from the birthday party that she has made last for almost a year.

"Go ahead. Kill my dreams. I feel it coming," she says dryly.

I snort at her little sarcastic mouth. She's going to be a pain in the ass when she's a teenager. I'll probably leave all of that to Beau. He's the patient one when it comes to Billy.

"Things around here are going to be changing. Change is good. Change is how we grow. You're growing, and sometimes when we grow, we have to allow change to happen and be willing to adapt.

"We're your family, Billy. Kyle, Andy, Emma, Beau, everyone here at the gym. You have people you can trust that just want to do things for you and see you happy," I say. "No strings attached."

Her eyes bounce around my face as she takes my words in. Tears gather as she bites down on her lip. The war inside of her spills to the surface, shadowing her features.

"Only time people every did anything for me is if they wanted something. Gabby gave me candy to be quiet. Wilson would bring me things… that family they'd buy me clothes and make feel bad for taking them… I stopped taking stuff. My *abuela* was the only one that took care of me… but th… they did stuff behind her back. I was too scared to tell her, and when I finally did, she was taken away," Billy whispers.

Now here's where my anger and heartache mix. Billy has lived through the shit I wish only happened in movies. Shit I heard my friends talk about in school but always thought they were exaggerating. That is until I got old enough and started hanging out in their hoods to see it for myself.

"Can I tell you something?" she says when I'm too busy beating back my anger to say a word. "I've never told anyone else."

I start to count in my head. I know Billy's story now. If she's about to open that fresh bag of shit, I'll need to ground myself right fucking now.

"Of course, I'm here anytime you want to talk," I say.

"My... my mom, she killed herself. It wasn't long after Daddy was murdered on the block. I was still really little, but I remember them. Daddy would play ball with me in the house. We had this little hoop. My mom... she always smelled like candy," she says with a wistful smile.

"I found her. I used her cell phone to call for help. Abuela came to get me. I stayed with her and Wilson until they broke up. That's when Abuela met Gabby. Gabby was her girlfriend; she moved in when I turned six. Gabby was nice, but she would leave me home alone while Abuela was working at the hospital," Billy looks down at her fingers and starts to twist them.

"She'd buy my favorite candy and give me pretty stuff not to tell. Wilson came over to see Abuela one night, but she got called into work.... Gabby never locked me in. After the first time he found me home alone, Wilson would come by the apartment to pay me visits.

"He would bring food and my favorite soda. He... he started to ask me to do stuff. I was seven, but I knew something was wrong about it. It felt wrong. I wouldn't do it, and the last time he tried to make me, I ran in the bathroom and locked the door. He begged me not to tell, made me promise not to. I said I wouldn't, but I did. I shouldn't have," she says sadly.

"You did the right thing. Telling was the right thing," I say.

She wipes at her tears and shrugs. Her eyes look past me, causing me to turn. Beau stands frozen by the door.

"I'm sorry. Take your time. I'll tell Emma you need a minute," he chokes out.

"You don't have to go," Billy says almost in a plea. "Um… I… I want you here too."

Beau nods and comes to take a seat on the floor with us. He places a comforting hand on my back or maybe it's an anchor for himself. His fingers curl into the fabric of my shirt.

"Abuela was so mad. She got in a big fight with Gabby and told her to leave. She waited for Wilson to come by. She didn't go to work for a couple of nights." Billy blows out a breath and wipes under her nose.

Beau and I give her time to get her words out. I get the sense she needs this cleansing. This is a lot for a girl her age to walk around holding.

"Abuela left the door unlocked like Gabby would, and one night Wilson walked right in. Abuela lost it. They were yelling, and he hit her. I've never seen her so mad. She kicked his butt, dragged him out the apartment, down the stairs, and beat him up some more on the street.

"Our friends and neighbors cheered her on. It pissed Wilson off. He told her… he told her he would get her back. The guys in the neighborhood stepped in. They made him leave. Everyone loved my abuela." She sniffles.

"Ms. Mary offered to babysit me after that. She was a nice old lady…." Her breath hitches.

What happened next makes me wish I knew Billy and her grandmother back then. I wish I could have protected them from the outcome of that terrible night. If only I could have been there.

From what reports say, after a few weeks, the pissed-off ex-boyfriend set the apartment on fire with Billy and the sitter inside. Billy barely made it out with her life, even suffered a few minor burns. The sitter wasn't as lucky.

"My abuela wasn't a bad person. She was good to me. She just had to work a lot," she whispers. "She was a good person."

Billy's grandmother was sentenced to twenty-five to life for putting a bullet in the ex-boyfriend's head. A year into her sentence, she committed suicide like her daughter, leaving Billy with no one.

"I had to stay in the hospital. They wouldn't let me see her. I never got to see Abuela again. I went to a foster home after that. They all used to beat me. The mom, the dad, and the two boys.

"They'd give me nice stuff, and then... I'd get hit for everything. Even things the boys did, and if I told it was them and not me, they'd jump me. I was so tired of it. A nice family moved in next door, and the mom and dad started to ask me questions. I didn't know he was a cop," she says into her lap. "I'm not a snitch."

I tighten my jaw. A snitch. No little girl should have to be silent about an entire family abusing her.

The officer that came to Andy's brother about Billy was the next-door neighbor. He'd just moved in and immediately grew suspicious. After observing an often frizzled and once bruised Billy, he stepped in. That's how she came to Savanna's House, with trust issues a mile long.

So when I say I want the best for Billy and she deserves it, I mean that shit. Beau was right when he told me I didn't want to know the truth about Billy's past. Hearing her tell it in her own words boils my insides even more. "Remember I promised you that I'd make sure no one ever hurt you again?"

"Yeah," she says softly and nods.

"We will never let anyone hurt you again," Beau says beside me. His hand in the back of my shirt is so tight, the shirt has tightened on my body. Billy lifts to her knees and crawls closer to hug us both. We each wrap an arm around her.

"Thanks for listening," she says, sitting back to look at Beau. "I'm sorry I got mad at you. I know what it's like not to want to talk about stuff. You'll do it when you're ready."

"Don't even sweat, darlin'," Beau says.

"Now, about those shoes and these clothes," I say. "We're taking you shopping, Billy."

She gives a small smile and wipes at her tears. "Okay, fine, but only because I trust you."

Just like that, she steals my heart all over again.

CHAPTER THIRTY-ONE

Still Learning

Beau

"You've been super quiet," I murmur as we lie in bed. It's our last week in the gym's loft. I'll be happy to get into the new place. I need that separation of work life and home again.

"Long-ass day," he mutters.

Today was emotional and rough. Like Angel, I'm not shaking it as easily as I would like. Part of that is because I haven't had the escape of going home. The other part is the weight of Billy's words. "I know what you mean," I say, thinking of my sparring session and walking in on Billy's confession.

I hadn't meant to eavesdrop on their conversation. Rustle had said he saw Angel step inside the classroom. Emma was ready to go, and I started to get concerned about Billy when we couldn't find her.

"I just can't get over all she's been through. Reading it was one thing. Hearing her small voice reveal all that shit— I just… I don't… I grew up with love. Yeah, I've seen things in my friends' homes. Then I thought I knew it all and got into shit, but my home was always a safe place. I think I forgot that somewhere along the line."

"We'll give her a safe place," I say.

"I can't wait to see the new place. I think we should take her out to dinner or something to tell her about the adoption."

"I sort of had a different plan. I want the two of you to see the place together. I was thinking that we could tell her over breakfast in our new place," I say. "Once she sees her new closet, she'll be excited to fill it."

He turns on his side to face me. Those dimples pop and his lips curl into a smile. I reach to tuck his hair behind his ear, happy I could get that smile to come back.

"I like the sound of that, but I think we need to take her shopping before next week. Those sneakers. *Dios*, I wanted to toss them in the trash." He frowns. "But I totally get why she doesn't want anything from anyone. Fuck, what I'd give to take all of that bad shit away."

"We'll do what we can with her future. Her past is the past."

"I know. It just pisses me off," he murmurs.

"Hey, today has been heavy enough. Why don't I take your mind off it all for a while," I say, reaching to run the backs of my fingers down his arm.

"Mr. Dalton-Hernández, are you offering the D, Papi, or are you trying to take this dick down like a good husband should?" he croons.

"Tell me what you're up for and I'm all over it."

"Oh, I got time for you, Beau. Question is… you got time for me?"

I take his lips and show him just how much time I have for him. Getting lost in each other is just what we need. We retreat into our bubble for a few hours of silence.

Angel

Beau's deep laugh fills the ring. Unable to sleep, we took a walk to the store for ice cream and fresh air. Now we're sitting in the center of the ring, chilling with our pints under the low lights above.

"Don't laugh, I legit felt like she was about to tear my clothes off," I say to Beau's teasing about our trip to the store. I've come across some aggressive females, but that woman tonight took the cake. I almost left the store without my purchase to put space between us.

"I'm not laughing at you. I'm laughing at the image of her face in my head," he says around a spoon full of ice cream. "When I walked up behind you and kissed your neck, her eyes popped right out of her head."

"Yeah, that was hilarious. She wasn't taking no for an answer before that. It's not like she didn't see the wedding band either."

"Definitely a woman after what she wants." Beau continues to laugh.

"Don't think I didn't see her friend watching you," I say and grin.

Beau shakes his head, placing his ice cream aside. I'm going to work his ass hard tomorrow morning for this little cheat. He might as well eat it all and make it worth it.

"That one was drunk talking to the chips," he says.

"Facts." I crack up laughing. I point at his ice cream with my spoon. "You might as well finish that."

"I don't think you want me to," he says and frowns down at the pint.

My brows wrinkle. "Why not?"

"I think I may have become lactose intolerant," he says and rips one.

I sit with my spoon frozen halfway to my mouth. My face twists when the smell reaches my nostrils. Picking up the bag that we brought the ice cream home in, I toss it at him. He dodges it while rubbing his stomach.

"Dude, the fuck did you eat today?" I gag.

Beau falls onto his back and groans. "It's the damn ice cream."

"Well, shit. Remind me not to give you any more in the future."

He turns those gray eyes on me, and they're full of mirth. I narrow my eyes at him. Before I can warn him not to, he cuts another.

"Beau," I bark.

I get up to leave the ring and head back upstairs. I don't even want to finish my pint anymore. I grumble to myself as I step out of the ring.

"Where you going, baby?" he drawls after.

"Away from you," I call over my shoulder. "Don't follow me."

I toss the warning over my shoulder as he scrambles on the canvas behind me. I turn back just as Beau rushes out of the ring. I shake my head. I'm still learning so much about my husband. We've been married almost a year, and he hasn't eaten ice cream once during that time.

He catches up to me, wraps his arms around me, burying his face in my neck. "What happened to for better or worse?" he says against my skin.

"This ain't the worse I signed up for," I mumble.

He snickers and pecks my skin. "Accept me as I am. I'm yours."

"Yo, B. Come on, the silent ones smell worse."

"Damn, I know," he groans. "Rub my tummy. It hurts."

I look at him over my shoulder. The puppy eyes almost make me feel sorry for him. Almost. "*Coño*, you're a big baby."

He pecks my lips. "Never said I wasn't. Now make it better, darlin'."

I shake my head, but I can't help smiling. A part of me wants nothing more than to take care of my husband, smelly gas and all. Soon I'll have a little girl to take care of too.

"You're thinking about taking care of Billy's tummy aches, aren't you?" Beau says with a smile.

"Yeah, it's crazy how much I can't wait to be her everything," I say with a huge grin.

"I know what you mean. Her first day of high school, college." He beams even more.

"Taking her to get her prom dress," I add.

He groans. "No. She's going to stay a tomboy. No boys."

"You keep telling yourself that. She was wearing nail polish yesterday."

"Shit, you saw that too?"

"Sure did."

"The next one will be a boy," he says.

I lift a brow. We never talked about more kids after Billy. Yet the huge grin on his face as he realizes what he just said has me thinking of a bigger family.

"We'll just have to make sure she doesn't put anyone in a choke hold when she finds out she has to share us," I say.

He bursts into laughter. "Yeah, that wouldn't be good."

But a big family with you, Beau, would be great. It would be perfect. I can't wait.

CHAPTER THIRTY-TWO

Realizations

Beau

"I think we're getting a total different kid than we signed up for," I whisper to Angel.

He turns to look at me and widens his eyes. "So it's not just me."

"Nope."

"That's an awful lot of pinks and purples," Angel says.

"And a few skirts and dresses. Did you see the dresses?"

I pull a hand down my beard while watching Emma, Mama, and Billy pull items from the racks. Billy grabs another pink dress, and I groan. This isn't how I thought this trip would go.

"Yup, I saw those," he says.

"Where are the basketball shorts and jeans?"

"Honestly, I think we assumed too much about her." Angel sighs.

Billy runs over and wraps her arms around my waist, then moves to do the same with Angel. Her eyes sparkle with happiness, causing my heart to swell. Just as soon as she runs over, she turns and runs back to Mama and Emma.

"Can I be honest?"

"You already know," he replies.

"She could ask for every dress in this store, and I'd buy it just to see that smile on her face. I love that kid. I want her to be who she wants to be. If that means dresses and pink, and cheerleading practice instead of basketball, I'm good with that," I say.

Angel folds his arms across his chest and leans into me as we watch an excited Billy make more choices. She's picked every item herself, showing her taste and personality. I think that's what's throwing me.

"I hear you, but I wouldn't go placing her on the cheerleading squad just yet. I just think this is a lesson. You know. Like last night at the store. Shorty hit on me because she perceived me to be straight.

"You can't judge a book by its cover. Nothing is ever black and white. We don't love her because she plays sports or because of the clothes she wears. We love her because she's Billy, and that can be defined so many ways," he says.

"I guess I'm just a little surprised, but you're right."

"Okay, boys. We're done here," Mama calls as the three walk over to the counter with their haul.

I reach for my wallet, and Angel narrows his eyes at me. I kiss his cheek and ignore him, moving to the counter. I let him pay in the last store.

"Thank you," Billy says as I hand over the card.

"You're very welcome, darlin'."

"I heard someone say that new families are coming this weekend. Maybe if I look nice one will want me," Billy says hopefully.

I bite my cheek to keep from saying anything. Mama gives me a knowing smile. I see Angel pinch Emma when she opens her mouth. My sister has been chomping at the bit to spill the beans. Angel and I made a bet that she'll slip up before we can have our big day.

"Something tells me you're about to find the perfect family," Mama says.

"I hope so. I'm tired of sharing a room. Shelly's feet stink. We've tried to tell her nicely, but she won't listen. Ugh, I just want a place to call home that's not stinky," she says, turning up her cute little nose.

"We can't have it all," Angel mumbles under his breath, glaring at me.

I purse my lips to keep from laughing. Turning my attention back to Billy, I watch her eyes shine as she keeps her eyes on her things going into bags. Yeah, next week can't arrive soon enough for me.

Angel

"You know, I was thinking. Maybe I don't want a family, you know. If I leave, then what happens to my horse? I wouldn't get to see you guys all the time or come to the gym," she rambles, as she bounces between Beau and me. "No, I don't think a family is a good idea."

We're walking up Madison, heading to a restaurant, and Billy hasn't stopped talking. It's adorable to see her so happy and excited. My mother-in-law and sister-in-law had to leave, but Beau and I decided to take Billy out to eat.

Beau had suggested we either have takeout at the gym or go to Kyle's, but I thought it would be nice to take Billy somewhere she hasn't been. She's always at the gym or the complex. From her excitement now, I'm glad we're going someplace different.

I go to reply to her, but several things happen at once. A group of teenagers rush out of a shop barking and hooting. A guy grabs his girl to shield her from the rowdy teens and bumps my shoulder. A motorcycle on the street revs and backfires.

It's too fast and too much. I'm not able to single them out or cancel them in my brain. The crowd around us grows too tight, closing in on me and raising my anxiety. My sight becomes unfocused, and just when my spiraling out hits its peak, the sound of glass shattering sends me right over.

"Someone talk to me!" I shout, but there's no returning answer. They're gone. They're all gone.

The smell of burning flesh and gunpower fills my nostrils. Yet I can't reconcile what that means. I refuse to connect the silence to the smell. My heart races.

"Come on, Bachman, say something, motherfucker. You talk to me," I shout.

Pain sears my right side. I shove the fallen debris off me, noting my dislocated shoulder. Closing my eyes and taking a deep breath, I roll hard, knocking it back into place. I bite back the scream that wants to erupt from my lips.

"Fuck," I gasp in a whisper.

After rolling onto my back, I push up. I have to move. I need to get to a safe location before this place collapses or, worse, goes up in flames. Once to my feet, I try to assess where I am and the best plan to exit.

The mission. It was an ambush. Something shifts, drawing my attention. I grab my blade just in time to slash out at the hostile coming toward me.

We struggle as I block out the pain. I fight with everything I have; the adrenaline kicks in to numb my body and my mind. In a quick move, I have his back to my front. I lift the blade to his neck as I hold him in a choke hold.

My arm and hand with the blade are shaking. It's the shoulder I just popped back in. His hold on my wrist is the only thing keeping me from dragging this knife across his throat. I'm stronger than him, but my damn injured side is allowing this to be a fight.

"Angel."

I look around. Someone's calling me. I blink as something about all of this feels off. The smoke thickens and my head feels clouded.

Everyone calls me Hernández or Truth because I'm always honest. Who's calling me by my name? I try to concentrate. Something's not right. The guy I'd been struggling with is gone. I'm alone and in the desert now.

My throat feels dry. I'm so thirsty. Where is everyone?

"Angel."

"Where are you? Who are you?"

"Angel."

Beau

"Stay back, Billy," I warn as I block her body with mine.

A crowd has surrounded us on the busy street. The man Angel was holding now sits pushed to the ground, looking on in confusion, but my focus is on Angel standing before me with his arms out at his sides. He's looking around him, but he's not seeing the scene before him.

"Where are you? Who are you?" he calls out.

"Angel," I call again.

He doesn't respond to me. His face twists with frustration and confusion. I don't want to risk getting closer. This isn't like at the wedding or our wedding reception. Something in his body language and expression give me pause.

"Angel," Billy calls out.

This time his head snaps in Billy's direction. She's behind me with her hands clasping my jacket as she peeks around my body. I want to tell her to get back, but this crowd is growing, and I don't want to lose her in it.

"Angel, it's me, Billy," she says.

"Angel, we're here right in front of you. Can you hear me?" I coax.

"Yo, Angel," Billy says.

That seems to do the trick. My shoulders sag in relief as he blinks at Billy and stumbles back a bit. His eyes clear, but they bounce between Billy still peeking from around my back and me. All of the blood drains from his face and his eyes widen.

"It's okay," I say.

However, it's not. Angel turns and takes off through the crowd. I go to take off after him, but I pause when I remember Billy.

"Where's he going?" she asks softly.

I run a hand through my hair and tug. I don't know where he's taking off to. I have a sinking feeling in the pit of my stomach. "I don't know."

CHAPTER THIRTY-THREE

Second Thoughts

Angel

I should've put more thought into this. Beau and I have been living in a bubble of our own creation, dreaming of things that can never be. Who was I kidding? "You're so fucking selfish," I bite out.

The look in Billy's eyes is burned in my head. I could see the fear in her gaze as she looked at me from around Beau's back. That little girl has had enough crap in her life. She doesn't need my fucked-up shit.

I have no business trying to adopt a kid. My worst nightmare is to fuck this up and ruin Billy's life. We should've thought ahead. Eric is wrong. I'm not mentally fit. I don't care what he says.

"Fuck," I breathe as I look out over the Hudson.

I needed to get away. I came here to think. I used to come here to get my head right when I lived on the streets. I've been here all night; dawn is just starting to break.

My phone rings in my pocket, grabbing my attention. I pull it out to send the call to voicemail. Beau has been calling all night. I just can't face him yet. However, when I look at the name on the screen, it's not Beau. I decide to pick up this time, needing a voice of reason. "Hello."

"Hello, Angel," Eric says into the phone. "Dar gave me a call. Your husband is very concerned about you. Do you want to talk?"

"This was all a mistake. I'll never be able to start a family like this," I say.

"Take a breath, Angel," he says. "Let's think this through."

"What's there to think through? I freaked out in front of the kid. I scared her. How can we adopt her when I could put her in danger at any moment?" I demand.

"You've been doing so well. This has been the first major episode you've had in almost a year. You've reduced your stress, and you've been sleeping more. So what makes you think you can't continue to progress?" he asks.

"I don't know. It just doesn't seem like enough," I whisper.

"Are we talking about your progress or you, Angel? You want to know what I've been hearing in our sessions?"

I take a moment to think over his words. Have I done enough to be worthy of Beau and Billy? I sigh, hoping he can point me to the answer. "Yeah, go on."

"You've become anxious in the last few sessions as you talked about getting ready to tell Billy that you and Beau want to adopt her. I see you beginning to stress about moving into the new apartment and taking this next step.

"Under this type of stress, you were bound to have an episode sooner or later. The outside triggers this time were just the catalyst to what was already building. We've talked about running away from your problems in the very beginning.

"I don't believe that's who you are. You're not a runner. I think you will be a great father to Billy. I wouldn't have put her life or care in danger by saying you were ready if you weren't. I take my job seriously. I stand by my recommendation," he says.

I close my eyes against the bright rising sun. As the warm rays hit my face, I allow his words to sink in. He's right. I'm not a runner. I've tried it in the past. Running only frustrates me in the end. I'd much rather confront my battles head on. "So what do I do?"

"Go home to your husband. Sit down with him and discuss what you felt before you took off. What's one of the biggest things you said you learned about yourself in the last year?" he asks.

I stop and think. I've shared so much with Eric over the last year. We've talked about everything. I've found more peace as I've revealed to him the things that lurk in my brain.

When I open my eyes, I see the answer. I know exactly what he's talking about. It's what shaped my life choices in the past.

"When I choose to run, I base the decision off my perception of other's feelings, but I'm not always right about how they feel," I say.

"Exactly. Go home. Put your husband's mind at ease. Then have a talk with Billy. See how the experience really affected her. Again, I wouldn't have cleared you or written the glowing letter that I did if I didn't think you were right for her. A bad day here and there shouldn't keep you and Beau from loving that child.

"Come see me in a few days. I think I have some new methods you might like to add on to your care plan. And, Angel?" he says.

"Yeah."

"Bad days help us gauge how we're doing in this life. You're doing better than you're giving yourself credit for," he says. "You're very lucky to have the support system you have. Don't take that for granted. Today is today; tomorrow is tomorrow. You live each as they happen. Not before and not after."

"I just need time to think," I say.

"That's fine. You're entitled to do that. Just make sure you consider what I've said," he says before we end the call and I power my phone down.

I do think on all he has said as I start to walk. Can I say for sure that I scared Billy? No. In my moment of panic, that's what I interpreted in the look on her face. Have I come a long way? Yes. I've been holding down two jobs, and I function in my home life with Beau. Is it perfect? No. I still get up in the middle of the night most nights, but it's not as bad as it used to be.

But I do know how serious Eric is about his work. When I thought he would just sign off on my mental health as a friend of Darwin and the family, he didn't. He actually increased my sessions and had me work through a few things before he did give me the all clear.

But there's one question that still looms in my head. The most important one in my opinion. The one I need to answer before I return home.

Am I enough?

Beau

I look at the clock again. It's nine in the morning. Darwin called over two hours ago to let me know that Eric finally got through to Angel. Yet my husband hasn't answered a single one of my calls. His phone has started to go straight to voicemail.

I can't lift another weight, throw another pitch, skip another rope. I've done it all in between calling Angel over and over. I'm exhausted and worried to my wits' end. I want to be out there searching for him, but Andres and Alejandro felt it would be better if I stayed here at the gym.

"Hey."

I whip around at the sound of Emma's voice. I didn't even hear her come into the gym. I wipe away the sweat from my forehead with the back of my arm. My muscles are screaming at me in protest of every move at this point. "Hey," I murmur.

I take the cup of coffee she hands me. I'll need it. I'm not going to rest until I can see with my own eyes that Angel is okay.

"We know how to pick 'em, don't we?" she says as we move to take a seat on the bleachers.

"Trouble in paradise?" I ask, not ready to talk about my own relationship.

"That's just it. I don't know. Andres has this way of shutting down. I don't know what I did or what's going on," she says and pouts.

"Want me to talk to him?"

"No." She sighs. "It'll be fine. I'm just going to give him some space for now."

I study her face. It's not fine, but I'll respect her decision for now. I honestly think Andres has fallen for her. I see the way he looks at her. I'm not really sure what his problem could be.

"Do you think he's just freaked out about becoming a dad?" Emma says, pulling me from my thoughts after a few moments pass.

"Em, I don't know what he's thinking. Angel... he has this way of seeing everyone else for who they are. It's one of the things that made me open up and fall for him so hard. But when it comes to him looking in the mirror, he doesn't see how amazing he is," I reply.

"Everything has happened sort of fast. I can see him needing time to think."

"He can have all the time in the world to think. I just want to know he's okay. This isn't all right," I explode. I clamp my mouth shut and reel it back in. "I love him. I want to be there for him when he needs me. I'm so damn pissed at him."

"Maybe you can step into his shoes for a second," she says. "You're so used to controlling your environment around you. It's one of the things you do best. You take care of everything, make sure everything goes the way it should.

"Oh my God, that apartment. It's perfect for both Angel and Billy. They're going to flip when they see it. Everything about that place speaks of how you take control.

"You and Angel are so alike in so many ways, but think about it, Beau. This is the one thing he can't control. He's trying so hard to. He's been working so hard. Add to that loving the stuffing out of Billy and being worried that he could lose her because of this. Could you imagine not having the control you always have over something that important to you?" she says.

I look down into the cup in my hands. No, I couldn't imagine that. It makes my head hurt trying. I never thought of it that way.

Angel and I bump heads about who gets the bill. We've learned to compromise control in so many areas, but that's still a challenge as one of us is always left grumbling about conceding. That's when we chose to give up control. I can't imagine involuntary giving up my power over my life.

Even in the ring, I'm making the choices that control my fight. I'm always driving the situation. Always weaving the outcome in some form. Making the choices.

"He doesn't get the choice when this happens," I think out loud.

"Exactly. Now think about how that must tear him apart," she says.

My anger begins to wean. I place my coffee aside and wrap my arm around my sister, kissing the top of her head. Her arms go around me and give a little squeeze.

"When did you get so wise?" I murmur.

"Always have been. I knew you'd notice one of these days."

"I love you, darlin'. Thanks."

"It's all going to be fine. I have a niece," she squeals.

I release a laugh and give her a squish. I hope it all works out. Too many hearts to be broken if we can't pull it together. "One thing at a time," I say.

"Yeah, I guess you're right. But I'm still so excited."

"No one can say we live a dull life."

I take out my phone and shoot Angel a text. I'm doing my best to be understanding and do just as Emma said. I'm placing myself in his shoes.

Me: *Take your time. I'm here when you're ready. I love you.*

CHAPTER THIRTY-FOUR

Love's Submission

Beau

I peel my eyes open and look around the loft. I don't remember coming up here or getting into bed. I spent the day locked in my office, waiting to hear back from Angel or someone who found his location.

I turn for the clock and see I must have passed out for a bit. I sit up and toss my legs over the edge of the bed. I lift my phone from the pillow to check for messages. I have a few text messages, but they're all from everyone except the person I'm looking for. As my head clears, I register the whine of the pipes from the gym below.

I get to my feet and head downstairs without a second thought. As I get to the lower level, the lights in the locker room draw my attention and the sound of the shower reaches my ears.

The knot in my chest that has been resting there since last night begins to loosen.

"Thank God," I drawl out.

I enter the showers to find Angel under the spray, standing the exact same way I found him that first night: his head bent between his shoulders with his hands braced against the tiles. Water cascades down his muscled brown back.

I step out of my shorts and pad the rest of the way in to stand behind him. I gently place a hand on his hip to warn him of my presence, so I don't alarm him. His muscles bunch, and his hands fist against the tiled wall.

I kiss his shoulder and cover his fists with my palms. He relaxes, flattening his hands beneath mine. Placing my forehead to the back of his wet hair, I soak him in. It's only been a little over twenty-four hours, but it feels like weeks. I relish the feel of him as the sound of the shower fills the silence.

"Are you okay?" I say into the quietness between us. "That's all that matters to me."

He nods, turning to face me. His arms go around me, and his face buries into my neck. I feel like I can breathe again as I hold him in my arms. I lend him my strength, willing his pain into my own body.

"I'm here," I say. "I'm here for whatever you need."

He raises his head, and those whiskey-colored eyes lift to meet mine. I think I fall in love with him all over again. His eyes speak of his concern for me, while I can feel his own pain. When he cups my face to search my eyes, the emotions I see are confirmed. His thumb strokes my cheek.

"You look tired. I'm sorry. I needed to clear my head, but I won't disappear like that again," he says.

"Don't worry about it. I just needed to know you were okay. That's all I wanted."

"Yeah, I'm good."

I search his eyes to see if that's the truth. I push his wet hair from his face. He turns his head to kiss my palm.

The simple gesture turns into heated, openmouthed kisses trailing from my palm to my wrist. I clench my teeth and stifle a groan, my gaze drawn to his mouth against my skin. "Angel—"

"I'm fine. At least, I will be," he cuts me off. "This is what I need for now."

He takes my lips, and I give in without protest. Emma's earlier words about Angel's need for control rings in my ears. I yield to him as his hands lock in the top of my hair, holding me to him.

Tonight, I'll be whatever he needs. Tomorrow we'll talk about what went wrong because losing him isn't an option. We can make it through as long as we do it together.

Angel

Normally I'd thrill in the fight between us, and I'd be pissed that Beau's giving in so easily. Not tonight. I need this, and the fact that he understands that makes me love him even more. It makes me feel worse for shutting him out.

I plan to make that up, though. I slide my tongue deeper into his mouth as my fingers run through his scalp. The groan that sounds from him is a soothing balm to my soul. A confirmation that I should've come home sooner.

"I love you," I breathe into his open mouth.

"I love you too," he says.

I break the kiss to look into his eyes. I brush my fingers across his collarbone. I love that I can pull shivers from him with the simplest touch.

My gaze follows as my hand travel down over his nipple, shifting course to run down his taut stomach. Another tremble rolls through his strong body. I grin as I watch his belly cave under my touch.

I claw my nails from the front of his waist around to his lower back. He releases a loud groan, and I bite down on my lower lip. I've learned so many things about this man. I know what turns him on. I know where he needs my touch most and when.

I know he trusts me. And that's what brought me home. That trust I see in his eyes even now.

"Angel," he breathes as I continue to caress and tease the skin along his lower back.

I cease the slow touch to lift my hand to his lips. His tongue comes out to play, licking my fingers as I brush his full lips. I stick my thumb into his mouth as my other fingers bury into his beard.

I'm transfixed by him sucking me into his mouth. A new thrill hits me as Beau begins his own seduction. I drag my finger from his lips as he begins to lower to his knees. I step forward a bit to come from under the spray of the showerhead.

He takes a pause, looking up at me for permission. I nod and he places his hands on my thighs. My dick is pointing straight at him, making it easy for him to take me right into his mouth.

"Mm," I hum as he takes me in slowly.

I fist the top of his hair and start to guide him as my hips take on a mind of their own, thrusting into his hot, waiting mouth. I throw my head back and get lost in the feel of his wet cavern. My lips part and my nostrils flare.

"Yes, just like that," I hiss out. "Suck that dick like you mean it. You know what I want you to do for me."

He releases me from his mouth and dips his head to take my balls between his lips instead. My eyes roll as the sensation of the shower at my back and his attention to my sac cause my spine to tingle. When I tighten the hold I still have on his hair, he shifts his attention back to my erection.

His hands caress up and down my thighs a few times before joining his mouth. It won't be too much longer, and he knows it. He glides one hand around to my ass to squeeze and knead the cheek.

"Suck harder," I command.

Those grays lock with mine, sending promises of a grand completion. He hollows his cheeks and takes me deep. His hand tightens at the base, and I explode with a loud call of his name.

Wrapping a palm around his neck, I gently guide him to his feet. When I take his lips, it's a punishing kiss. I want him to feel me. I want him to know how much I've fallen in love with him.

I swift our bodies until his back hits the shower wall. He bites my lip, drawing a hiss from me. I return the favor, licking away the sting. His fingers dig into my shoulder blades, clinging to me and holding me to him.

Slowing things down just a bit, I nip and sip from his mouth, tasting and tempting, as our sounds of pleasure ring out. When I have him where I want him, I draw back just out of his reach. Frustration lines his features as I tease him, lean in, but back away just before the connection.

After one time too many for his liking, his hands go into my hair, tugging me forward. I chuckle into his mouth and our tongues dance. Reaching for his hands, I pin them over his head. I explore him with my mouth. First, his lips and chin.

Then I move to his neck, licking and nipping at the moist soft flesh. I let my tongue glide across his collarbone, moving down to his nipple. His groans fill the air, pushing me forward. Releasing his wrists, I gently drag my hands down his arms, over his chest, his stomach, and back up his ribs.

I squat before him and just stare. His body is gorgeous. All of the training has only toned him to a greater level of perfection.

"I don't know what I did to deserve you," I choke out as the last twenty-four hours hit me hard.

He cups my face and lifts it until my eyes train on his. I can see the love he has for me in them. I close my lids as I realize what I have.

Am I perfect? No. Am I enough? Yes, for Beau I am, and that's all that matters.

Beau

Something shifts as Angel looks up at me. When he closes his eyes, peace washes over his features. A peace I've never seen before. It tugs at my heart and cracks it open.

He has become my peace, and I now believe that I can see that I'm his. I want this peace for him more than I want my next breath. I brush a hand over his wet hair, and he opens his lids. Water clings to those full long lashes, making him look like a true ethereal being. Simply beautiful.

However, this time when I look into his gaze, I see more than peace. Desire like I've never seen before stares back at me. It oozes from him, filling the shower stall to a point of stifling the air around us.

He wraps my length in his palms, his lips encasing me next. His lids are hooded as those dark lashes shadow his gorgeous eyes. I lick my lips, my own mouth watering at the sight of him sucking my cock.

"Angel," I whisper, damn near drooling on myself as he takes me in over and over.

I push a hand into the side of his hair. It's not a guiding hand, rather an anchor as my toes curl and my heart pounds. I want to throw my head back, but I don't want to tear my gaze from him.

Even like this he has control. It's the way he commands my body and demands my pleasure. He does it so effortlessly. I don't even try to fight my orgasm.

"Fuck, Angel," I roar as I release. I don't get to come down before he lifts to his full height and turns me swiftly. Pushing a hand between my shoulder blades, he presses me forward. I place my hands on the shower wall.

"I love you," he says as he begins to kiss and caress his way down my back.

I arch my back when he licks from the base of my spine up the center to my nape. He gently kicks my legs apart, grabbing and kneading my cheeks roughly. Anticipation builds in the pit of my belly.

His mouth and tongue are in command of my ass in the next motion. I grind my teeth and squeeze my eyes shut as pleasure seizes me and my sanity. Although it's not quickly, when he does pull away, it's much too soon.

Taking the shower gel from my right in his hand, the sound of the cap clicking open echoes in the space. His breath fans my ass as he works the soap over his cock. He pours some of the soap down my back, smoothing it over my skin.

Lifting to his full height, he leans into my back. His chest presses against me and he places his lips close to my ear. "*Te amo.*"

Cupping my throat, he tugs my head to the side carefully and takes my lips in a slow kiss. This kiss speaks. It tells a story of his love for me. I take it with understanding of the language that has become our own.

"I love you, Beau," he repeats as he starts to inch into me.

He takes his time as the soap becomes our only lube. I need him so much I welcome him without hesitation. I grunt and take him, growing hard again as he begins to ease in and out of me. His free hand goes to my waist, guiding me to his rhythm. Not too fast, not too slow.

"Ah, Angel, yes," I groan out as he releases my lips to watch my face.

"Tell me how you want this dick," he says in my ear. "Tell me how much you need me."

I reach to lace my fingers with his on my hip. He backs up, guiding me with him until I'm arched farther forward in front of him. Now that I'm more open to him, he drives in harder, faster.

"Just like that," I call out. "Fuck, Angel. Just like that."

He slaps my ass not once, not twice, but three times, alternating between both cheeks, and keeps thrusting. I reach for my cock and start to stroke. I half expect him to knock my hand away, but he covers it with his instead. We work together to push me over the edge as he grows near.

Chests heaving, legs buckling, we sag forward and fall to the floor. Angel reaches up to turn the water off. His arms go around me as he shifts our bodies. His back to the shower wall, me cradled between his legs.

"Thank you," he says, kissing my shoulder.

I nod. No words need to be said. I already understand.

CHAPTER THIRTY-FIVE

Right Perspective

Angel

"Okay, ladies. That's a wrap for today. Enjoy the rest of your day," I call out to my self-defense students. They begin to pack up, and I start to clean and set up for the next class. I'm lost in thought as I work until cheers from outside of the classroom grab my attention. Some of the guys are gathered in the ring, horsing around.

I smile. No anxiety, no episode. I've been in a good place the last few days. I've noticed a few times that things that would've triggered me in the past are rolling right off me. Eric was right. I've come a lot further than I'd been giving myself credit for.

"Angel!"

Billy rushes into the self-defense classroom and wraps her arms around my waist. I'm surprised at first, but I shake it off and return the embrace. She breaks the hug and backs away, her little brown cheeks glowing.

"Hey, kid."

"I'm glad you're okay," she says softly.

"I'm sorry if I scared you," I say.

She looks at me and tilts her head. Her brows furrow.

"I wasn't scared of you. I was worried," she says. "Those people don't understand. Some of them looked angry. I didn't want anyone to try to touch you or hurt you."

My shoulders sag. Eric was right again. I'd made assumptions about how others felt. I didn't stick around to hear her actual thoughts. I just reacted off what I thought she felt. "They were probably in more danger than I was," I say.

Beau told me about the man I grabbed and knocked on his ass. I wish I knew how to find him to apologize. Beau said he did apologize on my behalf, and Eric says I need to let that one go. I have for the most part.

"I'm just glad you're here," she says.

I reach to palm the top of her head and shake it from side to side, earning a grin. "Where else would I be?"

She joins me in the completion of my setup for the next session. My mind wanders to my conversation with Beau this morning. We're trying to figure out the best way to ask her to hang out with us so we can do the big reveal.

I think we're both making something so simple into much more than it is. Yet we still hadn't come up with an answer by the time we finished our breakfast and Beau's morning training session. I'll text Emma for ideas later.

"You guys still owe me dinner, by the way," Billy says, pulling my attention.

She has a little twinkle in her eyes. Her teasing reminds me that we did miss going to dinner that night. It also gives me the door I need to solve our little issue. I smile and wrap an arm around her shoulders.

"How about we have breakfast?"

"Really?"

"Yup." I nod. "Beau and I will pick you up Friday."

Her face lights up, and my chest swells. We'll be making this official on Friday. Billy will know that we want her as a part of our family.

"That's what's up, I'll be ready."

Beau

I walk up beside Angel as he packs the last of his things into the boxes that will be delivered to the new place. Placing a hand on his back, I start to rub soothing circles. He turns to look at me with a smile on his lips.

"So Friday," I say and draw in a deep breath.

"Friday." He grins. "She was excited. I mean, she has no idea, but she was so excited to have breakfast with us."

"Is it just me, or are you scared shitless that she'll say she doesn't want us?" I speak my latest fears aloud.

Angel stops, tossing down the shirts in his hands. He turns to look at me with the same worry I feel. It actually allows me to take a breath.

"Dude, I'm not going to lie. I've thought that shit so many times it's making me twitchy. We've gone through all of this, and she could say she doesn't want to be our little girl. I think… nah, I know I'd be crushed," he says.

"You and me both." I grunt. "She's so independent minded, and you never know what she'll do next. In the back of my mind, I know she's asked us about being her family, but I just can't shake the doubts."

He wraps his arms around my waist and tugs me in closer. We enter in a slow, lazy kiss that soothes some of my nerves. When our lips separate, he places his forehead to mine.

"I think we both need to relax." He laughs. "At the end of the day, her happiness is what matters. If she says no, it won't be the same, but we can look for another kid."

"It would take me a while to get to that point, I think. You know what I mean?"

"Sure do," Angel breathes. "It will be fine. We're just psyching ourselves out."

I rub my hands up and down his back, knowing his words are nothing but truth. We're worrying over nothing. Once Billy sees the home we've made for her, she'll be ready to move in right away.

"I can't wait for you two to see the place. It's nothing like before," I say with new excitement running through my bones.

"I'm sure it'll be popping," he says with those dimples showing.

My cell chimes in my pocket, drawing my attention. I pull it out and read the message. I can't help the frown that comes to my face.

"What's wrong?" Angel asks.

"It's nothing," I bite out harder than I mean to.

Angel places his fingers beneath my chin, lifting and turning my face to him. He searches my eyes for answers, but I slam the shutters closed. I chose not to worry him with this. Until this moment, I had pushed it to the back of my mind.

"Nah, we're not doing that. We just agreed the other night that we'd stop closing each other out. What's going on?" he says.

I pull away and start back over to the things I'd been placing in boxes. Angel stands with his arms folded across his chest, waiting. I'm not ready to talk about this because it makes my head want to explode, but he's right. We did agree to stop shutting down.

"Steve has been trying to sell off rights he feels he has to me," I ground out.

"Steve?" Angel asks, then realization hits. "Your old promoter?"

"Yeah, in my old contract, there was a clause that guarantees him a stake in my future earnings. I was young and stupid. Mama never trusted him, but I thought I was a man and knew it all. I signed that contract anyway. There was a shit-ton wrong with it." I snort and draw a hand down my face.

"I'm no lawyer or anything, but if the agreement is with him, doesn't it die with him if he sells it?" Angel asks with furrowed brows.

"No, he's packaging the sale as his promotion business. The contract is an asset. Basically, my contract is the sum total of the value to his company," I reply.

"That's bullshit."

"He's desperate."

"Can we buy him out?" Angel asks thoughtfully.

"I'm not giving him a fucking dime, and neither is anyone else I know."

Angel moves across the bedroom to me, wrapping his arms around my neck, his touch causing some of the tension to release. I'm still fuming inside.

"So what do you want to do? I didn't like his ass from jump. I'm down for whatever," he says.

"Javi has put out the word that no one is to touch the deal. So far no one has. However, the fight is getting closer, and Steve's starting to make noise about the purse," I explain. "He's calling attention to himself in the press. Again, Javi is working to silence the stories, but this has to end."

"I don't want you to think about this. I'll talk to Javi in the morning and deal with it. You focus on the fight."

"Angel—"

"Nah, I know his type. I got this. Leave it to me. I'll take care of it," he says.

I purse my lips, but I don't argue. My plan was to go beat the shit out of Steve, but that wouldn't do me any good. When I give Angel a silent nod, he presses his lips to my forehead.

I pull him into a hug and hold him. I may need to feel like I'm the one always in control, having to be the one that handles things to keep us going. Still, it feels good to let go this once and have the man I love take care of things for me. I appreciate it more than he knows.

You're not alone, Beau. Not anymore.

CHAPTER THIRTY-SIX

Our Home

Beau

I have a lump in my throat the size of Texas. This is it. I get to give Angel and Billy a new home. On top of that, we're going to tell Billy what's going on. She gets to decide if she'll have us, if this is the home she wants to call her own.

"I thought you guys lived at the gym," Billy says as we step off the elevator on our floor.

I jingle the keys in my hand nervously as we move to the new entrance. I changed everything about this place. I moved the main entrance closer to the elevator to have central access. The entire floor is now our personal living space.

"We were just staying there while our place got a makeover," Angel says.

"Oh, cool. So like you painted the place or something?"

"More like expanded and redesigned," I say.

"I can't wait until I'm big enough to have my own place and do stuff like that," she says. "I'm going to have a huge room and a hoop in my living room."

I grin as I push the key into the lock and turn it. My heart stops as I push the door open and allow first Billy, then Angel to walk in ahead of me. The audible gasp from them both starts my heart again.

I shuffle in quickly and close the door behind me. Angel pulls off his sneakers and puts them in the cubbies I had designed by the front door. Billy slips off her sparkling pink flats and places them in a hole as well.

I didn't miss that she got dressed up for our breakfast. A pink blouse with ruffles and pressed black slacks. Her hair isn't in that braided bun. Instead, it's in two braids on either side of her head, hanging over her shoulders with pink ribbons at the ends.

I kick off my cowboy boots as the two wait expectantly for me. I am so caught up in their reactions, I almost forget to move. When I step forward, Billy places her small hands in ours, and I have to fight the tears that try to rush me.

This feels right.

"This place is… it's beautiful," she whispers.

"Beau… I don't know what to say," Angel chokes out.

"You've never been here before?" Billy asks as she looks up at Angel in confusion.

"Not since the renovations started," he says. "This is… it's totally different. *Nuestro pedazo de cielo.*"

"Our piece of heaven?" I interpret, hoping I got it right.

Angel looks at me, rising a questioning brow. I grin like a kid caught with his hand in a cookie jar. I can feel the blush on my cheeks.

"I've been brushing up on my Spanish," I say and wink at him.

"You're full of surprises today," he says.

I lead them farther into the apartment. I don't know what to show them first. I'm too nervous to start with Billy's room, so I decide to show Angel one of the things I've done for him first.

"Your ceilings are so cool," Billy says as she looks up at the frosted glass. It looks like artwork with the veining as if it's made of marble.

"You haven't seen a thing yet, darlin'," I say and move to the digital panel on the wall.

I switch the settings, and again they both gasp. The once-frosted ceilings are now clear and see-through. The sunlight shining into our new little world.

"You can adjust it anyway you like. If it gets too bright or you want to shut out the rain or snow, we can shade it or frost it back," I say, watching Angel's face.

His Adam's apple bobs several times. I gather that his emotions are too much for him to speak. He nods and looks around at the open floor plan of our home. The walls of windows wrap the apartment on one side, bringing in more natural lighting and views of the city around us.

"You have a hoop in the living room," Billy says with excitement. "This place is amazing."

I remembered her telling Angel that she played hoops with her dad in their home. I know we'll never replace her dad, but I wanted to give her a piece of him to remember. However small it might be.

"Mama sent us blueberry muffins for breakfast. You guys want to sit and talk?" I say nervously.

"I'm eating anything Ms. Daphne made," Billy says.

I shake my head after her as she goes and makes herself comfortable on one of the barstools at the kitchen island. I reach for Angel's hand and squeeze it. We follow Billy, Angel taking a seat beside her while I get us orange juice to wash down our muffins.

I watch with a smile as Billy tears into her baked treat. Angel has a huge smile on his face as well. If all goes well, our new chef will start on Monday. I wanted to have someone who will be able to cook something for the three of us since I'm on a special diet that's not ideal for a growing nine-year-old. Angel loves to cook, but he's been busy while training me, and working.

"This is so good." Billy hums.

"Mama makes the best muffins," I say.

Billy places the muffin down and looks around the place. Her eyes go from sparkling with awe to something else. Disappointment... longing... hope.

"How many bedrooms do you have here?" she asks as she looks up at me.

"Three on this side of the apartment, four on the other," I reply.

Hope blooms a bit more. She brushes her hands off in front of her, then places them in her lap. She turns to Angel and her shoulders sag. "Did you ever fix your head?" she murmurs to him.

"I got my life together as best I could. My head isn't perfect, but it's better," he replies.

"Oh... that's good, right?"

The hope in her voice could take on a physical presence, it's so strong. I round the island to sit on the other side of her. She looks between us with a plea in her eyes.

"It's very good, darlin'," I tell her. "It's actually why we want to bring you here. We wanted to see if you like our home. If maybe… it's your decision. But we'd like for you to come live with us."

Tears start to spill down her cheeks. I look at Angel, not knowing what to do. I didn't expect to make her cry.

"Yes, please," she says softly. "I've been praying you guys would come get me. You're the family I want to want me. Yes, please."

Angel and I wrap our arms around her, and she breaks down into sobs. My own tears wet my cheeks. Her little arm wraps around me and clings to my shirt.

"We were coming for you, darlin'. We just had to build you the right home," I say over her sobs.

Slowly, Angel and I release her. I brush a hand over one of her braids, and she smiles. I know we still have two months before it's final, but I've never felt more complete in my life.

"How about we go take a look at your room?"

"I have a room?" she asks as she beams and sniffles.

"You sure do."

Angel

She's ours. Or at least she will be. Of all the ways I imagined this day going, I never imagined this reaction at all. When she broke down in tears, I thought my heart would fall out.

Now as we climb the gorgeous staircases with glass railings, Billy has a tight hold on each of our hands. There's so much to absorb in this moment, I don't know what to focus on. The cool concrete of the stairs beneath my feet brings a smile to my face.

Beau really listened to the things I told him I would love to have and mixed that with making a place perfect for us as family. I'm so full right now. From living on the streets off and on to having a family and this beautiful home. The place is so huge I don't know if it's possible for me to feel closed in.

The ceilings, though! Beau is the fucking man for that shit. God, I love him.

"Okay, Angel and I are down the hall," Beau says. "This here is your room. Go on. Go in."

Billy reluctantly releases our hands and reaches to turn the knob. She pushes into the room and freezes in place. When I step inside, I see why.

I turn and grab Beau by the front of his shirt, drawing him to me. I place my forehead to his, trying to say it all without the words I can't get through my emotion-clogged throat. He cups me by the back of my head and nods his understanding.

"All of this is for me?"

I turn to see the look of disbelief on Billy's face. Hell, I'm in awe myself. Beau couldn't have captured a more perfect room.

"It's all yours," he replies because I still can't say shit. I don't know where to take in first. It's a room fit for a princess all right, but not just any princess. This one is for Princess Billy.

From a huge window overlooking the city with a bench seat beneath it, pink and purple pillows make the space look inviting; bookshelves line either side of the window, stuffed with books; to a huge bed fit for a queen that anchors the center of the room, it's draped in sheer fabrics and covered in beautiful matching bedding. It's waiting to cradle the dreams of the most precious little girl in the world.

Then there's the hangout spot. A seating area for Billy and her friends. A TV is mounted to the wall in front of an accent mat, two accent chairs, and a little couch. A built-in harbors every gaming system known to man. On one side of the TV is a mini basketball hoop; on the other is a dart board and mini cooler beneath.

Framed MMA posters line the walls, boasting Billy's favorite fighters. Yet the frame that stands out most to me is the one over her desk. It's a picture of the three of us from her birthday party last year. I hadn't known Beau even owned such a picture.

Beau has Billy wrapped in a hug as she laughs with a pretty smile on her face. I'm standing with them, making a goofy face that I'm sure is the reason behind her laughter. We look like a family.

"When can I come home?" Billy asks, pulling me from taking in the room.

My chest fills to the point of bursting. She's already calling it her home. Beau takes my hand and gives it a squeeze.

"It's up to you. As soon as you like. We have the okay," Beau says.

"We can go get my things? I'm ready to come home now. I… I just wanted to go home with you guys. I didn't know you would do all of this for me. *Es perfecto, gracias*," she says.

"You're welcome," Beau and I say in unison.

We look at each other and I know. Nothing can stop me from making this work. This was what I prayed for too—my heart's desire as Beau put it—what seems like forever ago.

CHAPTER THIRTY-SEVEN

Becoming Family

Beau

"This place is so cool," Billy says as she munches on popcorn.

Angel and I decided to share our movie garden with Billy. It's been two weeks, and we've been having family night every single night. Today we're making a day of it.

Billy wanted to see the new Marvel movie that comes out next month, so I'm surprising her with an advanced copy. The surrounding trees are in full bloom, so we don't have to worry about sharing this private viewing. The trees are also providing just the shading we need to view the movie against the blackened brick wall.

"It is," Angel says. "I love this place."

He gives me a look, his eyes twinkling. I still remember our first date here. I can't believe how much has changed since then.

We all get our snacks arranged and make ourselves comfortable. It's the perfect day for this. I inhale and relax to enjoy the day with my family.

"So what are we watching?" Billy asks as she shifts to settle in between us.

"You'll see," I say as I start the movie.

Billy nearly turns over her popcorn in excitement when the opening to the movie starts. I beam with pride. I'll never get tired of making this little girl happy.

"I can't wait to tell the kids at school I got to see this," she gushes.

We didn't pull Billy from her school even though we're outside its jurisdiction. Andy was more than willing to allow us to keep her enrolled in the academy on the complex. Her teachers are saying that she's excelling even more than usual, and she's a much happier kid overall.

In just two weeks, I know that's more than we could've asked for. Sure, there have been adjustments that Angel and I didn't think of, but we're working our way through them. Things like our 5:00 a.m. runs. We can't leave a nine-year-old home alone while we go running.

I went alone the first few days. Then Emma started to come by in the mornings to take Billy to school. She offered to come earlier to allow Angel to run with me since it's a part of my training. Emma is always up at the crack of dawn anyway.

Honestly, we've been making it over a lot of obstacles with the help of our family. Kyle and Andy keep Billy after school on days we both have to work. Mama plans to make Billy fat with cookies as she shows up on the weekends to spoil her.

"You guys are the best," Billy says when the movie ends. "That was awesome."

"It was pretty good," I say. "What do you guys want to do next? We're not due at Mama's until seven."

"Do you think Mas and his dads can play ball with us?" she asks hopefully.

"I think we can make that happen," I say and wink at her.

"Cool. Maybe next time they can watch a movie with us," she muses.

"Sounds good. We'll ask them next time."

Next time.

I'm still getting used to knowing there will be a next time. I fire off a text before we all start to clean up. Kyle replies, confirming that we can meet up for a game.

"Let's go home and change. We have a game," I say.

"Yes," she whoops and pumps her fist.

Now making that smile there happen will never get old.

Angel

"That was a good game," I say as we all walk into Daphne's.

We all rode over together for dinner since everyone had plans to be here tonight. I grin down at Billy who's dressed up in a pretty pink T-shirt and skirt to come over here. I'll admit we're failing in the hair department. She has so much, and after sweating it out in the game, it just turned into a puffy mass.

"Dear Lord, what have you done to my grandbaby?" Daphne says when she gets a look at Billy.

Billy giggles and brushes a lock of hair out of her face. Yeah, it's bad. The tie I had put in it popped somewhere between the game and us getting ready to come here.

"Hey, Grandma." Billy says the word grandma as if she cherishes it.

"Hey, sugar," Mama says. "Let's see if Grandma can help you at least see."

Daphne takes her by the hand, and they disappear into the house. I head straight for the cookies. We all laugh as we seem to have the same idea as we stumble over each other. Kyle snatches up two, handing one to Mas.

"So how are things going? Other than you two failing at doing hair?" Kyle asks.

"It's been great," Beau says. "We're adjusting. She's independent and helpful, so she fits right in with us. We're all simple and easy."

"Yeah, that about sums it up. We've been having fun. I love seeing that smile on her face," I say.

"And you guys, how are you doing as a couple?" Andy asks. "Parenting can be a strain on a relationship."

I look at Beau and smile. I think having Billy around has increased our bond. I know I will forever love him for the apartment and how well he nailed everything for the both of us. Our bedroom is perfect. A wall of windows just like the living room and the best part is the unique design. It's closed off, but with the frosted glass the ceiling is made of, if I ever need the place to feel open I have options.

"We're doing great," I say.

"Good, I'm glad to hear that," Kyle says. He smiles at Beau. "Only seven weeks until the fight. You guys sure do have a full plate but you look happy. That's what's up."

"Where's Aunt Emma?" Mas asks while munching on his cookie. He's reaching for another before he's done with the first.

Just as the words hit the air, my brother and Emma enter the kitchen. Emma has a huge smile on her face, and Andres looks like he's sitting on top of the world. Something is definitely up with the two.

"Where's Mama?" Emma asks.

"Trying to do something with Billy's hair. Beau broke her already," I tease.

Kyle and Andy snicker. Beau tosses a napkin at me. I shrug and laugh.

"I can probably help. I had to learn how to do Aryanna's hair on the weekends I have her," Andres offers.

Emma grabs him by the hand and drags him off. I turn back toward the cookies. A few moments later, squeals come from the back of the house.

"What's that about?" Beau grumbles looking in the direction they just disappeared in.

"Have no idea," I reply.

Soon enough the four return to the kitchen where the five of us are snagging our third cookie. We can at least see Billy's smiling face now as the front of her hair is brushed up into a top knot and the back remains wild, hanging free. It's when Emma reaches to brush the side of Billy's hair that I see the big-ass rock on her finger.

Emma has a beaming smile, and my brother is grinning like a fool. I can feel his happiness oozing from him. I break into a face-splitting smile as I rush my brother and lift him into a bear hug.

"Congratulations," I croon.

"We're getting married," Emma squeals, wiggling her hand out for the others.

"Go on tell them the rest now," Andres says with his chest poked up.

"I had no idea that he was acting all weird because he was going to propose. I decided to keep this a secret from everyone because I thought we were about to break up, but... I'm pregnant," she says.

Daphne squeals and tugs Emma into a hug. I grab my brother for another embrace and rock him back and forth. I couldn't be happier for him. His divorce was hard on him. There was a time I didn't think he'd recover.

"I'm so happy for you," I say in his ear. "So proud of you, *mi hermano.*"

"Same here, Angel. I'm so fucking proud of you. You guys made me get my shit together to propose. I had no idea about the baby," he whispers back.

"I love you, 'Dres. None of this would have happened for me without you," I reply.

"Yes it would. You're the stronger twin. You make shit happen," he says, cupping my face and squeezing. "I always knew you would do it."

I nod as my emotions take over. Stepping out of the way, I let Andy and Kyle get in for their hugs and congratulations. I move across the kitchen and look around at all of the smiling faces and realize I'm in a room full of people and love. A room I don't want to claw my way out of.

"I'm going to be a big cousin," Billy says, placing her hand on Emma's still-flat belly.

"You sure are," Em replies.

"She's not my cousin," Mason says under his breath.

I only hear it because he's so close to me. I look down at him, making a sour face as he looks at Billy. Kyle reaches to pinch him.

"We talked about this," Kyle hisses.

"Nope, I'm not trying to hear that, Uncle Kyle. I don't care what Capys and Themiste did. I'm not marrying my cousin," Mason says. "That's just gross."

I'm stunned, not knowing what just happened here. Kyle tosses his head back and blows out a breath. When he turns back to Mas, he levels him with a glare. Mas looks back at him unfazed.

"You're ten. You're not marrying anybody," Kyle says.

"The gods have chosen my path," Mason points to Billy. "She was created for me. For the love of Zeus, she's not my cousin."

He storms off out of the room, leaving me and Kyle staring after him with open mouths. I turn to Kyle, and he pulls a hand down his face as he shakes his head. I don't even know what to say.

"I miss the days when his only obsession was Greek mythology," Kyle says.

"Did he just claim my daughter as his wife in the name of Zeus?"

"That would be a yes," Kyle replies. "Your daughter. That sounds good on you."

Kyle smiles and pats me on the back, walking to go find my future son-in-law it seems. Beau walks over looking at me curiously. I'm still trying to wrap my head around what just happened.

"What did I miss?"

"I don't think you want to know." I burst into laughter.

CHAPTER THIRTY-EIGHT

Decisions

Beau

I look down at Billy tucked underneath my arm and kiss the top of her head. "It's past your bedtime, sugar," I say.

It's been a long but good weekend. Billy has school in the morning, and I have to be on site for the final inspection at the new development. We're finally wrapping things up there after having to flatten the existing buildings and rebuild.

"But my toes are still drying," she yawns and wiggles her toes on Angel's lap.

I look at a proud Angel. He painted her toes and managed to stay on the actual nails. Angel was damn sexy to watch with those dimples showing as he polished and sang to Billy in Spanish. I have the video to remember it by.

"Come on, *cariño*. I'll carry you up and tuck you in," Angel says as he stands.

"Okay." Billy yawns again.

I lift my arm, and she turns to give me a hug good night. Angel lifts her onto his hip and starts for upstairs. I grab my phone to get some notes down for my day tomorrow. As the screen lights up, an alert for an appointment with Eric pops up.

I sigh and sit back on the couch. I have a decision to make. I made the appointment because Angel begged me to. I'm still not fighting optimally. Yet I still have reservations about digging into why.

Billy's giggles float down the stairs. I have so much more to think about now than I did eight years ago. When I step in the ring this time, it's to feed my husband and daughter. I have a little girl to put through college someday.

I want to give her that first car at sixteen like I had. If I can help it, Billy will never want for anything. Then there's Angel. We've talked about him letting the job at Refuge go. He doesn't work there half as much as he used to, and he has taken on so much at the gym with me.

I think the only reason Angel hasn't left the club is because he's too proud to have me take care of everything around here. Yet I want to make it where he can do whatever he chooses. I love having him in my corner. I rub at my chest. A lot is riding on this fight.

"What are you thinking so hard about?" Angel asks as he returns.

"I'm supposed to see Eric tomorrow evening," I reply.

"It's the right thing to do, Beau." He sighs. "I don't like what's going on in the ring. I wish we would've taken longer to find you a fight. If I would've seen you hesitate back then, I wouldn't have let you do this."

"I'm not saying you're wrong," I say.

Angel runs his hand through my hair and I turn to look at him. I purse my lips, and I think over what I want to say. This has been weighing heavily on me.

"Just say it," he says. "No shutting down, remember."

"That night feels like it will forever haunt me. I have prided myself on making right decisions. I knew it was the wrong one to get in that ring," I say. "There was a time where I didn't feel I deserve absolution from what I did. You know. I killed him. It was on me. The blood was on my hands."

"Beau, it wasn't your fault—"

"I know. I know that now. At least I've been trying to tell myself that. I have you and Billy and I want to change how that night has haunted my life. I want to be free from that darkness. I'm just afraid to go digging in the shit and stirring the pot," I finally admit out loud.

"Take it from someone that knows. Sometimes you have to shovel the shit, Papi. It's the only way to get to the other side."

I reach to pull the tie from his hair and run my fingers through his locks. The front spills forward, covering one side of his face. Tucking the wayward locks behind his ear, I lean in and kiss his lips.

We don't deepen the kiss, but we keep the connection. I turn and he nuzzles the side of my face with his nose. This is all the comfort I need in the world. If I could have this feeling in the ring every time I stepped in, I'd be a champion.

"I'll sleep on it," I say.

"I'll take that. But, Beau?"

"Yeah, darlin'."

"If you don't start looking like you're all in by the week of the fight, you're not getting in that ring. I can promise you that. I don't give a fuck what anyone says. You step in with your whole heart or not at all," he says.

"I hear you, baby. I hear you."

Angel

I can't sleep. I've been thinking about Beau's words from earlier. I wish I could reach his tortured soul and heal it. I want nothing more than to see him and Billy happy.

Billy.

I stand in the doorway of her room, leaning against the jamb as I watch her sleep. She looks so peaceful. She's safe and happy. Not at all the same little girl I met at the gym.

I see the way she looks at us. We're her entire world. Everything I do I do for these two. Each day I wake with them on my mind. Fighting to live, to want to be here, to overcome my daily challenges, I do it because I love them.

What I'll do tonight is no different. My phone vibrates, letting me know my ride is here. I push off the door, flip my hoodie over my head, and jog down the stairs. After shoving my feet into my sneakers, I slip out the front door. When I get to the garage, I slip into the back of the car waiting for me.

"Thanks for doing this, Javi," I say to the man waiting in the back of the car for me.

"Not a problem, but you won't be leaving your family tonight," he replies.

"What do you mean?"

"We won't need to visit our friend this evening. It has been handled."

I turn in my seat to really look at him. I want to see if he's telling me the truth or changing his mind about helping me with this. When I told Beau I'd take care of this, I meant it.

"Care to explain?"

"There's something I need you to know. It's my job to protect my brothers, *sí*. Something they don't ask me to do. *No significa nada*. It's what I do." He waves a hand nonchalantly.

"Okay, I think I've picked that up about you," I say.

"There are things we didn't tell Beau about what happened that night. The six of us decided he didn't need to know. He was already destroyed. I'm telling you this now because you have become a part of our brotherhood.

"The autopsy revealed that Roman had *cocaína* in his system. Beau isn't with that shit. He hates the garbage. As you probably know by now, he won't even take a simple aspirin. It would've ripped him apart to know Roman got mixed up in the trash," he says.

I give a low whistle. Leaning forward, Javi reaches into the pocket of the back of the driver's seat and pulls out a manila envelope, handing it over to me.

"Steve is a *sucio diablo*. I've always had my suspicions about that fight. I believe he had something to do with Roman getting into drugs. I couldn't prove it then, but I have always blamed him for Roman's death.

"Steve has always been shady. I just needed to wait for the *cabrón* to slip up. He's desperate now, and he's making all the right mistakes," Javi croons.

I flip through the pictures I pull from the envelope. My brows rise at the images before me. Steve handing a well-known fighter as suspicious-looking baggy. The same fighter that was just banned for substance abuse. More pictures of him in questionable situations that make my stomach turn. The last photo is of him in a leopard print robe being led out in cuffs.

"Looks like Stevey boy got into promoting some other things in the last few years," I say.

"*Sí*, you would be right. It makes it so much sweeter to shove him into the hands of justice. I have friends in high places. I'm sure you've noticed at Refuge. I've sent them an air-tight case. He won't be trying to distract Beau with his bullshit anytime soon," Javi says with a bright smile.

"Thanks."

"*De nada.*" Javi waves me off. "I told Beau I would take care of this. However, I did want to see you beat the shit out of Steve first. Unfortunately I got the call this evening just after they picked him up."

I laugh and shake my head. A ton of pressure has been lifted from my shoulders. I wanted to have a meet with Steve and let him know he was barking up the wrong tree coming for my husband. I should've known the all-seeing Javier was on top of this.

"I wanted to talk to you," I say.

"You will be leaving my employment," he replies, reaching into his suit jacket. "I've seen this coming. It is good. Here is a parting gift. I've enjoyed having you as an employee. My members will miss seeing your face."

"I can't take that," I say, pushing his hand back toward him.

"*Si, mi amigo*, you will. It is a gift and insurance. I always give parting gifts. It tends to serve as a reminder," he says.

"You're my family. No reminder needed."

"Which is why you will take it. You're family. I take care of my family. Buy the little *princesa* something. I will not take no for an answer," he says.

"Thanks, Javi. For everything," I reply.

"*De nada.* Just make sure Beau never finds out what we've kept from him. We don't keep many secrets, but that one was a necessity," he says.

"You should rethink that one. It may change how he feels about that night, but he won't hear it from me. It's not my story to tell. Not my facts to prove," I say.

Javi regards me thoughtfully. I get the feeling he's looking at something deeper, trying to grasp a bigger picture. He nods and pats my knee. "This is why he fell for you. You're wise, Angel. Maybe it is time we have a talk with him."

CHAPTER THIRTY-NINE

Family Terrors

Angel

I sit with my back to the headboard, watching Beau in his sleep. We had our first major fight, and it was a huge one. We're less than two months out from this fight, and I can literally see him thinking while in the ring.

This has to stop. If he's not going to face this by talking to Eric, he needs to do something. For two weeks now, I was under the impression that he actually went to his appointment and has continued to go. I only found out that he hasn't because I tried to schedule our appointments around the same time.

"I'm sorry, Mr. Hernández-Dalton, your husband doesn't have an appointment for this week," the receptionist said.

"Okay, well, can you make two appointments around his usual time? My schedule is more flexible," I said.

"Um... I think I should put you on the phone with Dr. Levine," she replied.

I was so pissed by the time I got off the phone with Eric, but I was going to let it slide. However, when it was time to spar, and Beau got in that ring looking like an amateur, I lost my shit.

I release a sigh and brush a lock of hair from his face. I know I need to be more understanding. Everyone deals differently. I get that. I just want him to actually deal.

Beau's face tightens in his sleep. He starts to shift restlessly. I frown, knowing he's having one of his nightmares. I don't want to wake him too abruptly, so I give his shoulder a gentle shake.

"Beau," I call softly. "Beau."

He tosses and pulls away, murmuring something in his sleep. I reach for him again, but he bolts out of his sleep at the same time a piercing scream fills the air.

Beau

"You want to forget me," Roman says.

I stumble back. I look between the body lying in the ring and the man standing in front of me. Shaking my head to clear it, I look to see the canvas beneath my feet is soaked in blood.

"I don't want to forget you. I want to forget the pain," I reply.

"Is that not the same, amor? *You choose to forget me," he says sadly.*

I push a hand through my hair in frustration. It's not that same. I will never forget the love I had for Roman.

"I just need to let this—" I point around the ring. "—go. It has to end. I can't keep coming back here."

"Then go, don't come back," he says like a perpetual child.

It reminds me of how childish he could get. It wasn't one of my favorite traits of his. Many of our arguments came from his childish behavior.

"It's not right," I seethe. "It's not right that I feel guilty for this all my life. Even now, you're trying to make me feel guilty."

He turns his hazel eyes on me. Sorrow, denial, and torture—all feelings I've carried over the years.

In the next breath, my father is standing before me. My knees buckle, and I fall to the canvas, but it's no longer blood-stained. Instead, the ring is filled with water.

"You carry the weight of the world, son. You have to decide when to let all of that go. You can't keep bringing all of that in this here ring. What did I used to tell you?" he says.

"I don't know," I whisper.

"Yes, you do, son. You're responsible for you when you step in here. What the other fighter does isn't your business. You fight your fight. You be your best."

"I don't know what my best is."

"Bullshit, Beau James. You're hiding your best."

"Daddy—"

I look up and he's gone. Roman is lying before me again, and the crowd's laughing and pointing. I have blood on my hands. It's the same old dream again.

"No!"

I pop up from my sleep. I'm disoriented. Somewhere in the distance, I can hear crying and screaming. It takes me a few seconds to realize it's Billy. I go to rush to her room, but something is off.

I turn on the lights to find Angel standing with that look on his face. "Bachman, cover me," he calls out.

"Fuck, fuck, fuck, fuck," I grind out as I continue to hear Billy's cries.

I have to think quickly. Angel shifts and knocks over the bedside lamp. Shit, I can't leave him here alone, barefoot stumbling in broken glass.

I pick up my phone, trying to think of who to dial. I need someone to come for Billy and make sure she's okay. Emma and Mama are too far away. Andy! Andy has a way with kids. I place the call.

Kyle has a key to my place just as I have one to his. He'll be able to get in. I'm gutted that I can't just go up the hall to my little girl, but Angel could seriously injure himself.

"Angel," I call while I wait for Andy to pick up on the other end. "Angel, baby."

"Hello," Andy's sleepy voice carries to me.

"And', I need you. Billy's having a nightmare or something, but I can't go to her because Angel's having an episode. There's glass everywhere. I think we triggered him," I ramble into the line as I panic.

"I'm on the way. We'll be there in five," he says.

I look at the clock. There shouldn't be any traffic. They're not that far away.

I turn my focus back to Angel as my heart squeezes from the sound of Billy's cries. If I can get Angel out of the glass, I can get to her. Shit.

"Angel, come on, baby. I need you to come back to me. You're here with me in our home," I coax.

"Get down, get down," he bellows.

"No!" I yell, grabbing the spread from the bed and tossing it to the floor over the broken glass.

He drops and rolls seconds after the fabric is in place to shield him. My heart is in my throat. Blood begins to trickle from his shoulder, but it's not a lot.

I continue to try to pull him back into the present. When I hear the front door alarm sound through the apartment, relief washes over me. Silence falls from the hallway outside our bedroom. I think it's enough to allow me to call Angel back.

"Angel, come on. Focus." He turns to me and stares for a few moments.

Suddenly, I see the look of clarity I've been seeking. His eyes move around the bedroom and his shoulders sag. I move to wrap him in my arms and slide to the floor with him.

Kyle appears in the bedroom doorway, but I give him a nod to let him know I've got this one. He returns the nod and exits the way he came. As I focus back on Angel, my heart starts to slow and sweat drips down my back.

"Holy shit," I murmur to myself.

This isn't something I saw coming. I thought to soundproof the rooms in the design, but I didn't want to deaden all sound with a kid in the home. I'm second-guessing that decision.

"What did I do?" Angel says brokenly.

"Nothing, darlin'. Nothing but show me I need to get my head right." I sigh.

I'll be going to see Eric. This can never happen again. It's time I face my nightmares.

CHAPTER FORTY

Getting Help

Beau

"I thought if I ignored it all, it would go away," I say into my lap. "My life is busy. That usually pushes the nightmares back."

"Suppressing the dreams under the stress of exhaustion of the body and brain doesn't send them away for good nor does it deal with them. You're just tricking the mind and body to focus on other things for a bit," Eric says as he sits in his armchair.

"So what do I do?"

"You were on the right track a few years ago. Do you remember any of the tools we were using to get you there?"

"Yeah, some mediation and a lot of writing about my feelings," I say with a frown.

"Do you still have your journals?"

"Yeah, I have them."

"Beau, what happened?"

I shift in my seat and look up at Eric sitting across from me. What frustrates me about Eric is that he never gives you the answers. He makes you work it out for yourself. That's when you're in his office. I've been around him in casual settings and know for a fact he's bound to tell you what he thinks without concern for a filter. I wouldn't mind him getting to the point now.

"What do you mean?"

"You were making progress, then you started making up excuses not to come to see me. I never pressure clients to come in, especially not those close to Darwin. But I was disappointed you chose to stop. You were right at the cusp of a breakthrough," he replies. "What happened?"

I blow out a breath and rub my temples. I could say it was life. I got busy with the complex and things started to change as Kyle gained custody of Mason and later started dating Andy. Those are all excuses.

"The truth, I didn't feel I deserved it," I confess.

"What didn't you deserve?"

"My freedom. Redemption. It wasn't mine to have."

Eric places his pen and notebook down. He leans forward and places his forearms on his knees. I brace myself for what's to come out of his mouth next.

"Have you watched that fight? I remember asking you to try," he says.

"No." I shake my head. "I can't."

"I want you to try. I need you to see what happened that night. It's important you put that fight into perspective. If you

can see what we saw, I think you'd have a different take on...
everything."

I tear my gaze away from his. Everyone has told me that I
wasn't responsible, but I was there. I threw the punch. I don't
know what watching the fight will do to change that. It will only
bring more pain to see what I've done.

"I don't know if I can do that, Eric," I drawl.

"So let's unpack this a bit differently, while keeping that
option on the table for your consideration. You've stepped back
into the ring. Does that mean you're now seeking out your
redemption?"

My brows furrow. Is that what I'm looking for? I don't
know. "I want to provide for my family," I say.

"Come on, Beau. You don't have to box another day in your
life to provide for those two. Telling yourself that is just piling
shit on top of the heaping pile of shit you've been feeding
yourself," he says.

I lean back. I guess the kid gloves have officially come off.
Leave it to Eric to know how to call me on my shit.

"Answer me this, Beau. Why are you fighting again?"

"I don't know," I say.

"Beau, please. Of all of you guys, you're the most forward
and direct about your feelings and getting things done. It was
one of the first things Darwin told me about you, and he was
spot on. You don't do anything without knowing why. You may
avoid the why, but it's always there.

"You're not showing up in the ring. Why? What's stopping
you? Is it fear? If it is... what are you afraid of? You need to step
into the ring in your head before you step into the ring for this
fight in five weeks," he says.

"What if I step in that ring and can't fight my way through the shit in there?" I bite out in frustration.

"Ah, now we're getting somewhere. Whether you like it or not, you're already in the midst of the fight. Your subconscious is at war, calling you out in your dreams and now in the ring.

"It's for you to decide who will win this battle. I want you to think about what's most important to you. Your why. What's making you box again? I believe that answer will carry you to your restoration."

"My why," I repeat.

"Yes, your why. And, Beau?"

I purse my lips and look him in the eyes. So many things are going on in my head. I don't know which to put first.

"Yeah."

"When you find your absolution, know this… you deserve it."

Angel

"How are you feeling?" Eric asks, tilting his head at me.

No matter how many times I come to this office, it always takes me a moment to settle in. Eric may sit casually in that leather armchair, but his mind is always at attention. He's assessing every word, every move. It's unnerving to have someone look into your life, but this is what I'm here for.

"Other than frustrated and embarrassed? My shoulder has been a little sore from the glass I apparently dove into," I say and frown.

Eric nods. "I have these for you. They're earbuds. You told me once Beau is a light sleeper. I believe it will be safe for you to block out sound without compromising Billy's safety. Your husband will be able to hear her just fine," he says, sitting forward to give the buds to me.

"But Beau had a nightmare as well. It wasn't just Billy's screaming." I huff.

"Angel, have you ever been triggered by Beau's nightmares before?"

"No."

He gives me a pointed look. I just want to be sure. I was gutted when I realized Kyle and Andy had to rush over to take care of Billy while Beau took care of me.

"I've mentioned to Beau that I'd like to continue seeing Billy regularly. If the three of you are open to it, we can do a family session as well. How are you doing with the alternative methods your father has been offering you?"

"They help. I thought it was some BS. Stones and oils and shit, but I've been less anxious and more focused," I reply.

"I'll let you in on a secret. I use a lot of those methods in my personal life. I actually believe in a holistic approach to any type of healing. A blend of it all. It's all a part of the process to get the best results," he says.

"I have a question," I say, leaning forward.

He folds his arms across his chest and cups his chin with one hand. I take it as him offering his attention. I lick my suddenly dry lips.

"Do you think we'll make it?" The words burst out.

Eric drops his hand and gives me a smile. It seems like hours float by before he responds.

"Angel, I'm watching the three of you make it. These are bumps in the road that you're making into mountains. I'm not in any way downplaying what are real mental health concerns for you, Billy, or Beau.

"What I am saying is that I'm in awe of the three of you. Each of you are determined to live a full life and put your demons behind you. You've come such a long way. Will there be a time when you're never triggered or when your anxiety ceases to exist? I can't promise you that, but I do believe you'll make it. Your entire family will," he says softly.

I can live with that.

CHAPTER FORTY-ONE

Our Brand

Beau

Angel is up to something. Mama has come by to sit with Billy for the day, and Angel has been bouncing around with tons of nervous energy. I narrow my eyes at him as he stops in front of me, dressed in black jeans with the thighs shredded, a white T-shirt, and tan construction boots.

His hair is loose around his shoulders, and his dimples are showing as he tries but fails at hiding his smile. I'm distracted for a moment as I devour his sexy look. I arch a brow.

"What exactly are you up to? Where are we going?"

"I've been wanting to do something. I thought maybe we could do it together," Angel croons.

"What exactly is that?"

"You have to come with me to find out," he says.

"We're not getting a dog," I whisper.

Angel rolls his eyes at me. Billy has asked for a dog twice in the last month. We're not home enough to get one. Although Eric thinks it's a good idea.

"No, we're not going to get a dog. Besides, she asked for a cat this morning." He snorts.

"Please, no. She can have the dog." I groan.

"Kid is smarter than we give her credit for. I think that was the plan all along."

"I bet."

We start out of the apartment and down to the garage. When we get into the elevator, Angel crowds my space, placing his hands on either side of my head. Leaning in, he flicks his tongue over my bottom lip.

"Have I told you how much I love you?" he breathes.

"Not much lately. You've been cursing my ass out in the ring." I snort.

"I know I've been hard on you," he says, pecking my lips. "Four more weeks, and we'll have this one behind us."

"Then on to the next one." I hear the lack of conviction in my own voice.

"If that's what you want. Yes," he says, searching my face. "Is it?"

The elevator dings, saving me from answering that question. Angel lets it go, pushing off the wall and threading his fingers through mine as we walk to the car. When we get to the car, he holds the passenger side door open for me.

"You're driving?"

"Yup, cowboy. Get in."

My curiosity soars as I climb in. I watch him round the car with that confidence that belongs to Angel and Angel alone. My heart fills at the sight of his ease and good mood. Seeing Angel like this is becoming a regular occurrence. One I can get used to.

He climbs in behind the wheel and starts the car. He pulls my shades from the console and puts them on. They look good on him. I can't keep myself from grasping the back of his neck and pulling him to me.

I place a demanding kiss on his lips before releasing him and settling in my seat. He shoots a blinding smile at me and shifts the car into gear. That confidence drips off him in waves.

"Hope this doesn't take too long," I mutter and reach to adjust myself.

Angel laughs and takes off. I turn on the radio, and we fall into a light banter. It's an easy forty-five-minute drive. Soon Angel's pulling into a parking spot in front of some shops in Brooklyn.

"I wanted to bring you to check this spot out first. I told you a while back that Brooklyn has some hidden gems of its own. You haven't lived until you've had curry oxtail and roti," he says.

"What makes you think I've never had roti and oxtails?"

Angel pulls back and places his hand on his chest. "Well, excuse me, Beau. My bad. Let me take that back. You haven't lived until you had it from this spot," he says.

"Let's go, then," I say as I grin at him.

We get out of the car and head inside. The place is packed and smells great. My mouth starts to water as I look at all of the choices.

"Where'd you first get your hands on roti?" Angel says.

My cheeks heat in a blush. I was hoping he didn't ask that. It was a long time ago.

"I had a crush on this guy, freshman year in college. He was West Indian and Latino. His family owned a restaurant. We hung out a few times," I reply.

"What happened? You two didn't date?"

"I begged Kyle to sing to him for me. Found out Sebastian was hanging with me because he had a crush on Kyle," I say and shrug.

"Oh, damn. That sucks." He winces.

"Not really. We got free food whenever we went to the restaurant."

"Did Kyle date him?"

"No." I purse my lips. "Kyle wasn't out. So poor Sebastian would just drool over him."

Angel nods, placing a hand on my back as our turn comes up at the counter. We order, and although my hand itches to reach for my wallet, I bite the inside of my mouth and let him pay. There's nowhere to sit inside the little storefront, so we head back to the car.

I start with one of the beef patties that look so good. It's even better than it looks. I hum and bob my head as I chew. "This is delicious," I say around another bite.

"Told you this place was the truth. You can always tell when the food is going to be popping by the flavors in the patties. Trust. You're going to go crazy over that roti."

He's right. As soon as I dig in, I'm in heaven. We sit and eat, having an animated conversation about our youth.

"We really are city boy verse country boy." Angel laughs.

"We're not that different at all," I reply, reaching to squeeze his thigh.

"I have someplace I want to take you next," he says, looking a bit nervous. "I thought about bringing Billy, but... let's see how this works out."

"I'm with you."

"Yeah, I know." He grins.

Angel

I don't know why this has become so important to me, but I want to do this. I want to show Beau where I grew up. I pull up in front of the little Brooklyn home I shared with my family for most of my life. I don't remember the days Mommy and Papi talk about before we moved here. This has always been home to me.

"Is this your parents' house?" Beau asks.

"Yeah."

"Why didn't we wait to eat your mother's cooking? Man, I've been waiting for her to stop by and cook." He pouts.

"B, if you don't get your ass out of this car—" I laugh and shake my head. "She'll be sure to send us home with plenty of food. Mark my words."

We get out of the car and walk to the front gate. My father has the door open before we get up the three steps. He looks around us, then mumbles to himself.

"What? We're not good enough company?" I tease.

"No, I like Billy better," he tosses back but pulls me into a bear hug. "Good to have you home, *m'ijo*."

"Good to be here, Papi."

"Ah, Beau, we finally got you to Brooklyn. *Bienvenido a mi casa*," Papi says to Beau.

"*Gracias*," Beau replies.

Papi beams at Beau and pats him on the shoulder. We all enter the house. I take a deep breath once inside. Anxiety tries to claw at me, but I rub the stone inside my jean pocket as I count backward. When we enter the living room, the smell of my mom's cooking and scent of what I know as the Hernández home hits me, and I start to fully relax.

"Angel," Mommy sings as she comes out to join us.

"Hey, Mommy."

"Where's Billy?"

"Ay, is Billy all anyone cares about these days?" I groan playfully.

"You can't blame me for wanting to spend time with my granddaughter. How is she?" she says.

"She's doing good. Daphne is watching her for the day. I wanted to see if I could do this… you know. Hang out here before we bring her over."

"Ah, *sí*. I understand. Are you boys hungry?"

"No, we ate before we came over," I reply.

"I'll make you something to take home for you two and Billy. No worries," she says rushing off to the kitchen.

I turn to Beau and give him a look to say, *I told you so*. He looks back at me, grinning and patting his belly. I shake my head at him and take a seat on the couch. I look around the place and marvel at how nothing has changed over the years.

Beau takes a seat next to me as Papi sits in his recliner. A baseball game is playing on the television. Not unusual in the Hernández home on a Saturday afternoon.

"These boys today don't play like they used to," Papi says, frowning at the TV.

"You say that about everything," I say, humor lacing my words.

"It's the truth. In my day, you valued your sport. You put work into it. Now—" He waves his hand. "There's no dedication."

"I can see that," Beau says. "Things weren't as easy back then. A lot of entitlement colors multiple professions these days. I try to teach my fighters better."

"You're old-school. Your father raised you the old way. I can tell. It makes a difference, you know. A pitcher, boxer, driver, it doesn't matter. Your values show in your performance. I like a boxer with integrity. It makes for a better fight," Papi says.

"I hear you," Beau adds, placing his arm behind me on the back of couch.

"Four weeks. How are you feeling about this fight?" Papi asks.

"I honestly don't know." The words pour out of Beau's mouth, seeming to surprise even him. "I mean, physically I'm ready. I don't think I'll have a problem going twelve rounds. Beyond that, I'm still working some things out for myself."

"I will tell you like I've been told and like I've told every fighter I've worked with. A man decides a fight's outcome in his heart before he steps in the ring. Your heart will guide you to the end of the fight. We will all be here to see what that outcome will be," Papi says.

The struggle happening within is written all over Beau's face. I didn't bring him here to stress out about the fight. This was supposed to be a day to chill and relax.

"Come on, I'll show you my old room," I say to Beau. "We'll be back."

Papi waves us off and turns back to his game. Beau and I go upstairs. I smile at the memories lining the walls. Photo, awards, and degrees are all displayed proudly. Beau stops midway up to the landing.

"You have a master's in social science?"

"Yeah, that would be me," I say. "World of good it has done me."

"What else don't I know about you?"

"Come on." I wave him forward. "Let's see what you can learn about me in my room."

I have my fluorite stone in my hand as we step into my old room. I think I'm more anxious about having him in here than I am about being in the tightly spaced house. Although my room seems so much smaller with the two of us in here. We can fit this room into our bedroom at least four times.

"Check you out. You were a lady's man in high school," he teases as he looks at old pictures tacked to my wall.

"How do you know that's me and not Andres?"

There are a number of pictures with me and my twin, but there are some that are of one or the other. Most people have to ask which of us is in which. The picture in question is one I've been asked about a million times. Most people assume it's Andres.

He shrugs. "I know you. It's… I don't know how to describe it. You just have this way about you."

He turns and looks me over from head to toe. The desire in the appraisal is palpable. I move closer and wrap my arms around his waist. "You're the first boy I've ever had in my room," I say and bite my lip.

"Your father still has a great right hook. You're not getting my ass kicked and my mama called," he says with mirth dancing in his eyes.

"Whatever." I laugh. "I have a few photo albums. Come here."

I lead him to sit on the bed, and we get lost in the albums. We're laughing about a few old photos of Andres and me, when music starts to blare up the stairs. Excitement hits and memories flood my brain. Good memories.

"Come on, you have to see this," I say, closing the album and tucking it away.

I jog down the stairs as Marc Anthony's version of "Mi Gente" plays. Just as I knew I would, I find Papi dancing Mommy around the small living room. They still have it. I've loved watching this since I was a little boy.

Papi twirls Mommy and it's like watching them fifteen years ago. They haven't aged in my eyes. Mommy bursts with laughter and joy as she stops spinning. Of course my father shows off, dipping my moms and kissing her throat.

The song changes and my parents really show off as they start to bachata to Prince Royce singing "La Carretera." It's a beautiful song of a lost love and seeking that lover once more. My parents do the melody justice as they move in a sensual dance like only they can.

"Come on, *m'ijo*. Teach Beau how it's done," Papi croons.

I laugh, but I reach for Beau's hand and pull him to me. Beau's cheeks turn pink as he starts to stumble through the first few steps. He's adorable.

"Let me lead," I say as I place a hand on his hip and guide him.

"Ay, no, no," Papi says, coming to stand behind Beau. "Move with the music, *hijo mio*."

In this moment my heart swells. My father just called my husband his son, and he's legit showing Beau how to bachata with me, moving his hips to the alluring rhythm of the music and everything. I turn to my moms, and she has a shaky hand covering her mouth as tears well in her eyes.

"Now you have it. *Sí, sí*, you're a Hernández yet," Papi says, cupping Beau's face and kissing his check. "*Síguele, síguele.*"

"Good job, Beau," Mommy says. "Very good."

"Not bad at all, cowboy," I tease.

"You're not bad yourself," he says, wiping at the tears that have slipped free. He leans into my ear. "He has always been proud of you. No matter what. Have no regrets, your choices brought you to me."

I purse my lips and nod. Beau kisses me, and I spin him, not able to say all the things I'm feeling. We dance in the small living room, with my parents, and for once, I'm present in my childhood home. Nothing else can tear me away.

Beau

"Ready to get into some real trouble?" Angel asks, placing the car in park.

I lean in to kiss his nose. "As long as it's with you, I'm ready."

Angel gives me that breathtaking smile that I've had the pleasure of seeing all day, and gets out of the car. When he leads us into our next destination, I'm a little caught off guard. I wasn't expecting the next stop to be a tattoo parlor. I turn to Angel with a mix of amusement and curiosity.

Angel's smile turns mischievous. Before I can question him, a guy comes from the back, heading for us. The two clasp hands and pull each other in for a shoulder tap.

"What's good, Angel? I was hyped to get your text. Good to see you, bro," the guy says.

"Nothing much. Good to see you too. Beau, this is Dexter. He did most of my work," Angel says.

"What's up? Nice to meet you," Dexter says, giving me a knowing grin and clasping my hand to pull me in for the same shoulder bump he gave Angel.

"Nice to me you too," I reply.

"I have that artwork if you're ready," he says to Angel.

"Let's go."

Angel locks our fingers together, and we follow Dexter to the back. Once in the private room, Angel pulls his shirt off. My gaze follows the fluid ripple of his muscle. I'm surprised when Angel sits in the chair with his back to Dexter. I'd assumed he was getting something on his chest since his back is covered.

"You can have a seat right here, bro." Dexter points to the seat placed next to where Angel is.

I sit, searching Angel's grinning face. Dexter moves to get to work. Angel winks at me but doesn't give away what he's up to. I cock a brow at him, and he shrugs.

"I'm going to need you to loosen your jeans and push them down a bit," Dexter says.

Now I'm really curious. Angel releases his belt and pushes his pants down his hips a bit. Dexter bobs his head to himself as he places the sheet of paper with the design on Angel's lower back.

"All right, you want to take a look at the position and design before I get started?" Dexter says.

Angel gets up and turns his back to the mirror, looking over his shoulder. Dexter holds up a second mirror to help Angel see it better. When I see what the design is, I can't stop smiling.

"You're getting my name tatted on your back?"

"Pretty much," he croons. "You've been my strength. You always have my back, my support when I need it most."

I just sit and stare. Today has been a day full of simple things that have meant so much. It encompasses the simplicity of who we are. But this… in all its simplicity has driven home our love in a new way.

"Can you put his name in that exact same style?" I ask Dexter.

"Sure can. Same spot?"

"No, mine belongs over my heart."

CHAPTER FORTY-TWO

Completion

Beau

"You guys ready for this?" Emma says, holding her hands over her little baby bump as she walks over to me and Angel.

My sister is glowing. Pregnancy looks good on her. Across the open apartment a happy Andres is tickling both Billy and Aryanna. Our home is full of family, making the vast open space seem warm and cozy. Even with the view open to the city skyline, the setting has become intimate and homey with all of our loved ones.

I couldn't be more ready for today. It seems like it has taken forever to get here. Yet we made it.

"Are you kidding? We've been waiting for long enough," Angel says, speaking my exact thoughts. He moves to throw an arm around Emma's shoulders. She moves her hand to allow him to rub her bump, bringing a smile to my face.

"I know, but you guys have been a family since the day she moved in," Emma says.

Her words hit home. We have. No court, no judge, no documents can change what we've known in our hearts. We've been a family from a lot longer than the day Billy moved in.

"What about you? Are you getting ready for this little one to arrive?" Angel asks, releasing her.

"Ugh, I'm just happy the morning sickness stopped. Like, it came out of nowhere. As soon as I told everyone, it was like *bam.*"

We laugh at her as she rolls her eyes and shakes her head. Morning sickness or not, we both know that hasn't slowed my sister down. She has been planning her wedding full steam ahead.

"You just let me know if there's anything we can do for you," I say, tucking her under my arm and kissing her forehead.

"Oh, you guys are totally babysitting. No worries. I'm making a schedule for rotation," she says.

"Darlin', I'm there. Just call."

Mama walks over with a glass of ice-cold water for Emma. I don't think my mama could be happier with the new additions to her life. I do believe Billy's cheeks have gotten chubbier because of Mama.

"She's having such a great time," Mama says as she beams.

Billy is now talking animatedly to Kyle and Andy across the room. She's probably talking them into another game. I think we've been playing once a week now.

"She's going to be so excited when you guys tell her," Emma says.

"You boys make me so proud," Mama says. "I think we should go ahead and cut the cake. How about you?"

"I'm ready," I say and look at Angel. "You ready, baby?"

"Let's make this official," he says.

Mama rushes off to get the cake she baked for Billy. She insisted we let her make it and not buy one like we wanted. When Angel and I couldn't decide if we wanted to get a princess cake or one shaped like a basketball, we relented and let Mama take care of it.

"Showtime," Angel says and goes to get our gift to Billy.

Before he can get too far, Billy runs over to him and wraps her arms around his waist. Whatever Angel says to her makes her laugh that beautiful laugh. I take out my phone and capture the moment.

"You're going to run out of space soon," Emma teases. "I love the photos you text me. I can see how much you love her. Daddy would be so proud of you."

This time as my sister says those words, they don't have a bitter taste. I feel them and take them to heart. I think my daddy would've been proud of my family. Although it aches that he'll never meet Angel or Billy, I can honestly say I'm doing right by my daddy.

"I think you're right," I say and cover her bump with my hand. "He'd be proud of you too."

"Yeah, I think so," she says as she tears up.

"Come on, everybody, let's sing Billy happy birthday," Mama says as she comes out with the candles already lit. "Get over here and have a seat, sugar."

Billy releases Angel and runs over to take a seat. As she runs over with her ponytails bouncing, I swear I can see the years play forward: her sweet sixteen, her prom, graduation, her wedding day, the day she becomes a mom—I want to be there for them all. I send up a prayer that I am.

Angel

"Happy birthday, dear Billy. Happy birthday to you," we all sing as we surround a smiling Billy.

She blows out her candles and everyone cheers. Beau and I move to her side, and I hand her the envelope we put together for her. I stand with bated breath as she opens it, Beau clutching my hand tightly in his.

"Dear Billy," she reads and looks up to grin at us. "We couldn't be happier to announce that you are officially Bienvendia Desiree Hernández-Dalton. Our Billy. Happy tenth birthday, baby girl. Welcome home for good. Love, Angel and Beau."

Bienvenda.

Billy's given name means welcome. It's fitting for who she is and what she means in our life. With a shaky hand, she flips the page to the officially signed documents. My heart melts when her nail polish catches my eye. I painted her nails for her this morning. I also did her hair. I puff my chest out. I'm learning, and I did a damn good job.

Billy lifts her head to look at the two of us. Tears roll down her cheeks. She stands in the chair she's been sitting in and wraps her arms around our necks.

"This is the best birthday present ever," she chokes out.

"You're the greatest thing that's ever happened to us," I say.

I give her a gentle squeeze and bite back my laugh as Emma sobs ridiculously loud. Yeah, those hormones are getting to her.

Mas has a mix of emotions on his face. I look away from him so my laughter doesn't slip free.

I take in everyone, and I'm breathless. This is our huge corky family. I have a little girl and a husband I love to life and beyond.

This… is my normal. I'm living again.

Beau

"This was the best day ever," I hear Billy say in the living room as she sits with Angel.

I'm trying to tend to a few contracts I need to get out first thing in the morning, along with documents I want to get in order now that Billy's adoption is final. I learned from my father that you take care of business and make sure those you love are always taken care of. Even after you're gone.

With the planning of the birthday party, I got a little behind on a few things. I'm trying to finish up to join them, but I pause at the change in conversation. I'm not expecting the words that come out of Billy's mouth.

"The fight is coming. Do you think he'll show up?" she says to Angel.

"I don't know, kid. He's been looking good lately," he says.

"But not as good as you guys want him too," she replies. "He's holding back on the right-handed punches. Where all his power is."

"You're a smart kid, you know that?" Angel says. "Yeah, he's still holding back."

"Is that going to be a bad thing? Do you and abuelo still think you should call the fight?"

I blow out a breath and place my pen down. Paperwork forgotten, I go to sit with them. Angel reaches to run a hand through my hair.

"They won't have to call the fight off. I'm going to be fine," I say.

"You don't have to do this if you don't want," Billy says.

I laugh. "No one is forcing me to fight. It's something I need to do for me. It'll be fine."

She eyes me warily, her little face twisting as she thinks. Moving to wrap her arms around my neck, she holds me tight.

"*Estás listo*," she whispers.

CHAPTER FORTY-THREE

Heavy Minds

Beau

"You having a bad night?" I say into my pillow as Angel goes to climb out of the bed.

"Yeah, sorry," he replies, leaning to kiss my shoulder before he gets up.

I turn onto my back. His naked body comes into view. I smile when my gaze falls on the tattoo of my name at the base of his spine. He bends to step into a pair of shorts, and I groan.

"Dude, carry your horny ass back to sleep." He laughs.

I grunt and squeeze my cock. It's not like we didn't fall asleep after making love already. I've just had more adrenaline pumping through me the last few days as we draw near the fight. It feels like my entire fate will be determined in two weeks.

Although, as I watch my husband stretch his arms over his head, I can't just blame wanting him on my building anxiety about this fight. How can I not appreciate this sexy-ass man? Every inch of him is perfect in my eyes.

He walks out onto the balcony and drops down into push-ups. I sigh. It's one of those nights. His dreams are riding him. He doesn't have the nightmares often, but when he does, they take a toll.

It's interesting. We've come a long way, but that doesn't mean that all of our problems have just magically gone away. There are nights I still wake in a cold sweat. Before Angel can comfort me, Billy's cries pierce the air. We haven't had a mess like that one night. The earbuds Eric gave Angel help.

Still, even that was our mess, and I wouldn't trade either of them for the world. We're learning to cope as a family. Billy is happy, and that's our main concern. I smile as I stare at the ceiling, trying to go back to sleep. Only it doesn't come as easily tonight.

I stand and pull on my own shorts. I walk toward the balcony and lean in the doorjamb. Angel is now leaning on his forearms against the railing, his hair blowing loosely in the wind. I take a few moments to relish watching him.

After pushing off the doorjamb, I saunter over to stand behind him and cage him in with my arms, my hands on the rails. He stiffens for a moment but relaxes when I kiss between his shoulder blades. I shift to rest my chin on his shoulder.

"I hate when I wake you. You have training in the morning and press stops after." He sighs.

"I'll be fine. I've run off of less sleep."

"So much has changed, and yet so much is still the same."

"I was thinking that not too long ago. We take the good with the bad, though. We're lucky to have a great support system," I say.

"We sure are. Not everyone can say that."

"What's on your mind?"

"I got a call from an old buddy today. His wife can't take it. She's leaving him," he says, his voice filled with so much pain.

Angel is so compassionate. When you look at him you may see the rough and tough exterior, but he has a big soft heart. He draws you in with it.

I give a low whistle. "That has to hit hard for them both." Turning my face into his neck, I inhale him. "But that's not us. I'd chase you to the ends of the earth to make sure you know I love you, and our little girl is crazy about you."

"I hate it when you read my thoughts," he grumbles.

I chuckle and nuzzle his neck. "Just returning the favor. I think that's when I knew we were meant to be together. You were in my head from the beginning."

"I think I knew when I turned to find you watching me take a shower in your gym. You didn't call the cops or try to knock my ass out," he says with a laugh.

"This house is full of fighters. We're not leaving you, Angel. Just like you wouldn't leave us," I say.

"*Para decirle a mi cabeza lo que mi corazón sabe.*"

"To tell my head what my heart knows," I repeat.

"*Sí*, you're getting good. Billy loves that she can speak Spanish to us both now."

"I love it too."

He turns in my embrace to face me. I slide my arms around his waist and pull him close. There will never be a time where

I'm close enough to him. I'll always want to be closer. If I could, I'd pour myself into him and rest there for life.

"You're going to win the fight," he says. "It's your fight. It's your time. It was meant to be."

"From your lips to God's ears." I snort.

He runs his hand through the front of my hair. Those whiskey-brown eyes scan mine from beneath those long dark lashes. He cups my face in his hands.

"It's your fight to win. The only thing that will stop you is you. Leave the baggage outside the ring. You've spent over a year getting ready for this. No one deserves this win more than you," he says with such sincerity I feel it in my bones.

"How do you always know just what I need to hear?"

"You're the other half of my soul. I am the other half of yours. It's why you're always able to call me back to you," he says against my lips.

We both complete the connection at once. It's not a hungry kiss, but a tender one that speaks of the patience we have learned with each other and life. Our kiss tells a story of us—going somewhere, it just doesn't always have to be fast.

"*Te amo.*"

"I love when your country ass speaks Spanish," he laughs.

"*Te amo*, Papi. Come, let's go to bed."

CHAPTER FORTY-FOUR

Should've Told Me

Beau

I'm vibrating with rage as I storm into Refuge. I have the documents that arrived at the gym clinched in my hand, burning a hole through my palm. I still can't believe what I read on them. I need to hear this from Javier himself.

"*Beau*, hey, gorgeous," Darwin sings as I approach the table.

I ignore him and slam the papers in my hand down on the table in front of Javier. My palm slaps the glass so hard, the drinks on it shake and a bottle of champagne turns over. Javier's gaze takes me in and his smile falls. He lifts the papers to see what I've placed before him.

"What the fuck is that, Javi?" I demand.

The blood drains from his face. He swallows hard and looks back up at me. I feel the betrayal cut deep. It's clear by his expression that he's seen these documents before. He's no stranger to what they are.

"Where did these come from?" he asks.

"Answer my damn question."

"Beau, calm down," Chris says.

I turn to him and glare. It dawns on me that a few of my friends are here. Daniel takes the papers from Javier, and the look on his face tells me this betrayal runs deeper than I thought.

"Ah, fuck," Kyle says when he gets his hands on the pages.

"You knew about this?" I say to my brother, feeling the most hurt by him having knowledge of this and keeping it from me.

I consider them all my brothers, but Kyle might as well be my own flesh and blood. This hurts so much, I feel like I'm going to explode. I can't believe they hid this from me.

"How did you get these?" Javier asks again.

"They were delivered to my damn front door," I seethe. "I was heading out of the gym when a carrier dropped them off."

"Un-fuck-real," Kyle snarls. "So what? This is Steve's final play. Payback?"

Kyle looks at Javier as he says this. It pisses me off that they're still excluding me from something that clearly involves me. I snatch the papers back as if I can snatch back the past and do it over again.

"Exactly what I was thinking," Javi says as he looks me in the eyes. "Your fight is tomorrow. You don't find it strange that these would appear now?"

"I don't give a fuck about that. I care that you requested these documents and never thought to share what they revealed. You buried this shit without coming to me."

"You were not in the right state of mind to find these things out," Javi says.

"I absolutely agree," Kyle says. "We didn't do this to hurt you. It was to protect you. I'd do it again too."

"It's been years. You could've told me at some point," I growl.

"In all fairness, Beau, you just turned your life around and came out of the funk you were in after all of that. There has never been a right time to tell you. This damn sure wasn't the right time either," Chris says.

The others gathered around the private booth nod in agreement. I tighten my fist with the papers in it. I'm fuming to the point I'm seeing red.

"You moved on with your life. I didn't see the point in dumping that shit on your doorstep. Shit, you wouldn't get in the ring before Angel. Now you're about to have a professional bout," Ray says.

"Beau, you can't be angry with them. They always had your best interest in mind, always," Darwin says.

I stumble to take the empty seat between Javi and Kyle. I drop my head into my hands, still clenching the papers. My head hurts.

"He was high," I murmur to no one in particular.

"As a fucking kite," Chris says.

"If you watch the fight, you'll see something was off. It was more than his usual showboating," Kyle says.

"How did this happen?" I say, feeling lost and confused. "We were always together. He didn't use. We were tested before the fight. Nothing was in his system."

"Which is why I put all my eggs in the basket that says Steve gave it to him right before the fight," Javi says.

"He was a better fighter than that. He should've known better," I say hoarsely.

"He was young. Steve was selling him all kinds of dreams and shit." Kyle snorts. "Man, you can't beat yourself up for any of that."

"He died. He died on my watch," I say.

Javi places his hand on my back. I turn to look into his eyes. Regret weighs heavily in them.

"I'm sorry you found out this way. I had planned to tell you after you win this fight. You didn't need this on your head. Please, don't take this on, my friend. Roman made several bad choices that led to his fate.

"He and Steve didn't think about you or what all of this would do to you. I ask you not to throw your future away for people that never cared enough to protect it. We all want what's best for you. We're always here to protect you," he says.

I close my eyes and turn away. I'm angry, but I honestly don't think it's with them. I don't know who to truly be angry with.

Hell, I don't know how knowing any of this should make me feel. It doesn't make me feel any better. If anything, I'm back to square one. The blood has stained my hands all over again.

"I need you to stop whatever's going on in your head, Beau," Kyle says. "I know you like the back of my hand. You've jumped over a huge hurdle in the last few weeks. Don't let this set you back."

"I need to go," I say.

I don't look back as I stumble from the club and drive home numb to everything. I don't know if I'll ever be free of that fight. Roman's death is hellbent on haunting me for the rest of my damn life.

Angel

I've been pacing the apartment since Beau stormed out of here with that letter clenched in his hand. It was delivered to the gym just before we left for the night. Beau didn't get to open it until after we fed Billy and tucked her in.

If I'd known what was in that envelope, I'd never have let him open it. I felt it in his body as I held him. When I started to read over his shoulder, I felt sick. It killed me that I couldn't tell him that I knew.

The alarm sounds below, alerting me to the return of my husband. I leave the balcony and move to the hallway, jogging down the stairs. Beau is on the couch with his head thrown back against the cushions and his arms crossed over his face.

I sit on the coffee table in front of him. I inhale deeply as I still myself to tell the truth. I want him to know that I knew.

"I asked Javi to get me access to Steve. I knew Javi had the reach and knowledge to get me to him. However, Javi had it handled before I got to put the pressure on that loser. That night I had planned to confront Steve, while you were sleeping, Javi had come to tell me the job was done. He also told me about the drugs in Roman's system—"

I pause when Beau's head snaps up and he gives me a death glare. I sigh. I knew he wasn't going to take this well. I just don't want this between us. Not after I saw how upset he was earlier.

"Don't," he warns. "Don't add to this shitstorm."

"I wanted you to know. It wasn't my place to tell you. I heard it secondhand, and as your present husband, I didn't feel it right to tell you that type of thing about your ex," I say and wince.

"You know. I can't be mad at you for that. You haven't known me half as long as them. You weren't there when it happened," he bites out.

"They meant well," I reply.

"That's not even what has me so damn pissed off," he says. "I killed him, Angel. Those drugs in his system just helped that right along."

I fall into a blinding rage. This is what those motherfuckers want. Steve is in jail, but he's still fucking with Beau. I know in my gut this is because of him. I won't let Beau let that asshole win.

"Oh, no," I bark. "I see what you're about to do. That's just what whoever sent that shit wants. Don't you dare. Don't make this a crutch."

His jaw works, his nostrils flare, and his eyes flame with fury. He needs to save all that shit for the ring. I'm not trying to hear it.

"A crutch." He snorts.

"Yes, a crutch. Come on, Beau. You were ready. You've been in the zone for the last two weeks. Until you opened that fucking envelope you had this," I say.

He stands. "I'm going to bed. I have a long day ahead of me. Good night," he says.

I sigh in frustration. I want to tear my hair out. I have no idea what tomorrow will bring. This could be a damn disaster.

"Fuck."

CHAPTER FORTY-FIVE

Redemption

Angel

This is the night Beau has worked over a year for. Yet this locker room feels like we're about to walk out to a funeral. I don't know how I feel. Do I think he can win this thing? Fuck, yeah. He has worked his ass off and could take this fight in his sleep.

However, I don't think his mind is here. I don't know if my fighter is going to appear tonight, and that both scares the shit out of me and pisses me off. He put in too much work for this. Both physically and mentally.

"Can everyone give us a minute?" I say to our team.

Everyone begins to shuffle out. I heave a heavy breath. Today has been a long day. I received a text from Javi that Steve and Norwack's promoter were in fact behind those documents that were delivered. All of that will remain with me until this fight is over.

I know, I know. Another secret, but the last thing Beau needs is that shit in his head. I'll protect him no matter what.

I take over taping Beau's hands. He won't look at me. It's been this way all day. I finish up and reach under his chin to lift his gaze to mine. Those troubled gray eyes nearly slay me from inside out.

"You told me that Eric told you to figure out your why? I don't know if you've done that yet, but it's a good time to lock on to that and not the past. I'm here no matter what.

"All of this means nothing if you're not happy at the end of it. To be truthfully honest, if you say fuck this shit let's go home right now, I'm with you. We're out. No questions asked. As long as we do what makes you happy," I say.

"I'm no quitter," he says emotionlessly.

I sigh and shake my head. He's so damn stubborn. I go to lay into him, but I reel it in. I'm not going to stress him out before he gets in the ring.

I reach to massage his shoulders. I don't know what else to say. This is all on him now.

I kiss his forehead, willing my strength and love into him. If anyone can make a comeback, it's Beau. I believe in him. It's time he believes in himself.

"You've got this, Beau. I know you do."

I can't get my head into the ring. It's all of our worst nightmares. I've been mind-fucked thoroughly.

"Come on, Beau. Start punching," Angel bellows into the ring. "Move your fucking feet."

I'm down on the score cards. I know I am. I haven't been throwing nearly as many punches as I should. I'm on the defense, and this guy is taking advantage of that.

I dance out of his way again as he tries to steer me toward the ropes. The one thing I have going for me is my stamina. This guy is getting tired, and I'm not even panting.

He throws another combination, but only lands a weak jab. Still that jab is one more punch landed, one more on the score card. The bell rings.

"To your corners," the ref calls.

I turn and walk to my corner, knowing I'm losing this fight. The lump in my throat feels like it's going to choke me. He's not even the better fighter. The old me would've taken him out rounds ago.

I can feel the tears stinging my eyes, but I fight them back harder than I'm fighting Gordon. I flop down in my seat, and Angel pulls my guard out of my mouth. Frustration lines his face.

"What the fuck, B? Where's your head? You're throwing this fight away. All that hard work to get in here and not fight?"

"I'm fighting," I say, knowing it's a lie.

"Fuck out of here. If that's fighting, I'm married to Apollonia," he says and frowns.

I'd laugh if I weren't drowning in the cesspool in my head. So many thoughts, so many emotions and I don't know how to get ahold of them. The hinge has been blown off, and just as I thought I'm not dealing well with reining it all in on the most important night. "What do you want me to do?"

"*Ay coño*, Beau. I want you to fight. Throw a damn punch for Christ's sake. *Dios.*"

"If you don't start throwing some serious punches in the next three rounds, this fight is over," Andres says as he wipes my face.

"Come on, Beau, you can do this," Billy says, holding up my water bottle from outside the ring.

I look her in the eyes. There's pleading there. I'm failing her. I drop my head and stare at the canvas. Angel moves to place his lips to my ear as he massages my shoulders.

"Stop thinking. You've overcome all your shit to be here. Now you're here. Go get him, Papi. Don't give him your fight," he says.

I nod just as the bell rings. I stand, not feeling any more certain that I can turn this fight around. I'm more distracted by the pleading look in Billy's eyes. So much so, the first few haymakers Gordon throws connect and stun me.

"Wake up, Beau," Angel calls.

I shake it off and move. I throw a couple of halfhearted punches. I need to make it out of this round with more punches on my score card, but I'm just not taking them. Instead I'm drowning in the roar of the crowd. It's as if I can hear their disappointment as well. I haven't shown up to give them the fight I promised.

In the moment when defeat grasps me around the throat, Billy's little voice carries over everything. Above the crowd, over Angel and Andres, above my father-in-law fussing at me in Spanish, and over my own thoughts—I hear her.

"Come on, Daddy!" Billy says. "Come on! You can do this! Make Grandpa proud. Kick his butt!"

Suddenly everything goes silent, the arena stills, and it all falls into place. My thoughts clear and my why is revealed. Billy has never called me her daddy before. The truth of who I am to her slams into me.

I'm doing this for my little girl. I wanted to show her that she's right. You don't ever give up on what you love. You don't run from who you are.

Something shifts inside me. I'm thrown back in time to one day when I trained with my own daddy. He was extra tough on me that day.

"You know why I'm so hard on you, Beau James?" he said.

"No, sir."

"Because you're the best. I don't question if you can be. I know you are. When I can get you to see what I see, you're going to be unstoppable. You just have to believe in yourself like I do. Now let's go. Get those arms up and show me some real punches."

And that's what I do. I square up and take this fight back because Angel was right. It's mine. I take this fight because I was born to do this and I'm the best. Boxing is in my blood and I love it.

This is who I am.

Angel

The moment the words come out of her mouth, I feel the atmosphere change. It's like Billy breathed life into Beau just when he needed it. His entire posture changes, and he shifts the fight. I know this is a wrap when he changes to southpaw.

Gone are the timid punches. He starts to throw precise blow after blow. He's amazing in the ring. Right now, he's looking more like a fighter in the first round rather than the ninth. His opponent is winded from punching himself out in the first half of the fight.

The crowd gets to their feet and starts to chant Beau's name. Beau James, they call, electrifying the arena, but I don't think he hears any of that. He's in the zone.

He's taking this fight back with everything he's got. It's like watching poetry dance in the ring. Fluid and rhythmic. The body blows smack like music.

"Yes," Billy cheers as she stands on her chair. "He's doing it."

I place a hand on her head and shake it. "All for you," I choke out.

"Not for me. It's for all of us. For the broken," she says. "He's the hero I can be. The hero you are."

The glow on her face says a million words. Just then the bell rings. I shake off my awe of this kid and get in the ring. I can't stop smiling, but the best part is, neither can Beau.

"Now that's what I'm fucking talking about," I say, playfully slapping him in the side of the head.

He looks me in the eyes, and I see something I've never seen before. It's a cocksureness that's oozing off him. It's sexy as fuck and well placed.

This is Beau.

"I need the knockout," he says.

"Yeah, to seal this without question. You do."

He nods. "Then let's finish this."

I palm the back of his head and kiss the top. I don't care. I'm so fucking proud of him.

Beau

The pride in Angel's eyes when he releases me and places my guard back in my mouth makes me feel like I'm ten feet tall. I'm ready to finish this fight. Doubts and fears try to creep in, but I shove them down hard.

I turn to wink at Billy, and she beams back at me, giving a thumbs-up. Her excitement is palpable. A quick scan of the crowd, and I see my family and friends there with the same pride on their faces. Friends that always have my back.

The bell rings and I'm up and charging. Gordon is winded. He's a big boy and I'm going to need all my power to knock him on his ass, but I know I can.

I size him up with a few jabs, just waiting for my opening. He sways left when I throw a combination. He's weak on that side. Then it happens: I see it before it occurs—he exposes his left side, trying to compensate with his dominant right.

I hear my daddy's voice as clear as if he were in the ring with me.

Take it, Beau. Use your uppercut now.

It's like it happens in slow motion. I shift out of southpaw and step forward. I throw my force into the punch, coming right under his chin. All two hundred and fifty-five pounds of Gordon Norwack drop to the canvas.

My hands drop to my sides, and I hold my breath. Flashes of Roman's lifeless body rush me. I stumble forward.

No, not again.

Silence surrounds me. You can hear a pin drop. My chest starts to rise and fall erratically. The panic attack begins to build; my vision blurs. A few seconds pass as they wave the smelling salt. Then I see it. He starts to stir.

The crowd goes wild, and the next thing I know, Angel has me in the air off my feet. I'm stunned. I just won and he's alive. Reality hits, and I throw my fists in the air.

"You did it, Papi. I told you," Angel croons. "I love you so much."

I bend to kiss the top of his head. "I love you," I murmur into his hair.

Angel places me back on the canvas and hugs me while people around me pat me on my back. Andres and Alejandro work to get my gloves off as people shout questions and congratulations at me. Yet, the greatest moment is when I feel a little body wiggle between me and Angel.

I lift Billy into my arms. She wraps hers around my neck, squeezing as hard as she can. I kiss the top of her head.

"You did it, Daddy. You did it."

"I sure did, sugar. Thanks to you guys."

"I love you," she says as she cups my face in her small hands.

"I love you too, darlin'."

And just like that, I win something greater than a fight. I won the heart of a little girl that was afraid to trust. A little girl who thought no one would love her.

I pull Angel in and hold my family tight. I repeat my words of love to them both. Angel and Billy were just what I needed. Their love was worth the journey.

It's my redemption.

Family

Angel

"You're such a good boy," I coo.

Cody smells like all things sweet and sunshine. I love my nephew. Or should I say nephews. Andres and Emma had twins, Cody and Christian. I feel for their parents. If these two end up anything like 'Dres and me... I shake my head at the thought. My brother doesn't deserve half the shit we did behind our parents' back.

"You guys come to Uncle Angel. I'll show you how to have fun without making your Papi lose his hair," I whisper into Cody's ear and laugh, kissing the top of his head.

Looking around the gym, I can't help the smile that comes to my face. The entire family is here. Mason and Billy are going for their orange belts today. No one, not even our extended family was willing to miss this.

"I wish we had Billy when she was this small," Beau says as he walks over to me standing by the ring with Christian in his arms.

"B, I was think the same thing."

"Maybe we should think about adopting again or a surrogate." The light in his eyes as he makes the suggestion warms my heart.

However, I shake my head at him as I smile. Our lives are so full at the moment. Billy has ballet, martial arts, the school choir—that kid is in everything. I've taken over managing the gym and helping with the latest development Beau and Kyle have in the works. I don't go on site much, but I handle most of the logistics behind the scenes to take a load off Beau.

"Between trying to rebuild the city and training for this next fight when do either of us have time for a newborn?"

He grins. "Who knows. This next fight could be my last."

"You don't even sound like you believe that crap," I snort.

Cody begins to wail in my arms, causing Emma to jump up from her conversation with Jordan as they sit on the bottom bleacher. She rushes over to scoop the baby from my arms. Cody makes his demands known as he grabs for his mom's boob.

Emma's cheeks turn red. "I'm still not used to that," she giggles. "I'll take Christian too, Beau. Might as well get them both fed."

"You can use my office," Beau offers.

"Thanks," she says and rushes off.

Beau turns to me, his brows furrowed. "Okay, maybe not a newborn."

I bark out a laugh and wrap an arm around his waist. I nod at Jordan now talking to Javi. So much has changed in the last few months.

"He looks good. Is he any closer to getting back on the ice?" I ask.

Beau purses his lips and narrows his eyes. "He's ready for something but I don't know if it's getting back on the ice. Time will tell."

"Yo, Papi, Daddy," Billy runs over and wiggles between the two of us.

My heart swells whenever she calls me that. She has gotten into the habit of calling Beau Daddy and me, Papi. Our little family has found the perfect balance. We work for us.

"Hey, darlin'," Beau replies.

"What's up?" I say.

"Mas and Aryanna want to go for ice cream later. Can I go?"

"Sure," Beau and I say in unison.

I grin at my husband. We spoil this kid. I don't even know why she bothers to ask. She even got her dog. We're going to have to learn to say no one day.

I think about Billy's request and narrow my eyes. I may not know how to tell her no, but Beau is another story. "You're not touching that shit," I say low in warning to Beau.

He rumbles with laughter. I'm not laughing at all. I will not be up with him groaning over his stomach all night. Nope, not going to happen.

"By the way Papi, Abuela said we better be in Brooklyn tomorrow," Billy informs me.

I laugh and look over to where my parents are sitting in the bleachers. Both my parents are looking at us with wide smiles. My moms gives me a pointed look.

"We'll be there," Beau says patting his belly.

Yeah, I love my family and my life. This is my normal. My prayers have been answered.

Beau

I remember once praying to have a normal life back. As I look at my little girl pumping her fist as her uncle hands over her orange belt, my chest fills with pride. My daddy would've loved this. All these people here in his gym showing love and support.

All this family.

"We have a lot to be grateful for," Javi says. "Come by the club tonight. We can all catch up."

"I'll be there," Chris says from his stretched out position on the bleachers above me.

Daniel sitting to my right, puts his phone away before responding. "I have to fly out, but I'll stop in for a sec."

Jordan gives a silent nod, pulling my attention as he sits in the row below me. His usual humor is absent, this is way too quiet for him. In all honesty, he's been somewhere else all day. Before I can pry, Kyle's words pull my attention.

"The kids want to go for ice cream, but if you're down, Beau, we can ride together."

"I'll see if Angel's okay with putting Billy to bed," I say.

"I overheard them plotting on a sleepover at your in-laws," Ray says.

I look at my friend as he smiles. Ray still likes to tease us about Billy and Mason. I'm not entertaining his ass. There will be no boys. Not even Mas.

Kyle laughs. "Facts. Mas already asked."

Javi stand to stretch. "The offer was to all my family. It's time Andy and Angel begin to join our toasts," he says with a smile. "I'm off, amigos. See you this evening."

My heart swells. These are my brothers. Hearing the acceptance of my husband into our brotherhood at this level chokes me up. We've never allowed anyone else into our bond. Not even Dar joins in for our toasts and bonding.

We all wave as Javier jogs down the bleachers to go hug Billy and Mas goodbye. Seeing how much love my extended family has for my new family is just a cherry on top. These guys spoil Billy almost as much as Angel and I do.

Angel lifts Billy and spins her, causing her laugh to fill the gym. I can't help the face-splitting smile that takes over my face. My life has become complete. Normal was my prayer, phenomenal is my answer.

"You ready for this next fight?" Ray asks, pulling me from my thoughts.

"I was born ready."

ACKNOWLEDGMENTS

Hello again! So glad you shared your time with me to spend a little more in my head. Beau, Angel, and Billy stole my heart, and I hope they were able to capture a bit of yours. I absolutely love what I do, and I'm grateful for the opportunity to share that with you.

Again, I want to thank all of those who have supported me as both Royal Blue and Blue Saffire. Thank you to all of you awesome readers. You are now family in my brain. You've been adopted, and I'm not turning you loose. LOL. Thank you for your support, kind words, and every email, comment, post, shout out. It's heartwarming and always on time. Something to make me love this even more.

As always thank you to my husband. You're the best. Your support means everything.

Only God can bless me with the life I have. He fosters the openings that I'm able to move through. I thank Him for my blessings. Forever grateful and giving praise. To God be all the Glory.

ABOUT THE AUTHOR

The color blue is known for trust and healing as are the words of author Royal Blue. Blue started writing books to heal herself after losing her mother to breast cancer in 2007, followed by a miscarriage only eight months later. Books and words were one of the things that held her together.

As a young girl, Blue's mother introduced her to the world of love and music through movies like Seven Brides for Seven Brothers, Bye Bye Birdie, and Neptune's Daughter. Once she got her hands on books that sucked her into the magic that pages bring, an authoress was born. A story here, a few songs there, but she actually didn't complete a manuscript until 2009.

However, books were piling up and collecting dust as fear clung and whispered evil thoughts. Yet, fear was silenced in 2015. Needing to write in order to breathe and wanting to share, Blue Saffire, Royal's alter ego, rose from the ashes and entered the world.

The self-proclaimed hermit was born in Far Rockaway, NY, but is now a Long Island resident with her loving and supportive husband. The two work round the clock creating music and characters. There is no shortage of laughter or creativity in their home.

Never in a million years did she think the passion that saved her sanity would allow her to walk around with blue hair and spend her days dreaming of hot men to put on paper. After all, an MBA in Marketing and Project Management, as well as a MED in Curriculum Design and Instructional Technology, tell a very different story. Although, it's safe to say Royal would rather be doing something Blue with her time.

Links

Email: AuthorRoyalBlue@gmail.com
Website: AuthorRoyalBlue.com
Twitter: @authorroyalblue
Facebook: www.facebook.com/authorroyalblue/
Instagram: @authorroyalblue

Wait, there is more to come! You can stay updated with my latest releases, learn more about me, the author, and be a part of contests by subscribing to my newsletter at
www.RoyalBlue.com
If you enjoyed Beau's Redemption, I'd love to hear your thoughts and please feel free to leave a review. And when you do, please let me know by emailing me AuthorRoyalBlue@gmail.com
or leave a comment on Facebook
https://www.facebook.com/authorroyalblue/
or Twitter @AuthorRoyalBlue

Other books by Blue Saffire
Kyle's Reveal
Jordan's Commitment...*Coming 2020*

www.ingramcontent.com/pod-product-compliance
Lightning Source LLC
Chambersburg PA
CBHW070911260626
47162CB00007B/2636